Fritz Leiber, the son of a noted stage and screen performer, was born in the United States in 1910. A former actor, he has written many fantasy and science fiction stories, and contributed to *Weird Tales* before the Second World War. Leiber is well known and held in high regard by readers of both science fiction and fantasy: he has received several Hugo and Nebula awards for the former, and he is seen as the doyen of fantasy writers, as the man who practically invented the sword and sorcery genre as it is known today. Most of the leading writers in the field acknowledge their debt to him, but, as is often pointed out, what makes Leiber's fantasy adventures superior to those of the many writers who have followed in his footsteps is the strong vein of dry wit that permeates his work.

By the same author

Novels

Gather Darkness
Conjure Wife
The Green Millennium
Two Sought Adventure
Destiny Times Three
The Big Time
The Silver Eggheads
The Wanderer
Tarzan and the Valley of Gold (based on the film)
A Spectre is Haunting Texas
Our Lady of Darkness
Swords and Deviltry
Swords Against Death
Swords Against Wizardry
The Swords of Lankhmar
Swords and Ice Magic

Collections of stories

Night's Black Agents
The Mind Spider
Shadows with Eyes
Ships to the Stars
A Pail of Air
The Night of the Wolf
Secret Songs
Night Monsters
You're All Alone
The Best of Fritz Leiber
The Book of Fritz Leiber
The Second Book of Fritz Leiber
The Worlds of Fritz Leiber

FRITZ LEIBER

Swords in the Mist

BOOK 3 IN THE SWORDS SERIES

GRAFTON BOOKS

A Division of the Collins Publishing Group

LONDON GLASGOW
TORONTO SYDNEY AUCKLAND

Grafton Books
A Division of the Collins Publishing Group
8 Grafton Street, London W1X 3LA

A Grafton Paperback Original 1979
Reprinted 1986, 1987

The Cloud of Hate was first published in *Fantastic*, May 1963. *Lean Times in Lankhmar* was first published in *Fantastic*, November 1959. *Their Mistress, the Sea* was newly written for this book. *When the Sea-King's Away* was first published in *Fantastic*, May 1960. *The Wrong Branch* was newly written for this book. *Adept's Gambit* was first published in *Night's Black Agents*, Arkham House, 1947; copyright Fritz Leiber 1947. A shorter version, abridged by the author, was published in *Fantastic*, May 1964.

ISBN 0-583-13088-7

Printed and bound in Great Britain by
Collins, Glasgow

Set in Intertype Plantin

Contents

That evil, far from being the illusion mystics deem it, is the dark glittering power that shapes the World Show. How the Gray Mouser and Fafhrd discoursed of watchmanship and of the keen joys the simple life affords, especially to penniless men, but were interrupted by something that walked though it had no legs and flew though it had no wings.

Showing how lack of money leads to lack of love, even between sworn comrades. How when adventure cloys and risky enterprises become wearisome, there are two chief paths to take: that of godless rapine and that of holiness. With interesting sidelights on the uses which can be made of scrawny nymphs and doddering priests, if only their diets be first improved. Of the Second Coming of Issek of the Jug, together with notes on a thousand other gods. And of how blood-brothership, and also the adventure-itch, are allergies or ills not easily arrested and never cured.

Of a tempestuous paramour whom Fafhrd and the Mouser could share without jealousy. The means whereby heroes get back into battle trim after grievous debauchery or self-denial. Including the piquant encounter of Ourph the passionate Mingol with five defenseless witchwomen of his tribe.

Of the delusions and lascivious imaginings of seamen athirst and erotically starved – or else of a magic mightier than the weight of all the world's waters. Of land tunnels and sea tunnels, of water wells in earth and air wells in water, of cliffs paper-thin and oceans at war. Of the Triple Goddess at work in Nehwon, or at play. Of a masked black sea-witch and her magical toys. Of two luscious sea-queens and their outre harem guard. Together with a compendium of practical information useful to those who must walk, not on water, but – without diving garb – down, through, and under the aqueous element.

V: THE WRONG BRANCH   96

The devious workings of the Sea-King's curse. A swimming race between men and sharks and how it was betted on. Of noisome Ilthmar. Of Doors between distant worlds. A warning to all to avoid side-paths when visiting Ningauble of the Seven Eyes in his caverns, and of how this wise rule was broken upon one occasion.

VI: ADEPT'S GAMBIT   103

In his gambits, a chess-player sacrifices pawn or piece to checkmate his adversary. But in *his* games, a black magician, in order to triumph, may sacrifice living pieces and even himself the player.

1. *Tyre* Of a humiliating enchantment which robbed Fafhrd and the Gray Mouser of all girls, except Chloe the cross-eyed Greek. And of how the Mouser fell into love, though not with Chloe.

2. *Ningauble* Of a visit by the two heroes to the Gossiper of the Gods, to find a cure for their girl-denying enchantment. Of a word-war of maneuver between Ningauble and the Mouser, with mention of four infamous handmaidens of Ishtar and a dwarf who was richly compensated for his deformity, of the Friday concubine of the satrap Philip, and of like matters.

3. *The Woman Who Came* How on Ningauble's advice and to make a magic to restore them, Fafhrd and the Mouser went on a multiple quest to procure the Shroud of Ahriman, aphrodisiacal mummie of the Demon Pharaoh, the Cup from which Socrates drank the hemlock, a sprig from the primal Tree of Life, and The Woman Who Would Come When She Was Ready.

4. *The Lost City* Of the heroes' cautious courting of shy, sly Ahura. Of the rift she naughtily digged between them. Of the journey they made, all three together. Of the Mouser's theory of Ahura's sex, and of how he felt it disproved in the moment of proving it. Of a saving gale, a messenger-bat, and the making of a great magic.

5. *Anra Devadoris* Of a fastidious stranger named the Dark Gift of Demons. Of the most taxing sword fight in the Gray Mouser's duel-starred life. Of the stranger's filthy bed.

6. *The Mountain* Of a demon peak that preyed on its countryside, and of a demon castle atop that peak. Of the follies of heroes and of a quest resumed.

7. *Ahura Devadoris* The spoken story of the Bright Gift of Demons. Of a tyranny more intimate and absolute than that of a wizard over his concubine-acolyte. Of the mixings of magics and whoredoms. Of a Tyrian orgy and its frightful close.

8. *The Old Man Without a Beard* Ahura's weird tale concluded. Of a sorcerer, his student, and their evil curriculum. Of an especially close confinement suffered by Ahura.

9. *The Castle Called Mist* Of a vast edifice alive or stretching into other dimensions. Horrors innumerable. End of Ahura's tale. Fate of the Old Man. A final duel and a final revelation. Lankhmar once more in view.

1: THE CLOUD OF HATE

Muffled drums beat out a nerve-scratching rhythm and red lights flickered hypnotically in the underground Temple of Hates, where five thousand ragged worshipers knelt and abased themselves and ecstatically pressed foreheads against the cold and gritty cobbles as the trance took hold and the human venom rose in them.

The drumbeat was low. And save for snarls and mewlings, the inner pulsing was inaudible. Yet together they made a hellish vibration which threatened to shake the city and land of Lankhmar and the whole world of Nehwon.

Lankhmar had been at peace for many moons and so the hates were greater. Tonight, furthermore, at a spot halfway across the city, Lankhmar's black-togaed nobility celebrated with merriment and feasting and twinkling dance the betrothal of their Overlord's daughter to the Prince of Ilthmar, and so the hates were redoubled.

The single-halled subterranean temple was so long and wide and at the same time so irregularly planted with thick pillars that at no point could a person see more than a third of the way across it. Yet it had a ceiling so low that at any point a man standing tall could have brushed it with his fingertips – except that here all groveled. The air was swooningly fetid. The dark bent backs of the hate-ensorceled worshipers made a kind of hummocky dark ground, from which the nitre-crusted stone pillars rose like gray tree trunks.

The masked Archpriest of the Hates lifted a skinny finger. Parchment-thin iron cymbals began to clash in unison with the drums and the furnace-red flickerings, wringing to an unendurable pitch the malices and envies of the blackly enraptured communicants.

Then in the gloom of that great slit-like hall, dim pale tendrils began to rise from the dark hummocky ground of the bent backs, as though a white, swift-growing ghost-grass had been seeded there. The tendrils, which in another world might have been described as ectoplasmic, quickly multiplied, thickened, lengthened, and then coalesced into questing white serpentine shapes, so that it seemed as if tongues of thick river-fog had come licking down into this sub-cellar from the broad-flowing river Hlal.

The white serpents coiled past the pillars, brushed the low ceiling, moistly caressed the backs of their devotees and source, and then in turn coalesced to pour up the curving black hole of a narrow spiral stairway, the stone steps of which were worn almost to chutelike smoothness – a sinuously billowing white cylinder in which a redness lurked.

And all the while the drums and cymbals did not falter for a single beat, nor did the Hell-light tenders cease to crank the wooden wheels on which shielded, red-burning candles were affixed, nor did the eyes of the Archpriest flicker once sideways in their wooden mask, nor did one mesmerized bent soul look up.

Along a misted alley overhead there was hurrying home to the thieves' quarter a beggar girl, skinny-frail of limb and with eyes big as a lemur's peering fearfully from a tiny face of elfin beauty. She saw the white pillar, slug-flat now, pouring out between the bars of a window-slit level with the pavement, and although there were thick chilly tendrils of river-fog already following her, she knew that this was different.

She tried to run around the thing, but swift almost as a serpent striking it whipped across to the opposite wall, barring her way. She ran back, but it outraced her and made a U, penning her against the unyielding wall. Then she only stood still and shook as the fog-serpent narrowed and grew denser and came wreathing around her. Its tip swayed like the head of a poisonous snake preparing to strike and then suddenly dipped toward her breast. She stopped shaking then and her head fell back and the pupils rolled up in her lemur-like eyes so that they showed only great whites, and she dropped to the pavement limp as a rag.

The fog-serpent nosed at her for a few moments, then as though irked at finding no life remaining, flipped her over on her face, and went swiftly questing in the same direction the river-fog itself was taking: across city towards the homes of the nobles and the lantern-jeweled palace of the Overlord.

Save for an occasional fleeting red glint in the one, the two sorts of fog were identical.

Beside a dry stone horse-trough at the juncture of five alleys, two men curled close to either side of a squat brazier in which a little charcoal glowed. The spot was so near the quarter of the nobles that the sounds of music and laughter came at intervals, faintly, along with a dim rainbow-glow of light. The two men might have been a hulking beggar and a small one, except that their tunics and leggings and cloaks, though threadbare, were of good stuff, and scabbarded weapons lay close to the hand of each.

The larger said, 'There'll be fog tonight. I smell it coming from the Hlal.' This was Fafhrd, brawny-armed, pale and serene of face, reddish gold of hair.

For reply the smaller shivered and fed the brazier two small goblets of charcoal and said sardonically, 'Next predict glaciers! – advancing down the Street of the Gods, by preference.' That was the Mouser, eyes wary, lips quirking, cheeks muffled by gray hood drawn close.

Fafhrd grinned. As a tinkling gust of distant song came by, he asked the dark air that carried it, 'Now why aren't we warmly cushioned somewhere inside tonight, well drunk and sweetly embraced?'

For answer the Gray Mouser drew from his belt a rat-skin pouch and slapped it by its drawstrings against his palm. It flattened as it hit and nothing chinked. For good measure he writhed at Fafhrd the backs of his ten fingers, all ringless.

Fafhrd grinned again and said to the dusky space around them, which was now filled with the finest mist, the fog's fore-runner, 'Now that's a strange thing. We've won I know not how many jewels and oddments of gold and electrum in our adventurings – and even letters of credit on the Guild of the Grain Merchants. Where have they all flown to? – the credit-letters on parchment wings, the jewels jetting fire like tiny red and green pearly cuttlefish. Why aren't we rich?'

The Mouser snorted, 'Because you dribble away our get on worthless drabs, or oftener still pour it out for some noble whim – some plot of bogus angels to storm the walls of Hell. Meantime I stay poor nursemaiding you.'

Fafhrd laughed and retorted, 'You overlook your own whimsical imprudences, such as slitting the Overlord's purse and picking his pocket too the selfsame night you rescued and returned him his lost crown. No, Mouser, I think we're poor because—' Suddenly he lifted an elbow and flared his nostrils as he snuffed the chill moist air. 'There's a taint in the fog tonight,' he announced.

The Mouser said dryly, 'I already smell dead fish, burnt fat, horse dung, tickly lint, Lankhmar sausage gone stale, cheap temple incense burnt by the ten-pound cake, rancid oil, moldy grain, slaves' barracks, embalmers' tanks crowded to the black brim, and the stink of a cathedral full of unwashed carters and trulls celebrating orgiastic rites – and now you tell me of a taint!'

'It is something different from all those,' Fafhrd said, peering successively down the five alleys. 'Perhaps the last . . .' His voice trailed off doubtfully and he shrugged.

Strands of fog came questing through small high-set street-level windows into the tavern called the Rats' Nest, interlacing curiously with the soot-trail from a failing torch, but unnoticed except by an old harlot who pulled her patchy fur cloak closer to her throat.

All eyes were on the wrist game being played across an ancient oaken table by the famed bravo Gnarlag and a dark-skinned mercenary almost as big-thewed as he. Right elbows firmly planted and right hands bone-squeezingly gripped, each strained to force the back of the other's wrist down against the ringed and scarred and carved and knife-stuck wood. Gnarlag, who scowled sneeringly, had the advantage by a thumb's length.

One of the fog-strands, as though itself a devotee of the wrist game and curious about the bout, drifted over Gnarlag's shoulder. To the old harlot the inquisitive fog-strand looked redly-veined – a reflection from the torches, no doubt, but she prayed it brought fresh blood to Gnarlag.

The fog finger touched the taut arm. Gnarlag's sneering look turned to one of pure hate and the muscles of his forearm seemed to double in thickness as he rotated it more than a half turn. There was a muffled snap and a gasp of anguish. The mercenary's wrist had been broken.

Gnarlag stood up. He knocked to the wall a wine cup offered him and cuffed aside a girl who would have embraced him. Then grabbing up his two swords on their thick belt from the bench beside him, he strode to the brick stairs and up out of the Rats' Nest. By some trick of air currents, perhaps, it seemed that a fog-strand rested across his shoulders like a comradely arm.

When he was gone, someone said, 'Gnarlag was ever a cold and ungrateful winner.' The dark mercenary stared at his dangling hand and bit back groans.

'So tell me, giant philosopher, why we're not dukes,' the Gray Mouser demanded, unrolling a forefinger from the fist on his knee so that it pointed across the brazier at Fafhrd. 'Or emperors, for that matter, or demigods.'

'We are not dukes because we're no man's man,' Fafhrd replied smugly, settling his shoulders against the stone horse-trough. 'Even a duke must butter up a king, and demigods the gods. We butter no one. We go our own way, choosing our own adventures – and our own follies! Better freedom and a chilly road than a warm hearth and servitude.'

'There speaks the hound turned out by his last master and not yet found new boots to slaver on,' the Mouser retorted with comradely sardonic impudence. 'Look you, you noble liar, we've labored for a dozen lords and kings and merchants fat. You've served Movarl across the Inner Sea. I've served the bandit Harsel. We've both served this Glipkerio, whose girl is tied to Ilthmar this same night.'

'Those are exceptions,' Fafhrd protested grandly. 'And even when we serve, we make the rules. We bow to no man's ultimate command, dance to no wizard's drumming, join no mob, hark to no wildering hate-call. When we draw sword, it's for ourselves alone. *What's that?*'

He had lifted his sword for emphasis, gripping it by the scabbard just below the guard, but now he held it still with the hilt near his ear.

'It hums a warning!' he said tersely after a moment. 'The steel twangs softly in its sheath!'

Chuckling tolerantly at this show of superstition, the Mouser drew his slimmer sword from its light scabbard, sighted along the blade's oiled length at the red embers, spotted a couple of dark flecks and began to rub at them with a rag.

When nothing more happened, Fafhrd said grudgingly as he laid down his undrawn sword, 'Perchance only a dragon walked across the cave where the blade was forged. Still, I don't like this tainted mist.'

Gis the cutthroat and the courtesan Tres had watched the fog coming across the fantastically peaked roofs of Lankhmar until it obscured the low-swinging yellow crescent of the moon and the rainbow glow from the palace. Then they had lit the cressets and drawn the blue drapes and were playing at throw-knife to sharpen their appetites for a more intimate but hardly kinder game.

Tres was not unskillful, but Gis could somersault the weapon a dozen or thirteen times before it stuck in wood and throw as truly between his legs as back over his shoulder without mirror. Whenever he threw the knife so it struck very near Tres, he smiled. She had to remind herself that he was not much more evil than most evil men.

A frond of fog came wreathing between the blue drapes and touched Gis on the temple as he prepared to throw. 'The blood in the fog's in your eye-whites!' Tres cried, staring at him weirdly. He seized the girl by the ear and, smiling hugely, slashed her neck just below her dainty jaw. Then, dancing out of the way of the gushing blood, he delicately snatched up his belt of daggers and darted down the curving stairs to the street, where he plunged into a warmhearted fog that was somehow as full of rage as the strong wine of Tovilysis is of sugar, a veritable cistern of wrath. His whole being was bathed in sensations as ecstatic as those strong but fleeting ones the tendril's touch on his temple had loosed from his brain. Visions of daggered princesses and skewered serving maids danced in his head. He stepped along happily, agog with delicious anticipations, beside Gnarlag of the Two Swords, knowing him at once for a hate-brother, sacrosanct, another slave of the blessed fog.

Fafhrd cupped his big hands over the brazier and whistled the gay tune sifting from the remotely twinkling palace. The Mouser, now re-oiling the blade of Scalpel against the mist, observed, 'For one beset by taunts and danger-hums, you're very jolly.'

'I like it here,' the Northerner asserted. 'A fig for courts and beds and inside fires! The edge of life is keener in the street — as on the mountaintop. Is not imagined wine sweeter than wine?' ('Ho!' the Mouser laughed, most sardonically.) 'And is not a crust of bread tastier to one an-hungered than lark's tongues to an epicure? Adversity makes the keenest appetite, the clearest vision.'

'There spoke the ape who could not reach the apple,' the Mouser told him. 'If a door to paradise opened in that wall there, you'd dive through.'

'Only because I've never been to paradise,' Fafhrd swept on. 'Is it not sweeter now to hear the music of Innesgay's betrothal from afar than mingle with the feasters, jig with them, be cramped and blinkered by their social rituals?'

'There's many a one in Lankhmar gnawn fleshless with envy by those sounds tonight,' the Mouser said darkly. 'I am not gnawn so much as those stupid ones. I am more intelligently jealous. Still, the answer to your question: no!'

'Sweeter by far tonight to be Glipkerio's watchman than

his pampered guest,' Fafhrd insisted, caught up by his own poetry and hardly hearing the Mouser.

'You mean we serve Glipkerio *free*?' the latter demanded loudly. 'Aye, there's the bitter core of all freedom: no pay!'

Fafhrd laughed, came to himself, and said almost abashedly, 'Still, there is something in the keenness and the watchman part. We're watchmen not for pay, but solely for the watching's sake! Indoors and warm and comforted, a man is blind. Out here we see the city and the stars, we hear the rustle and the tramp of life, we crouch like hunters in a stony blind, straining our senses for—'

'Please, Fafhrd, no more danger signs,' the Mouser protested. 'Next you'll be telling me there's a monster a-drool and a-stalk in the streets, all slavering for Innesgay and her betrothal-maids, no doubt. And perchance a sword-garnished princeling or two, for appetizer.'

Fafhrd gazed at him soberly and said, peering around through the thickening mist, 'When I am *quite* sure of that, I'll let you know.'

The twin brothers Kreshmar and Skel, assassins and alley-bashers by trade, were menacing a miser in his hovel when the red-veined fog came in after them. As swiftly as ambitious men take last bite and wine-swig at a family dinner when un-expectedly summoned to the emperor's banquet board, the two finished their business. Kreshmar neatly bludgeoned a crater in the miser's skull while Skel thrust into his belt the one small purse of gold they had thus far extorted from the ancient man now turning to corpse. They stepped briskly outside, their swords a-swing at their hips, and into the fog, where they marched side-by-side with Gnarlag and Gis in the midst of the compact pale mass that moved almost indistinguishably with the river-fog and yet intoxicated them as surely as if it were a clouded white wine of murder and destruction, zestfully sluic-ing away all natural cautions and fears, promising an infinitude of thrilling and most profitable victims.

Behind the four marchers, the false fog thinned to a single glimmering thread, red as an artery, silver as a nerve, that led back unbroken around many a stony corner to the Temple of the Hates. A pulsing went ceaselessly along the thread, as nourishment and purpose were carried from the temple to the marauding fog mass and to the four killers, now doubly hate-enslaved, marching along with it. The fog mass moved purposefully as a snow tiger toward the quarter of the nobles and Glipkerio's rainbow-lanterned palace above the breakwater of the Inner Sea.

Three black-clad police of Lankhmar, armed with metal-capped cudgels and weighted wickedly-barbed darts, saw the thicker fog masses coming and the marchers in it. The impression to them was of four men frozen in a sort of pliant ice. Their flesh crawled. They felt paralyzed. The fog fingered them, but almost instantly passed them by as inferior material for its purpose.

Knives and swords licked out of the fog mass. With never a cry the three police fell, their black tunics glistening with a fluid that showed red only on their sallow slack limbs. The fog mass thickened, as if it had fed instantly and richly on its victims. The four marchers became almost invisible from the outside, though from the inside they saw clearly enough.

Far down the longest and most landward of the five alley-ways, the Mouser saw by the palace-glimmer behind him the white mass coming, shooting questing tendrils before it, and cried gayly, 'Look, Fafhrd, we've company! The fog comes all the twisty way from Hlal to warm its paddy paws at our little fire.'

Fafhrd, frowning his eyes, said mistrustfully, 'I think it masks other guests.'

'Don't be a scareling,' the Mouser reproved him in a fey voice. 'I've a droll thought, Fafhrd: what if it be not fog, but the smoke of all the poppy-gum and hemp-resin in Lankhmar burning at once? What joys we'll have once we are sniffing it! What dreams we'll have tonight!'

'I think it brings nightmares,' Fafhrd asserted softly, rising in a half crouch. Then, 'Mouser, the taint! And my sword tingles to the touch!'

The questingmost of the swiftly-advancing fog tendrils fingered them both then and seized on them joyously, as if here were the two captains it had been seeking, the slave-leadership which would render it invincible.

The two blood-brothers tall and small felt to the full then the intoxication of the fog, its surging bittersweet touchsong of hate, its hot promises of all bloodlusts forever fulfilled, an uninhibited eternity of murder-madness.

Fafhrd, wineless tonight, intoxicated only by his own idealisms and the thought of watchmanship, was hardly touched by the sensations, did not feel them as temptations at all.

The Mouser, much of whose nature was built on hates and envies, had a harder time, but he too in the end rejected the fog's masterful lures – if only, to put the worst interpretation on it, because he wanted always to be the source of his own evil and would never accept it from another, not even as a gift from the archfiend himself.

The fog shrank back a dozen paces then, cat-quick, like a vixenishly proud woman rebuffed, revealing the four marchers in it and simultaneously pointing tendrils straight at the Mouser and Fafhrd.

It was well for the Mouser then that he knew the membership of Lankhmar's underworld to the last semiprofessional murderer and that his intuitions and reflexes were both arrow-swift. He recognized the smallest of the four – Gis with his belt of knives – as also the most immediately dangerous. Without hesitation he whipped Cat's Claw from its sheath, poised, aimed, and threw it. At the same instant Gis, equally know-ledgeable and swift of thought and speedy of reaction, hurled one of his knives.

But the Mouser, forever cautious and wisely fearful, snatched his head to one side the moment he'd made his throw, so that Gis's knife only sliced his ear flap as it hummed past.

Gis, trusting too supremely in his own speed, made no similar evasive movement – with the result that the hilt of Cat's Claw stood out from his right eye socket an instant later. For a long moment he peered with shock and surprise from his other eye, then slumped to the cobbles, his features contorted in the ultimate agony.

Kreshmar and Skel swiftly drew their swords and Gnarlag his two, not one whit intimidated by the winged death that had bitten into their comrade's brain.

Fafhrd, with a fine feeling for tactics on a broad front, did not draw sword at first but snatched up the brazier by one of its three burningly hot short legs and whirled its meager red-glowing contents in the attackers' faces.

This stopped them long enough for the Mouser to draw Scalpel and Fafhrd his heavier cave-forged sword. He wished he could do without the brazier – it was much too hot, but seeing himself opposed to Gnarlag of the Two Swords, he contented himself with shifting it jugglingly to his left hand.

Thereafter the fight was one swift sudden crisis. The three attackers, daunted only a moment by the spray of hot coals and quite uninjured by them, raced forward surefootedly. Four truly-aimed blades thrust at the Mouser and Fafhrd.

The Northerner parried Gnarlag's right-hand sword with the brazier and his left-hand sword with the guard of his own weapon, which he managed simultaneously to thrust through the bravo's neck.

The shock of that death-stroke was so great that Gnarlag's two swords, bypassing Fafhrd one to each side, made no second stroke in their wielder's death-spasm. Fafhrd, conscious now chiefly of an agonizing pain in his left hand, chucked the brazier away in the nearest useful direction – which happened to be at Skel's head, spoiling that one's thrust at the Mouser, who was skipping nimbly back at the moment, though not more swiftly than Kreshmar and Skel were attacking.

The Mouser ducked under Kreshmar's blade and thrust Scalpel *up* through the assassin's ribs – the easy way to the heart – then quickly whipped it out and gave the same measured dose of thin steel to the dazedly staggering Skel. Then he danced away, looking around him dartingly and holding his sword high and menacing.

'All down and dead,' Fafhrd, who'd had longer to look, assured him. 'Ow, Mouser, I've burnt my fingers!'

'And I've a dissected ear,' that one reported, exploring cautiously with little pats. He grinned. 'Just at the edge, though.' Then, having digested Fafhrd's remark, 'Serve you right for fighting with a kitchen boy's weapon!'

Fafhrd retorted, 'Bah! If you weren't such a miser with the charcoal, I'd have blinded them all with my embercast!'

'And burnt your fingers even worse,' the Mouser countered pleasantly. Then, still more happy-voiced, 'Me thought I heard gold chink at the belt of the one you brazier-bashed. Skel . . . yes, alley-basher Skel. When I've recovered Cat's Claw—'

He broke off because of an ugly little sucking sound that ended in a tiny *plop*. In the hazy glow from the nobles' quarter they saw an horridly supernatural sight: the Mouser's bloody dagger poised above Gis's punctured eye socket, supported only by a coiling white tentacle of the fog which had masked their attackers and which had now grown still more dense, as if it had sucked supreme nutriment – as indeed it had – from its dead servitors in their dying.

Eldritch dreads woke in the Mouser and Fafhrd: dreads of the lightning that slays from the storm-cloud, of the giant sea-serpent that strikes from the sea, of the shadows that coalesce in the forest to suffocate the mighty man lost, of the black smoke-snake that comes questing from the wizard's fire to strangle.

All around them was a faint clattering of steel against cobble: other fog tentacles were lifting the four dropped swords and Gis's knife, while yet others were groping at that dead cutthroat's belt for his undrawn weapons.

It was as if some great ghost squid from the depths of the Inner Sea were arming itself for combat.

And four yards above the ground, at the rooting point of the tentacles in the thickened fog, a red disk was forming in the center of the fog's body, as it were – a reddish disk that looked moment by moment more like a single eye large as a face.

There was the inescapable thought that as soon as that eye

could see, some ten beweaponed tentacles would thrust or slash at once, unerringly.

Fafhrd stood terror-bemused between the swiftly-forming eye and the Mouser. The latter, suddenly inspired, gripped Scalpel firmly, readied himself for a dash, and cried to the tall northerner, 'Make a stirrup!'

Guessing the Mouser's stratagem, Fafhrd shook his horrors and laced his fingers together and went into a half crouch. The Mouser raced forward and planted his right foot in the stirrup Fafhrd had made of his hands and kicked off from it just as the latter helped his jump with a great heave – and a simultaneous 'Ow!' of extreme pain.

The Mouser, preceded by his exactly aimed sword, went straight through the reddish ectoplasmic eye disk, dispersing it entirely. Then he vanished from Fafhrd's view as suddenly and completely as if he had been swallowed up by a snow-bank.

An instant later the armed tentacles began to thrust and slash about, at random and erratically, as blind swordsmen might. But since there were a full ten of them, some of the strokes came perilously close to Fafhrd and he had to dodge and duck to keep out of the way. At the rutch of his shoes on the cobbles the tentacle-wielded swords and knives began to aim themselves a little better, again as blind swordsmen might, and he had to dodge more nimbly – not the easiest or safest work for a man so big. A dispassionate observer, if such had been conceivable and available, might have decided the ghost squid was trying to make Fafhrd dance.

Meanwhile on the other side of the white monster, the Mouser had caught sight of the pinkishly silver thread and, leaping high as it lifted to evade him, slashed it with the tip of Scalpel. It offered more resistance to his sword than the whole fog-body had and parted with a most unnatural and unexpected *twang* as he cut it through.

Immediately the fog-body collapsed and far more swiftly than any punctured bladder – rather it fell apart like a giant white puffball kicked by a giant boot – and the tentacles fell to pieces too and the swords and knives came clattering down harmlessly on the cobbles and there was a swift fleeting rush of stench that made both Fafhrd and the Mouser clap hand to nose and mouth.

After sniffing cautiously and finding the air breathable again, the Mouser called brightly, 'Hola there, dear comrade! I think I cut the thing's thin throat, or heart string, or vital nerve, or silver tether, or birth cord, or whatever the strand was.'

'Where did the strand lead back to?' Fafhrd demanded.

'I have no intention of trying to find that out,' the Mouser assured him, gazing warily over his shoulder in the direction from which the fog had come. 'You try threading the Lankhmar labyrinth if you want to. But the strand seems as gone as the thing.'

'Ow!' Fafhrd cried out suddenly and began to flap his hands. 'Oh you small villain, to trick me into making a stirrup of my burnt hands!'

The Mouser grinned as he poked about with his gaze at the nastily slimed cobbles and the dead bodies and the scattered hardware. 'Cat's Claw must be here somewhere,' he muttered, 'and I did hear the chink of gold . . .'

'You'd feel a penny under the tongue of a man you were strangling!' Fafhrd told him angrily.

At the Temple of the Hates, five thousand worshipers began to rise up weakly and groaningly, each lighter of weight by some few ounces than when he had first bowed down. The drummers slumped over their drums, the lantern-crankers over their extinguished red candles, and the lank Archpriest wearily and grimly lowered his head and rested the wooden mask in his clawlike hands.

At the alley-juncture, the Mouser dangled before Fafhrd's face the small purse he had just slipped from Skel's belt.

'My noble comrade, shall we make a betrothal gift of it to sweet Innesgay?' he asked liltingly. 'And rekindle the dear little brazier and end this night as we began it, savoring all the matchless joys of watchmanship and all the manifold wonders of—'

'Give it here, idiot boy!' Fafhrd snarled, snatching the chinking thing for all his burnt fingers. 'I know a place where they've soothing salves – and needles too, to stitch up the notched ears of thieves – and where both the wine and the girls are sharp and clean!'

II: LEAN TIMES IN LANKHMAR

Once upon a time in Lankhmar, City of the Black Toga, in the world of Nehwon, two years after the Year of the Feathered Death, Fafhrd and the Gray Mouser parted their ways.

Exactly what caused the tall brawling barbarian and the slim elusive Prince of Thieves to fall out, and the mighty adventuring partnership to be broken, is uncertainly known and was at the time the subject of much speculation. Some said they had quarreled over a girl. Others maintained, with even greater unlikelihood, that they had disagreed over the proper division of a loot of jewels raped from Muulsh the Moneylender. Srith of the Scrolls suggests that their mutual cooling off was largely the reflection of a supernatural enmity existing at the time between Sheelba of the Eyeless Face, the Mouser's demonic mentor, and Ningauble of the Seven Eyes, Fafhrd's alien and multi-serpentine patron.

The likeliest explanation, which runs directly counter to the Muulsh Hypothesis, is simply that times were hard in Lankhmar, adventures few and uninviting, and that the two heroes had reached that point in life when hard-pressed men desire to admix even the rarest quests and pleasurings with certain prudent activities, leading either to financial or to spiritual security, though seldom if ever to both.

This theory – that boredom and insecurity, and a difference of opinion as to how these dismal feelings might best be dealt with, chiefly underlay the estrangement of the twain . . . this theory may account for and perhaps even subsume the otherwise ridiculous suggestion that the two comrades fell out over the proper spelling of Fafhrd's name, the Mouser perversely favoring a simple Lankhmarian equivalent of 'Faferd' while the name's owner insisted that only the original mouth-filling agglomeration of consonants could continue to satisfy his ear and eye and his semi-literate, barbarous sense of the fitness of things. Bored and insecure men will loose arrows at dust motes.

Certain it is that their friendship, though not utterly fractured, grew very cold and that their life-ways, though both continuing in Lankhmar, diverged remarkably.

The Gray Mouser entered the service of one Pulg, a rising racketeer of small religions, a lord of Lankhmar's dark underworld who levied tribute from the priests of all godlets seeking to become gods – on pain of various unpleasant, disturbing and revolting things happening at future services of the defaulting godlet. If a priest didn't pay Pulg, his miracles were sure to misfire, his congregation and collection would fall off sharply, and it was quite possible that a bruised skin and broken bones would be his lot.

Accompanied by three or four of Pulg's bullies and frequently a slim dancing girl or two, the Mouser became a familiar and newly-ominous sight in Lankhmar's Street of the Gods, which leads from the Marsh Gate to the distant docks and the Citadel. He still wore gray, went close-hooded, and carried Cat's Claw and Scalpel at his side, but the dagger and slim curving sword kept in their sheaths. Knowing from of old that a threat is generally more effective than its execution, he limited his activities to the handling of conversations and cash. 'I speak for Pulg – Pulg with a *guh*!' was his usual opening. Later, if holy men grew recalcitrant or overly keen in their bargaining and it became necessary to maul saintlets and break up services, he would sign the bullies to take these disciplinary measures while he himself stood idly by, generally in slow sardonic converse with the attendant girl or girls and often munching sweetmeats. As the months passed, the Mouser grew fat and the dancing girls successively more child-slim and submissive-eyed.

Fafhrd, on the other hand, broke his longsword across his knee (cutting himself badly in the act), tore from his garments the few remaining ornaments (dull worthless scraps of base metal) and bits of ratty fur, forswore strong drink and all allied pleasures (he had been on small beer and womanless for some time), and became the sole acolyte of Bwadres, the sole priest of Issek of the Jug. Fafhrd let his beard grow until it was as long as his shoulder-brushing hair, he became lean and hollow-cheeked and cavern-eyed, and his voice changed from bass to tenor, though *not* as a result of the distressing mutilation which some whispered he had inflicted upon himself – these last knew he had cut himself but lied wildly as to where.

The gods *in* Lankhmar (that is, the gods and candidates for divinity who dwell or camp, it may be said, in the Imperishable City, not the gods *of* Lankhmar – a very different and most secret and dire matter) . . . the gods *in* Lankhmar sometimes seem as if they must be as numberless as the grains of sand in the Great Eastern Desert. The vast majority of them began as men, or more strictly the memories of men who led ascetic, vision-haunted lives and died painful, messy deaths. One gets the impression that since the beginning of time an unending horde of their priests and apostles (or even the gods themselves, it makes little difference) have been crippling across that same desert, the Sinking Land, and the Great Salt Marsh to converge on Lankhmar's low, heavy-arched Marsh Gate – meanwhile suffering by the way various inevitable tortures, castrations, blindings and stonings, impalements, crucifixions, quarterings and so forth at the hands of eastern brigands and Mingol unbelievers who, one is tempted to think, were created solely for the purpose of seeing to the running of that cruel gantlet. Among the tormented holy throng are a few warlocks and witches seeking infernal immortality for their dark satanic would-be deities and a very few proto-goddesses – generally maidens reputed to have been enslaved for decades by sadistic magicians and ravished by whole tribes of Mingols.

Lankhmar itself and especially the earlier-mentioned street serves as the theatre or more precisely the intellectual and artistic testing-ground of the proto-gods after their more material but no more cruel sifting at the hands of the brigands and Mingols. A new god (his priest or priests, that is) will begin at the Marsh Gate and more or less slowly work his way up the Street of the Gods, renting a temple or preempting a few yards of cobbled pavement here and there, until he has found his proper level. A very few win their way to the region adjoining the Citadel and join the aristocracy of the gods in Lankhmar – transients still, though resident there for centuries and even millennia (the gods *of* Lankhmar are as jealous as they are secret). Far more godlets, it can justly be said, play a one-night-stand near the Marsh Gate and then abruptly disappear, perhaps to seek cities where the audiences are less critical. The majority work their way about halfway up the Street of the Gods and then slowly work their way down again, resisting bitterly every inch and yard, until they once more reach the Marsh Gate and vanish forever from Lankhmar and the memories of men.

Now Issek of the Jug, whom Fafhrd chose to serve, was once of the most lowly and unsuccessful of the gods, godlets rather, in Lankhmar. He had dwelt there for about thirteen years, during which time he had traveled only two squares up the Street of the Gods and was now back again, ready for oblivion. He is not to be confused with Issek the Armless, Issek of the Burnt Legs, Flayed Issek, or any other of the numerous and colorfully mutilated divinities of that name. Indeed, his unpopularity may have been due in part to the fact that the manner of his death – racking – was not deemed particularly spectacular. A few scholars have confused him with Jugged Issek, an entirely different saintlet whose claim to immortality lay in his confinement for seventeen years in a not overly roomy earthenware jar. The Jug (Issek of the Jug's Jug) was supposed to contain Waters of Peace from the Cistern of Cillivat – but none apparently thirsted for them. Indeed, had you sought for a good example of a has-been god who had never really been anything, you could hardly have hit on a better choice than Issek of the Jug, while Bwadres was the very type of the failed priest – sere, senile, apologetic and mumbling. The reason that Fafhrd attached himself to Bwadres, rather than to any one of a vast number of livelier holy men with better prospects, was that he had once seen Bwadres pat a deaf-and-dumb child on the head *while* (so far as Bwadres could have known) *no one was looking* and the incident (possibly unique in Lankhmar) had stuck in the mind of the barbarian.

27

But otherwise Bwadres was a most unexceptional old dodderer.

However, after Fafhrd became his acolyte, things somehow began to change.

In the first place, and even if he had contributed nothing else, Fafhrd made a very impressive one-man congregation from the very first day when he turned up so ragged-looking and bloody (from the cuts breaking his longsword). His near seven-foot height and still warlike carriage stood out mountainously among the old women, children and assorted riff-raff who made up the odorous, noisy, and vastly fickle crowd of worshipers at the Marsh Gate end of the street of the Gods. One could not help thinking that if Issek of the Jug could attract one such worshiper the godlet must have unsuspected virtues. Fafhrd's formidable height, shoulder breadth and bearing had one other advantage: he could maintain claim to a very respectable area of cobbles for Bwardes and Issek merely by stretching himself out to sleep on them after the night's services were over.

It was at this time that oafs and ruffians stopped elbowing Bwadres and spitting on him. Fafhrd was not pacific in his new personality – after all, Issek of the Jug was notably a godlet of peace – but Fafhrd had a fine barbaric feeling for the proprieties. If anyone took liberties with Bwadres or disturbed the various rituals of Issek-worship, he would find himself lifted up and sat down somewhere else, with an admonitory *thud* if that seemed called for – a sort of informal one-stroke bastinado.

Bwadres himself brightened amazingly as a result of this wholly unexpected respite granted him and his divinity on the very brink of oblivion. He began to eat more often than twice a week and to comb his long skimpy beard. Soon his senility dropped away from him like an old cloak, leaving of itself only a mad stubborn gleam deep in his yellowly crust-edged eyes, and he began to preach the gospel of Issek of the Jug with a fervor and confidence that he had never known before.

Meanwhile Fafhrd, in the second place, fairly soon began to contribute more to the promotion of the Issek of the Jug cult than his size, presence, and notable talents as a chucker-out. After two months of self-imposed absolute silence, which he refused to break even to answer the simplest questions of Bwadres, who was at first considerably puzzled by his gigantic convert, Fafhrd procured a small broken lyre, repaired it, and began regularly to chant the Creed and History of Issek of the Jug at all services. He competed in no way with Bwadres, never chanted any of the litanies or presumed to bless in Issek's name; in fact he always kneeled and resumed silence while serving Bwadres as acolyte, but seated on the cobbles at the foot of the service area while Bwadres meditated between rituals at the head, he would strike melodious chords from his tiny lyre and chant away in a rather high-pitched, pleasing, romantically vibrant voice.

Now as a Northerner boy in the Cold Waste, far poleward of Lankhmar across the Inner Sea, the forested Land of the Eight Cities and the Trollstep Mountains, Fafhrd had been trained in the School of the Singing Skalds (so called, although they chanted rather than sang, because they pitched their voices tenor) rather than in the School of the Roaring Skalds (who pitched their voices bass). This resumption of a childhood-inculcated style of elocution, which he also used in answering the few questions his humility would permit him to notice, was the real and sole reason for the change in Fafhrd's voice that was made the subject of gossip by those who had known him as the Gray Mouser's deep-voiced swordmate.

As delivered over and over by Fafhrd, the History of Issek of the Jug gradually altered, by small steps which even Bwadres could hardly cavil at had he wished, into something considerably more like the saga of a Northern hero, though toned down in some respects. Issek had not slain dragons and other monsters as a child – that would have been against his Creed – he had only sported with them, swimming with leviathan, frisking with behemoth, and flying through the trackless spaces of air on the backs of wivern, griffin and hippogryph. Nor had Issek as a man scattered kings and emperors in battle, he had merely dumbfounded them and their quaking ministers by striding about on fields of poisoned

29

sword-points, standing at attention in fiery furnaces, and treading water in tanks of boiling oil – the while delivering majestic sermons on brotherly love in perfect, intricately rhymed stanzas.

Bwadres' Issek had expired quite quickly, though with some kindly parting admonitions, after being disjointed on the rack. Fafhrd's Issek (now *the* Issek) had broken seven racks before he began seriously to weaken. Even when, supposedly dead, he had been loosed and had got his hands on the chief torturer's throat there had been enough strength remaining in them alone so that he had been able to strangle the wicked man with ease, although the latter was a champion of wrestlers among his people. However, Fafhrd's Issek had not done so – again it would have been quite against his Creed – he had merely broken the torturer's thick brass band of office from around his trembling neck and twisted it into an exquisitely beautiful symbol of the Jug before finally permitting his own ghost to escape from him into the eternal realms of spirit, there to continue its wildly wonderful adventurings.

Now, since the vast majority of the gods *in* Lankhmar, arising from the Eastern Lands or at least from the kindredly decadent southern country around Quarmall, had been in their earthly incarnations rather effete types unable to bear more than a few minutes of hanging or a few hours of impalement, and with relatively little resistance to molten lead or showers of barbed darts, also not given overly to composing romantic poetry or to dashing exploits with strange beasts, it is hardly to be wondered that Issek of the Jug, as interpreted by Fafhrd, swiftly won and held the attention and soon thereafter also the devotion of a growing section of the usually unstable, gods-dazzled mob. In particular, the vision of Issek of the Jug rising up with his rack, striding about with it on his back, breaking it, and then calmly waiting with arms voluntarily stretched above his head until another rack could be readied and attached to him . . . that vision, in particular, came to occupy a place of prime importance in the dreams and daydreams of many a porter, beggar, drab scullion, and the brats and aged dependants of such.

As a result of this popularity, Issek of the Jug was soon not only moving up the Street of the Gods for a second time – a rare enough feat in itself – but also moving at a greater velocity than any god had been known to attain in the modern era. Almost every service saw Bwadres and Fafhrd able to move their simple altar a few more yards toward the Citadel end as their swelling congregations overflowed areas temporarily sacred to gods of less drawing power, and frequently late-coming and tireless worshipers enabled them to keep up services until the sky was reddening with the dawn – ten or twelve repetitions of the ritual (and the yardage gain) in one night. Before long the makeup of their congregations had begun to change. Pursed and then fatter-pursed types showed up: mercenaries and merchants, sleek thieves and minor officials, jeweled courtesans and slumming aristocrats, shaven philoso-phers who scoffed lightly at Bwadres' tangled arguments and Issek's irrational Creed but were secretly awed by the apparent sincerity of the ancient man and his giant poetical acolyte . . . and with these monied newcomers came, inevitably, the iron-tough hirelings of Pulg and other such hawks circling over the fowl yards of religion.

Naturally enough, this threatened to pose a considerable problem for the Gray Mouser.

So long as Issek, Bwadres and Fafhrd stayed within hooting range of the Marsh Gate, there was nothing to worry about. There when collection time came and Fafhrd circled the con-gregation with cupped hands, the take, if any, was in the form of moldy crusts, common vegetables past their prime, rags, twigs, bits of charcoal, and – very rarely, giving rise to shouts of wonder – bent and dinted greenish coins of brass. Such truck was below the notice of even lesser racketeers than Pulg, and Fafhrd had no trouble whatever in dealing with the puny and dull-witted types who sought to play Robber King in the Marsh Gate's shadow. More than once the Mouser managed to advise Fafhrd that this was an ideal state of affairs and that any considerable further progress of Issek up the Street of the Gods could lead only to great unpleasantness. The Mouser was nothing if not cautious and most prescient to boot. He liked, or firmly believed he liked, his newly-achieved security almost better than he liked himself. He knew that, as a recent hireling of Pulg, he was still being watched closely by the Great Man and that any appearance of continuing friendship with Fafhrd (for most outsiders thought they had quarreled irrevocably) might some day be counted against him. So on the occasions when he drifted down the Street of the Gods during off-hours – that is, by daylight, for religion is largely a nocturnal, torch-lit business in Lankhmar – he would never seem to speak to Fafhrd directly. Nevertheless he would by seeming accident end up near Fafhrd and, while apparently engaged in some very different private business or pleasure (or perhaps come secretly to gloat over his large enemy's fallen estate – that was the Mouser's second line of defense against conceivable accusations by Pulg) he would manage considerable conversations out of the corner of his mouth, which Fafhrd would answer, if at all, in the same way – though in his case presumably from abstraction rather than policy.

'Look, Fafhrd,' the Mouser said on the third of such occasions, meanwhile pretending to study a skinny-limbed pot-bellied beggar girl, as if trying to decide whether a diet of lean meat and certain calisthenics would bring out in her a rare gaminesque beauty. 'Look, Fafhrd, right here you have what you want, whatever that is – *I* think it's a chance to patch up poetry and squeak it at fools – but whatever it is, you *must* have it here near the Marsh Gate, for the only thing in the world that is not near the Marsh Gate is money, and you tell me you don't want that – the more fool you! – but let me tell you something: if you let Bwadres get any nearer the Citadel, yes even a pebble's toss, you will get money whether you want it or not, and with that money you and Bwadres will buy something, also willy-nilly and no matter how tightly you close your purse and shut your ears to the cries of the hawkers. That thing which you and Bwadres will buy is trouble.'

Fafhrd answered only with a faint grunt that was the equivalent of a shoulder shrug. He was looking steadily down past his bushy beard with almost cross-eyed concentration at something his long fingers were manipulating powerfully yet delicately, but that the large backs of his hands concealed from the Mouser's view.

'How is the old fool, by the by, since he's eating regularly?' the Mouser continued, leaning a hair closer in an effort to see what Fafhrd was handling. 'Still stubborn as ever, eh? Still set on taking Issek to the Citadel? Still as unreasonable about . . . er . . . business matters?'

'Bwadres is a good man,' Fafhrd said quietly.

'More and more that appears to be the heart of the trouble,' the Mouser answered with a certain sardonic exasperation. 'But look, Fafhrd, it's not necessary to change Bwadres' mind – I'm beginning to doubt whether even Sheelba and Ning, working together, could achieve that cosmic revolution. You can do by yourself all that needs to be done. Just give your poetry a little downbeat, add a little defeatism to Issek's Creed – even you must be tired by now of all this ridiculous mating of northern stoicism to southern masochism, and wanting a change. One theme's good as another to a true artist. Or, simpler still, merely refrain from moving Issek's altar up the street on your big night . . . or even move it down a little! – Bwadres gets so excited when you have big crowds that the old fool doesn't know which direction you're going, anyhow. You could progress like the well-frog. Or, wisest of all, merely prepare yourself to split the take before you hand over the collection to Bwadres. I could teach you the necessary legerdemain in the space of one dawn, though you really don't need it – with those huge hands you can palm anything.'

'No,' said Fafhrd.

'Suit yourself,' the Mouser said very very lightly, though not quite unfeelingly. 'Buy trouble if you will, death if you must. Fafhrd, what *is* that thing you're fiddling with? No, don't hand it to me, you idiot! Just let me glimpse it. By the Black Toga! – what *is* that?'

Without looking up or otherwise moving, Fafhrd had cupped his hands sideways, much as if he were displaying in the Mouser's direction a captive butterfly or beetle – and indeed it did seem at first glimpse as if it were a rare large beetle he

33

was cautiously baring to view, one with a carapace of softly burnished gold.

'It is an offering to Issek,' Fafhrd droned. 'An offering made last night by a devout lady who is wed in spirit to the god.'

'Yes, and to half the young aristos of Lankhmar too and not all in spirit,' the Mouser hissed. 'I know one of Lessnya's double-spiral bracelets when I see it. Reputedly given her by the Twin Dukes of Ilthmar, by the by. What did you have to do to her to get it? – stop, don't answer. I know . . . recite poetry! Fafhrd, things are far worse than I dreamed. If Pulg knew you were already getting gold . . .' He let his whisper trail off. 'But what have you *done* with it?'

'Fashioned it into a representation of the Holy Jug,' Fafhrd answered, bowing his head a shade farther and opening his hands a bit wider and tipping them a trifle.

'So I see,' the Mouser hissed. The soft gold had been twisted into a remarkably smooth strange knot. 'And not a bad job at all. Fafhrd, how you keep such a delicate feeling for curves when for six months you've slept without them against you is quite beyond me. Doubtless such things go by opposites. Don't speak for a moment now, I'm getting an idea. And by the Black Scapula! – a good one! Fafhrd, you must give me that trinket so that I may give it to Pulg. No – please hear me out and then think this through! – not for the gold in it, not as a bribe or as part of a first split – I'm not asking that of you or Bwadres – but simply as a keepsake, a presentation piece. Fafhrd, I've been getting to know Pulg lately and I find he has a strange sentimental streak in him – he likes to get little gifts, little trophies, from his . . . er . . . customers, we sometimes call them. These curios must always be items relating to the god in question – chalices, censors, bones in silver filigree, jeweled amulets, that sort of thing. He likes to sit looking at his shelves of them and dream. Sometimes I think the man is getting religion without realizing it. If I should bring him this bauble he would – I know! – develop an affection for Issek. He would tell me to go easy on Bwadres. It would probably even be possible to put off the question of tribute money for . . . well, for three more squares at least.'

'No,' said Fafhrd.

'So be it, my friend. Come with me, my dear, I am going to buy you a steak.' This second remark was in the Mouser's regular speaking voice and directed, of course, at the beggar girl, who reacted with a look of already practiced and rather languorous affright. 'Not a fish steak either, puss. Did you know there were other kinds? Toss this coin to your mother, dear, and come. The steak stall is four squares up. No, we won't take a litter – you need the exercise. *Farewell – Death-seeker!*'

Despite the wash-my-hands-of-you-tone of this last whisper, the Gray Mouser did what he could to put off the evil night of reckoning, devising more pressing tasks for Pulg's bullies and alleging that this or that omen was against the immediate settling of the Bwadres account – for Pulg, alongside his pink streak of sentimentality, had recently taken to sporting a gray one of superstition.

There would have been no insurmountable problem at all, of course, if Bwadres had only had that touch of realism about money matters that, when a true crisis arises, is almost invariably shown by even the fattest, greediest priest or the skinniest, most unworldly holy man. But Bwadres was stubborn – it was probably, as we have hinted, the sole remaining symptom, though a most inconvenient one, of his only seemingly cast-off senility. Not one rusty iron *tik* (the smallest coin of Lankhmar) would he pay to extortioners – such was Bwadres' boast. To make matters worse, if that were possible, he would not even *spend* money renting gaudy furniture or temple space for Issek, as was practically mandatory for gods progressing up the central stretch of the Street. Instead he averred that every tik collected, every bronze agol, every silver smerduk, every gold rilk, yes every diamond-in-amber glulditch! – would be saved to *buy* for Issek the finest temple at the Citadel end, in fact the temple of Aarth the Invisible All-Listener, accounted one of the most ancient and powerful of all the gods *in* Lankhmar.

Naturally, this insane challenge, thrown out for all to hear, had the effect of still further increasing Issek's popularity and swelled his congregations with all sorts of folk who came, at first at least, purely as curiosity seekers. The odds on how far Issek would get up the Street how soon (for they regularly bet on such things in Lankhmar) began to switch wildly up and down as the affair got quite beyond the shrewd but essentially limited imaginations of bookmakers. Bwadres took to sleeping curled in the gutter around Issek's coffer (first an old garlic bag, later a small stout cask with a slit in the top for coins) and with Fafhrd curled around him. Only one of them slept at a time, the other rested but kept watch.

At one point the Mouser almost decided to slit Bwadres' throat as the only possible way out of his dilemma. But he knew that such an act would be the one unforgivable crime against his new profession – it would be *bad for business* – and certain to ruin him forever with Pulg and all other extortioners if ever traced to him even in faintest suspicion. Bwadres must be roughed up if necessary, yes even tortured, but at the same time he must be treated in all ways as a goose who laid golden eggs. Moreover, the Mouser had a presentiment that putting Bwadres out of the way would not stop Issek. Not while Issek had Fafhrd.

What finally brought the affair to a head, or rather to its first head, and forced the Mouser's hand was the inescapable realization that if he held off any longer from putting the bite on Bwadres for Pulg, then rival extortioners – one Basharat in particular – would do it on their own account. As the Number One Racketeer of Religions in Lankhmar, Pulg certainly had first grab, but if he delayed for an unreasonable length of time in making it (no matter on what grounds of omens or arguments about flattening the sacrifice) then Bwadres was anybody's victim – Basharat's in particular, as Pulg's chief rival.

So it came about, as it so often does, that the Mouser's efforts to avert the evil nightfall only made it darker and stormier when it finally came down.

When at last that penultimate evening did arrive, signalized by a final warning sent Pulg by Basharat, the Mouser, who had been hoping all along for some wonderful last-minute inspiration that never came, took what may seem to some a coward's way out. Making use of the beggar girl, whom he had named Lilyblack, and certain other of his creatures, he circulated a rumor that the Treasurer of the Temple of Aarth was preparing to decamp in a rented black sloop across the Inner Sea, taking with him all funds and temple-valuables, including a set of black-pearl-crusted altar furnishings, gift of the wife of the High Overlord, on which the split had not yet been made with Pulg. He timed the rumor so that it would return to him, by unimpeachable channels, just after he had set out for Issek's spot with four well-armed bullies.

It may be noted, in passing, that Aarth's Treasurer actually was in monetary hot waters and really had rented a black sloop. Which proved not only that the Mouser used good sound fabric for his fabrications, but also that Bwadres had by landlords' and bankers' standards made a very sound choice in selecting Issek's temple-to-be – whether by chance or by some strange shrewdness co-dwelling with his senile stubbornness.

The Mouser could not divert his whole expeditionary force, for Bwadres must be saved from Basharat. However, he was able to split it with the almost certain knowledge that Pulg would consider his action the best strategy available at the moment. Three of the bullies he sent on with firm instructions to bring Bwadres to account, while he himself raced off with minimum guard to intercept the supposedly fleeing and loot-encumbered treasurer.

Of course the Mouser *could* have made himself part of the Bwadres-party, but that would have meant he would have had personally to best Fafhrd or he be bested by him, and while the Mouser wanted to do everything possible for his friend he wanted to do just a little bit more than that (he thought) for his own security.

Some, as we have suggested, may think that in taking this way out the Gray Mouser was throwing his friend to the wolves. However, it must always be remembered that the Mouser knew Fafhrd.

The three bullies, who did *not* know Fafhrd (the Mouser had selected them for that reason), were pleased with the turn of events. An independent commission always meant the chance of some brilliant achievement and so perhaps of promotion. They waited for the first break between services, when there was inevitably considerable passing about and jostling. Then one, who had a small ax in his belt, went straight for Bwadres and his cask, which the holy man also used as altar, draping it for the purpose with the sacred garlic bag. Another drew sword and menaced Fafhrd, keeping sound distance from and careful watch on the giant. The third, adopting the jesting, rough-and-ready manner of the master of the show in a bawdy house, spoke ringing warnings to the crowd and kept a reasonably watchful eye on *them*. The folk of Lankhmar are so bound by tradition that it was unthinkable that they would interfere with any activities as legitimate as those of an extortioner – the Number One Extortioner, too – even in defense of a most favored priest, but there are occasional foreigners and madmen to be dealt with (though in Lankhmar even the madmen generally respect the traditions).

No one in the congregation saw the crucial thing that happened next, for their eyes were all on the first bully, who was lightly choking Bwadres with one hand while pointing his ax at the cask with the other. There was a cry of surprise and a clatter. The second bully, lunged forward toward Fafhrd, had dropped his sword and was shaking his hand as if it pained him. Without haste Fafhrd picked him up by the slack of his garments between his shoulder blades, reached the first bully in two giant strides, slapped the ax from his hand, and picked him up likewise.

It was an impressive sight: the giant, gaunt-cheeked, bearded acolyte wearing his long robe of undyed camel's hair (recent gift of a votary) and standing with knees bent and feet wide-planted as he held aloft to either side a squirming bully.

But although indeed a most impressive tableau, it presented a made-to-order opening for the third bully, who instantly unsheathed his scimitar and, with an acrobat's smile and wave to the crowd, lunged toward the apex of the obtuse angle formed by the juncture of Fafhrd's legs.

The crowd shuddered and squealed with the thought of the poignancy of the blow.

There was a muffled *thud*. The third bully dropped *his* sword. Without changing his stance Fafhrd swept together the two bullies he was holding so that their heads met with a loud *thunk*. With an equally measured movement he swept them apart again and sent them sprawling to either side, unconscious, among the onlookers. Then stepping forward, still without seeming haste, he picked up the third bully by neck and crotch and pitched him a considerably greater distance into the crowd, where he bowled over two of Basharat's henchmen who had been watching the proceedings with great interest.

There was absolute silence for three heartbeats, then the crowd applauded rapturously. While the tradition-bound Lankhmarians thought it highly proper for extortioners to extort, they also considered it completely in character for a strange acolyte to work miracles, and they never omitted to clap a good performance.

Bwadres, fingering his throat and still gasping a little, smiled with simple pleasure and when Fafhrd finally acknowledged the applause by dropping down cross-legged to the cobbles and bowing his head, the old priest launched instantly into a sermon in which he further electrified the crowd by several times hinting that, in his celestial realms, *Issek was preparing to visit Lankhmar in person.* His acolyte's routing of the three evil men Bwadres attributed to the inspiration of Issek's might – to be interpreted as a sort of foretaste of the god's approaching reincarnation.

The most significant consequence of this victory of the doves over the hawks was a little midnight conference in the back room of the Inn of the Silver Eel, where Pulg first warmly praised and then coolly castigated the Gray Mouser.

He praised the Mouser for intercepting the Treasurer of Aarth, who it turned out *had* just been embarking on the black sloop, not to flee Lankhmar, though, but only to spend a water-guarded weekend with several riotous companions and one Ilala, High Priestess of the goddess of the same name. However, he *had* actually taken along several of the black-pearl-crusted altar furnishings, apparently as a gift for the High Priestess, and the Mouser very properly confiscated them before wishing the holy band the most exquisite of pleasures on their holiday. Pulg judged that the Mouser's loot amounted to just about twice the usual cut, which seemed a reasonable figure to cover the Treasurer's irregularity.

He rebuked the Mouser for failing to warn the three bullies about Fafhrd and omitting to instruct them in detail on how to deal with the giant.

'They're your boys, son, and I judge you by their performance,' Pulg told the Mouser in fatherly matter-of-fact tones. 'To me, if they stumble, you flop. You know this Northerner well, son; you should have had them trained to meet his sleights. You solved your main problem well, but you slipped on an important detail. I expect good strategy from my lieutenants, but I demand flawless tactics.'

The Mouser bowed his head.

'You and this Northerner were comrades once,' Plug continued. He leaned forward across the dinted table and drew down his lower lip. 'You're not still soft on him, are you, son?'

The Mouser arched his eyebrows, flared his nostrils and slowly swung his face from side to side.

Pulg thoughtfully scratched his nose. 'So we come tomorrow night,' he said. 'Must make an example of Bwadres – an example that will stick like Mingol glue. I'd suggest having Grilli hamstring the Northerner at the first onset. Can't kill him – he's the one that brings in the money. But with ankle tendons cut he could still stump around on his hands and knees and be in some ways an even better drawing card. How's that sound to you?'

The Mouser slitted his eyes in thought for three breaths. Then, 'Bad,' he said boldly. 'It gripes me to admit it, but this Northerner sometimes conjures up battle-sleights that even I can't be sure of countering – crazy berserk tricks born of sudden whim that no civilized man can anticipate. Chances are Grilli could nick him, but what if he didn't? Here's my reed – it lets you rightly think that I may still be soft on the man, but I give it because it's my best reed: let me get him drunk at nightfall. Dead drunk. Then he's out of the way for certain.'

Pulg growled. 'Sure you can deliver on that, son? They say

40

he's forsworn booze. And he sticks to Bwadres like a giant squid.'

'I can detach him,' the Mouser said. 'And this way we don't risk spoiling him for Bwadres' show. Battle's always uncertain. You may plan to hock a man and then have to cut his throat.'

Pulg shook his head. 'We also leave him fit to tangle with our collectors the next time they come for the cash. Can't get him drunk every time we pick up the split. Too complicated. And looks very weak.'

'No need to,' the Mouser said confidently. 'Once Bwadres starts paying, the Northerner will go along.'

Pulg continued to shake his head. 'You're guessing, son,' he said. 'Oh, to the best of your ability, but still guessing. I want this deal bagged up strongly. An example that will stick, I said. Remember, son, the man we're really putting on this show for tomorrow night is Basharat. He'll be there, you can bet on it, though standing in the last row, I imagine – did you hear how your Northerner dumped two of his boys? I liked that.' He grinned widely, then instantly grew serious again. 'So we'll do it my way, eh? Grilli's very sure.'

The Mouser shrugged once, deadpan. 'If you say so. Of course, some Northerners suicide when crippled. I don't think *he* would, but he might. Still, even allowing for that, I'd say your plan has four chances in five of working out perfectly. Four in five.'

Pulg frowned furiously, his rather piggy red-rimmed eyes fixed on the Mouser. Finally he said, '*Sure* you can get him drunk, son? Five in five?' ·

'I can do it,' the Mouser said. He had thought of a half dozen additional arguments in favor of his plan, but he did not utter them. He did not even add, 'Six in six,' as he was tempted to. He was learning.

Plug suddenly leaned back in his chair and laughed, signing that the business part of their conference was over. He tweaked the naked girl standing beside him. 'Wine!' he ordered. 'No, not that sugary slop I keep for customers – didn't Zizzi instruct you? – but the real stuff from behind the green idol.

Come, son, pledge me a cup, and then tell me a little about this Issek. I'm interested in him. I'm interested in 'em all.' He waved loosely at the darkly gleaming shelves of religious curios in the handsomely carved traveling case rising beyond the end of the table. He frowned a very different frown from his business one. 'There are more things in this world than we understand,' he said sententiously. 'Did you know that, son?' The Great Man shook his head, again very differently. He was swiftly sinking into his most deeply metaphysical mood. 'Makes me wonder, sometimes. You and I, son, know that these' – He waved again at the case – 'are toys. But the feelings that men have toward them . . . they're real, eh? – and they can be strange. Easy to understand part of those feelings – brats shivering at bogies, fools gawking at a show and hoping for blood or a bit of undressing – but there's another part that's strange. The priests bray nonsense, the people groan and pray, and then *something* comes into existence. I don't know what that something is – I wish I did, I think – but it's strange.' He shook his head. 'Makes any man wonder. So drink your wine, son – watch his cup, girl, and don't let it empty – and talk to me about Issek. I'm interested in 'em all, but right now I'd like to hear about him.'

He did not in any way hint that for the past two months he had been watching the services of Issek for at least five nights a week from behind a veiled window in various lightless rooms along the Street of the Gods. And that was something that not even the Mouser knew about Pulg.

So as a pinkly opalescent, rose-ribboned dawn surged up the sky from the black and stinking Marsh, the Mouser sought out Fafhrd. Bwadres was still snoring in the gutter, embracing Issek's cask, but the big barbarian was awake and sitting on the curb, hand grasping his chin under his beard. Already a few children had gathered at a respectful distance, though no one else was abroad.

'That the one they can't stab or cut?' the Mouser heard one of the children whisper.

'That's him,' another answered.

42

'I'd like to sneak up behind him and stick him with this pin.'

'I'll bet you would!'

'I guess he's got iron skin,' said a tiny girl with large eyes.

The Mouser smothered a guffaw, patted that last child on the head, and then advanced straight to Fafhrd and, with a grimace at the stained refuse between the cobbles, squatted fastidiously on his hams. He still could do it easily, though his new belly made a considerable pillow in his lap.

He said without preamble, speaking too low for the children to hear, 'Some say the strength of Issek lies in love, some say in honesty, some say in courage, some say in stinking hypocrisy. I believe I have guessed the one true answer. If I am right, you will drink wine with me. If I am wrong, I will strip to my loincloth, declare Issek my god and master, and serve as acolyte's acolyte. Is it a wager?'

Fafhrd studied him. 'It is done,' he said.

The Mouser advanced his right hand and lightly rapped Fafhrd's body twice through the soiled camel's hair – once on the chest, once between the legs.

Each time there was a faint *thud* with just the hint of a *clank*.

'The cuirass of Mingsward and the groin-piece of Gortch,' the Mouser pronounced. 'Each heavily padded to keep them from ringing. Therein lie Issek's strength and invulnerability. They wouldn't have fit you six months ago.'

Fafhrd sat as one bemused. Then his face broke into a large grin. 'You win,' he said. 'When do I pay?'

'This very afternoon,' the Mouser whispered, 'when Bwadres eats and takes his forty winks.' He rose with a light grunt and made off, stepping daintily from cobble to cobble.

Soon the Street of the Gods grew moderately busy and for a while Fafhrd was surrounded by a scattering of the curious, but it was a very hot day for Lankhmar. By midafternoon the Street was deserted, even the children had sought shade. Bwadres droned through the Acolyte's Litany twice with Fafhrd, then called for food by touching his hand to his mouth – it was his ascetic custom always to eat at this uncomfortable time rather than in the cool of the evening.

43

Fafhrd went off and shortly returned with a large bowl of fish stew. Bwadres blinked at the size of it, but tucked it away, belched, and curled around the cask after an admonition to Fafhrd. He was snoring almost immediately.

A hiss sounded from the low wide archway behind them. Fafhrd stood up and quietly moved into the shadows of the portico. The Mouser gripped his arm and guided him toward one of several curtained doorways.

'Your sweat's a flood, my friend,' he said softly. 'Tell me, do you really wear the armor from prudence, or is it a kind of metal hair-shirt?'

Fafhrd did not answer. He blinked at the curtain the Mouser drew aside. 'I don't like this,' he said. 'It's a house of assignation. I may be seen and then what will dirty-minded people think?'

'Hung for the kid, hung for the goat,' the Mouser said lightly. 'Besides, you haven't been seen – yet. In with you!'

Fafhrd complied. The heavy curtains swung to behind them, leaving the room in which they stood lit only by high louvers. As Fafhrd squinted into the semi-darkness, the Mouser said, 'I've paid the evening's rent on this place. It's private, it's near. None will know. What more could you ask?'

'I guess you're right,' Fafhrd said uneasily. 'But you've spent too much rent money. Understand, my little man, I can have only one drink with you. You tricked me into that – after a fashion you did – but I pay. But only one cup of wine, little man. We're friends, but we have our separate paths to tread. So only one cup. Or at most two.'

'Naturally,' purred the Mouser.

The objects in the room grew in the swimming gray blank of Fafhrd's vision. There was an inner door (also curtained), a narrow bed, a basin, a low table and stool, and on the floor beside the stool several portly short-necked large-eared shapes. Fafhrd counted them and once again his face broke into a large grin.

'Hung for a kid, you said,' he rumbled softly in his old bass voice, continuing to eye the stone bottles of vintage. 'I see four kids, Mouser.'

44

The Mouser echoed himself. 'Naturally.'

By the time the candle the Mouser had fetched was guttering in a little pool, Fafhrd was draining the third 'kid.' He held it upended above his head and caught the last drop, then batted it lightly away like a large feather-stuffed ball. As its shards exploded from the floor, he bent over from where he was sitting on the bed, bent so low that his beard brushed the floor, and clasped the last 'kid' with both hands and lifted it with exaggerated care onto the table. Then taking up a very short-bladed knife and keeping his eyes so close to his work that they were inevitably crossed, he picked every last bit of resin out of the neck, flake by tiny flake.

Fafhrd no longer looked at all like an acolyte, even a misbehaving one. After finishing the first 'kid' he had stripped for action. His camel's hair robe was flung into one corner of the room, the pieces of padded armor into another. Wearing only a once-white loincloth, he looked like some lean doomful berserk, or a barbaric king in a bath-house.

For some time no light had been coming through the louvers. Now there was a little – the red glow of torches. The noises of night had started and were on the increase – thin laughter, hawkers' cries, various summonses to prayer . . . and Bwadres calling 'Fafhrd!' again and again in his raspy long-carrying voice. But that last had stopped some time ago.

Fafhrd took so long with the resin, handling it like gold leaf, that the Mouser had to fight down several groans of impatience. But he was smiling his soft smile of victory. He did move once – to light a fresh taper from the expiring one. Fafhrd did not seem to notice the change in illumination. By now, it occurred to the Mouser, his friend was doubtless seeing everything by that brilliant light of spirits of wine which illumines the way of all brave drunkards.

Without any warning the Northerner lifted the short knife high and stabbed it into the center of the cork.

'Die, false Mingol!' he cried, withdrawing the knife with a twist, the cork on its point. 'I drink your blood!' And he lifted the stone bottle to his lips.

After he had gulped about a third of its contents, by the

45

Mouser's calculation, he set it down rather suddenly on the table. His eyeballs rolled upward, all the muscles of his body quivered with the passing of a beatific spasm, and he sank back majestically, like a tree that falls with care. The frail bed creaked ominously but did not collapse under its burden.

Yet this was not quite the end. An anxious crease appeared between Fafhrd's shaggy eyebrows, his head tilted up and his bloodshot eyes peered out menacingly from their eagle's nest of hair, searching the room.

Their gaze finally settled on the last stone bottle. A long rigidly-muscled arm shot out, a great hand shut on the top of the bottle and placed it under the edge of the bed and did not leave it. Then Fafhrd's eyes closed, his head dropped back with finality and, smiling, he began to snore.

The Mouser stood up and came over. He rolled back one of Fafhrd's eyelids, gave a satisfied nod, then gave another after feeling Fafhrd's pulse, which was surging with as slow and strong a rhythm as the breakers of the Outer Sea. Meanwhile the Mouser's other hand, operating with an habitual deftness and artistry unnecessary under the circumstances, abstracted from a fold in Fafhrd's loincloth a gleaming gold object he had earlier glimpsed there. He tucked it away in a secret pocket in the skirt of his gray tunic.

Someone coughed behind him.

It was such a deliberate-sounding cough that the Mouser did not leap or start, but only turned around without changing the planting of his feet in a movement slow and sinuous as that of a ceremonial dancer in the Temple of the Snake.

Pulg was standing in the inner doorway, wearing the black-and-silver striped robe and cowl of a masker and holding a black, jewel-spangled vizard a little aside from his face. He was looking at the Mouser enigmatically.

'I didn't think you could do it, son, but you did,' he said softly. 'You patch your credit with me at a wise time. Ho, Wiggin, Quatch! Ho, Grilli!'

The three henchmen glided into the room behind Pulg, all garbed in garments as somberly gay as their master's. The first two were stocky men, but the third was slim as a weasel

46

and shorter than the Mouser, at whom he glared with guarded and rivalrous venom. The first two were armed with small crossbows and shortswords, but the third had no weapon in view.

'You have the cords, Quatch?' Pulg continued. He pointed at Fafhrd. 'Then bind me this man to the bed. See that you secure well his brawny arms.'

'He's safer unbound,' the Mouser started to say, but Pulg cut in on him with, 'Easy, son. You're still running this job, but I'm going to be looking over your shoulder; yes, and I'm going to be revising your plan as you go along, changing any detail I choose. Good training for you. Any competent lieutenant should be able to operate under the eyes of his general, yes, even when other subordinates are listening in on the reprimands. We'll call it a test.'

The Mouser was alarmed and puzzled. There was something about Pulg's behavior that he did not at all understand. Something discordant, as if a secret struggle were going on inside the master extortioner. He was not obviously drunk, yet his piggy eyes had a strange gleam. He seemed almost fey.

'How have I forfeited your trust?' the Mouser asked sharply.

Pulg grinned skewily. 'Son, I'm ashamed of you,' he said. 'High Priestess Ilala told me the *full* story of the black sloop – how you sublet it from the treasurer in return for allowing him to keep the pearl tiara and stomacher. How you had Ourph the Mingol sail it to another dock. Ilala got mad at the treasurer because he went cold on her or scared and wouldn't give her the black gewgaws. That's why she came to me. To cap it, your Lilyblack spilled the same story to Grilli here, whom she favors. Well, son?'

The Mouser folded his arms and threw back his head. 'You said yourself the split was sufficient,' he told Pulg. 'We can always use another sloop.'

Pulg laughed low and rather long. 'Don't get me wrong, son,' he said at last. 'I *like* my lieutenants to be the sort of men who'd want a bolt-hole handy – I'd suspect their brains if they didn't. I *want* them to be sort of men who worry a lot about their precious skins, but only after worrying about *my* hide first!

47

Don't fret, son. We'll get along – I think. Quatch! Is he bound yet?'

The two burlier henchmen, who had hooked their crossbows to their belts, were well along with their job. Tight loops of rope at chest, waist and knees bound Fafhrd to the bed, while his wrists had been drawn up level with the top of his head and tightly laced to the sides of the bed. Fafhrd still snored peacefully on his back. He had stirred a little and groaned when his hand had been drawn away from the bottle under the bed, but that was all. Wiggin was preparing to bind the Northerner's ankles, but Pulg signed it was enough.

'Gilli!' Pulg called. 'Your razor!'

The weasel-like henchman seemed merely to wave his hand past his chest and – lo! – there was a gleaming square-headed blade in it. He smiled as he moved toward Fafhrd's naked ankles. He caressed the thick tendons under them and looked pleadingly at Pulg.

Pulg was watching the Mouser narrowly.

The Mouser felt an unbearable tension stiffening him. He must do something! He raised the back of his hand to his mouth and yawned.

Pulg pointed at Fafhrd's other end. 'Grilli,' he repeated, 'shave me this man! Debeard and demane him! Shave him like an egg!' Then he leaned toward the Mouser and said in a sort of slack-mouthed confidential way, 'I've heard of these barbs that it draws their strength. Think you so? No matter, we'll see.'

Slashing of a lusty man's head-and-face hair and then shaving him close takes considerable time, even when the barber is as shudderingly swift as Grilli and as heedless of the dim and flickering light. Time enough for the Mouser to assess the situation seventeen different ways and still not find its ultimate key. One thing shone through from every angle: the irrationality of Pulg's behaviour. Spilling secrets . . . accusing a lieutenant in front of henchmen . . . proposing an idiot 'test' . . . wearing grotesque holiday clothes . . . binding a man dead drunk . . . and now this superstitious nonsense of shaving Fafhrd – why, it was as if Pulg were fey indeed and performing some eerie ritual under the demented guise of shrewd tactics.

And there was one thing the Mouser was certain of: that when Pulg got through being fey or drugged or whatever it was, he would never again trust any of the men who had been through the experience with him, including – most particularly! – the Mouser. It was a sad conclusion – to admit that his hard-bought security was now worthless – yet it was a realistic one and the Mouser perforce came to it. So even while he continued to puzzle, the small man in gray congratulated himself on having bargained himself so disastrously into possession of the black sloop. A bolt-hole might soon be handy indeed, and he doubted whether Pulg had discovered where Ourph had concealed the craft. Meanwhile he must expect treachery from Pulg at any step and death from Pulg's henchmen at their master's unpredictable whim. So the Mouser decided that the less *they* (Grilli in particular) were in a position to do the Mouser or anyone else damage, the better.

Pulg was laughing again. 'Why, he looks like a new-hatched babe!' the master extortioner exclaimed. 'Good work, Grilli!'

Fafhrd did indeed look startlingly youthful without any hair above that on his chest, and in a way far more like what most people think an acolyte should look. He might even have appeared romantically handsome except that Grilli, in perhaps an excess of zeal, had also shorn naked his eyebrows – which had the effect of making Fafhrd's head, very pale under the vanished hair, seem like a marble bust set atop a living body.

Pulg continued to chuckle. 'And no spot of blood – no, not one! That is the best of omens! Grilli, I love you!'

That was true enough too – in spite of his demonic speed, Grilli had not once nicked Fafhrd's face or head. Doubtless a man thwarted of the opportunity to hamstring another would scorn any lesser cutting – indeed, consider it a blot on his own character. Or so the Mouser guessed.

Gazing at his shorn friend, the Mouser felt almost inclined to laugh himself. Yet this impulse – and along with it his lively fear for his own and Fafhrd's safety – was momentarily swallowed up in the feeling that something about this whole business was very *wrong* – wrong not only by any ordinary

49

standards, but also in a deeply occult sense. This stripping of Fafhrd, this shaving of him, this binding of him to the rickety narrow bed . . . wrong, wrong, wrong! Once again it occurred to him, more strongly this time, that Pulg was unknowingly performing an eldritch ritual.

'Hist!' Pulg cried, raising a finger. The Mouser obediently listened along with the three henchmen and their master. The ordinary noises outside had diminished, for a moment almost ceased. Then through the curtained doorway and the red-lit louvers came the raspy high voice of Bwadres beginning the Long Litany and the mumbling sigh of the crowd's response.

Pulg clapped the Mouser hard on the shoulder. 'He is about it! 'Tis time!' he cried. 'Command us! We will see, son, how well you have planned. Remember, I will be watching over your shoulder and that it is my desire that you strike at the end of Bwadres' sermon when the collection is taken.' He frowned at Grilli, Wiggin and Quatch. 'Obey this, my lieutenant!' he warned sternly. 'Jump at his least command! – save when I countermand. Come on, son, hurry it up, start giving orders!'

The Mouser would have liked to punch Pulg in the middle of the jeweled vizard which the extortioner was just now again lifting to his face – punch his fat nose and fly this madhouse of commanded commandings. But there was Fafhrd to be considered – stripped, shaved, bound, dead drunk, immeasurably helpless. The Mouser contented himself with starting through the outer door and motioning the henchmen and Pulg too to follow him. Hardly to his surprise – for it was difficult to decide *what* behavior would have been surprising under the circumstances – they obeyed him.

He signed Grilli to hold the curtain aside for the others. Glancing back over the smaller man's shoulder, he saw Quatch, last to leave, dip to blow out the taper and under cover of that movement snag the two-thirds full bottle of wine from under the edge of the bed and lug it along with him. And for some reason that innocently thievish act struck the Mouser as being the most occultly wrong thing of all the supernally off-key events that had been occurring recently. He wished there were some god in whom he had real trust so that he could pray to him for enlightenment and guidance in the ocean of inexplicably strange intuitions engulfing him. But unfortunately for the Mouser there was no such divinity. So there was nothing for it but to plunge all by himself into that strange ocean and take his chances – do without calculation whatever the inspiration of the moment moved him to do.

So while Bwadres keened and rasped through the Long Litany against the sighing responses of the crowd (and an uncommonly large number of cat-calls and boos), the Mouser was very busy indeed, helping prepare the setting and place the characters for a drama of which he did not know more than scraps of the plot. The many shadows were his friends in this – he could slip almost invisibly from one shielding darkness to another – and he had the trays of half the hawkers in Lankhmar as a source of stage properties.

Among other things, he insisted on personally inspecting the weapons of Quatch and Wiggin – the shortswords and their sheaths, the small crossbows and the quivers of tiny quarrels that were their ammunition – most wicked-looking short arrows. By the time the Long Litany had reached its wailing conclusion, the stage was set, though exactly when and where and how the curtain would rise – and who would be the audience and who the players – remained uncertain.

At all events it was an impressive scene: the long Street of Gods stretching off toward a colorful torchlit dolls' world of distance in either direction, low clouds racing overhead, faint ribbons of mist gliding in from the Great Salt Marsh, the rumble of far distant thunder, bleat and growl of priests of gods other than Issek, squealing laughter of women and children, leather-lunged calling of hawkers and news-slaves, odor of incense curling from temples mingling with the oily aroma of fried foods on hawkers' trays, the reek of smoking torches, and the musk and flower smells of gaudy ladies.

Issek's audience, augmented by the many drawn by the tale of last night's doings of the demon acolyte and the wild predictions of Bwadres, blocked the Street from curb to curb, leaving only difficult gangway through the roofed porticos to either side. All levels of Lankhmarian society were represented

– rags and ermine, bare feet and jeweled sandals, mercenaries' steel and philosophers' wands, faces painted with rare cosmetics and faces powdered only with dust, eyes of hunger, eyes of satiety, eyes of mad belief and eyes of a skepticism that hid fear.

Bwadres, panting a little after the Long Litany, stood on the curb across the Street from the low archway of the house where the drunken Fafhrd slept bound. His shaking hand rested on the cask that, draped now with the garlic bag, was both Issek's coffer and altar. Crowded so close as to leave him almost no striding space were the inner circles of the congregation – devotees sitting cross-legged, crouched on knees, or squatting on hams.

The Mouser had stationed Wiggin and Quatch by an overset fishmonger's cart in the center of the Street. They passed back and forth the stone bottle Quatch had snared, doubtless in part to make their odorous post more bearable, though every time the Mouser noted their bibbing he had a return of the feeling of occult wrongness.

Pulg had picked for his post a side of the low archway in front of Fafhrd's house, to call it that. He kept Grilli beside him, while Mouser crouched nearby after his preparations were complete. Pulg's jeweled mask was hardly exceptional in the setting; several women were vizarded and a few of the other men – colorful blank spots in the sea of faces.

It was certainly not a calm sea. Not a few of the audience seemed greatly annoyed at the absence of the giant acolyte (and had been responsible for the boos and cat-calls during the Litany). While even the regulars missed the acolyte's lute and his sweet tenor tale-telling and were exchanging anxious questions and speculations. All it took was someone to shout, 'Where's the acolyte?' and in a few moments half the audience was chanting, 'We want the acolyte! We want the acolyte!'

Bwadres silenced them by looking earnestly up the Street with shaded eyes, pretending he saw one coming, and then suddenly pointing dramatically in that direction, as if to signal the approach of the man for whom they were calling. While the crowd craned their necks and shoved about, trying to see what

Bwadres was pretending to – and incidentally left off chanting – the ancient priest launched into his sermon.

'I will tell you what has happened to my acolyte!' he cried. 'Lankhmar has swallowed him. Lankhmar has gobbled him up – Lankhmar the evil city, the city of drunkenness and lechery and all corruption – Lankhmar, the city of the stinking black bones!'

This last blasphemous reference to the gods *of* Lankhmar (whom it can be death to mention, though the gods *in* Lankhmar may be insulted without limit) further shocked the crowd into silence.

Bwadres raised his hands and face to the low racing clouds.

'Oh, Issek, compassionate mighty Issek, pity thy humble servitor who now stands friendless and alone. I had one acolyte, strong in thy defense, but they took him from me. You told him, Issek, much of your life and your secrets, he had ears to hear it and lips to sing it, but now the black devils have got him! Oh, Issek, have pity!'

Bwadres spread his hands toward the mob and looked them around.

'Issek was a young god when he walked the earth, a young god speaking only of love, yet they bound him to the rack of torture. He brought Waters of Peace for all in his Holy Jug, but they broke it.' And here Bwadres described at great length and with far more vividness than his usual wont (perhaps he felt he had to make up for the absence of his skald-turned-acolyte) the life and especially the torments and death of Issek of the Jug, until there was hardly one among the listeners who did not have vividly in mind the vision of Issek on his rack (succession of racks, rather) and who did not feel at least sympathetic twinges in his joints at the thought of the god's suffering.

Women and strong men wept unashamedly, beggars and scullions howled, philosophers covered their ears.

Bwadres wailed on toward a shuddering climax. 'As you yielded up your precious ghost on the eighth rack, oh, Issek, as your broken hands fashioned even your torturer's collar into a Jug of surpassing beauty, you thought only of us, oh, Holy Youth. You thought only of making beautiful the lives of the most tormented and deformed of us, thy miserable slaves.'

At those words Pulg took several staggering steps forward from the side of the archway, dragging Grilli with him, and dropped to his knees on the filthy cobbles. His black-and-silver striped cowl fell back on his shoulders and his jeweled black vizard slipped from his face, which was thus revealed as unashamedly coursing with tears.

'I renounce all other gods,' the boss extortioner gasped between sobs. 'Hereafter I serve only gentle Issek of the Jug.'

The weasely Grilli, crouching contortedly in his efforts to avoid being smirched by the nasty pavement, gazed at his master as to one demented, yet could not or still dared not break Pulg's hold on his wrist.

Pulg's action attracted no particular attention – conversions were a smerduck a score at the moment – but the Mouser took note of it, especially since Pulg's advance had brought him so close that the Mouser could have reached out and patted Pulg's bald pate. The small man in gray felt a certain satisfaction or rather relief – if Pulg had for some time been a secret Issek-worshiper, then his feyness might be explained. At the same time a gust of emotion akin to pity went through him. Looking down at his left hand the Mouser discovered that he had taken out of its secret pocket the gold bauble he had filched from Fafhrd. He was tempted to put it softly in Pulg's palm. How fitting, how soul-shaking, how *nice* it would be, he thought, if at the moment the floodgates of religious emotion burst in him, Pulg were to receive this truly beautiful memento of the god of his choice. But gold is gold, and a black sloop requires as much upkeep as any other color yacht, so the Mouser resisted the temptation.

Bwadres threw wide his hands and continued, 'With dry throats, oh, Issek, we thirst for thy Waters. With gullets burning and cracked, thy slaves beg for a single sip from thy Jug. We would ransom our souls for one drop of it to cool us in this evil city, damned by black bones. Oh, Issek, descend to us! Bring us thy Waters of Peace! We need you, we want you. Oh, Issek, come!'

Such was the power and yearning in that last appeal that the whole crowd of kneeling worshipers gradually took it up, chanting with all reverence, louder and louder, in an unendingly repeated, self-hypnotizing response: 'We want Issek! We want Issek!'

It was that mighty rhythmic shouting which finally penetrated to the small conscious core of Fafhrd's wine-deadened brain where he lay drunk in the dark, though Bwadres' remarks about dry throats and burning gullets and healing drops and sips may have opened the way. At any rate, Fafhrd came suddenly and shudderingly awake with the one thought in his mind: another drink – and the one sure memory: that there was some wine left.

It disturbed him a little that his hand was not still on the stone bottle under the edge of the bed, but for some dubious reason up near his ear.

He reached for the bottle and was outraged to find that he could not move his arm. Something or someone was holding it.

Wasting no time on petty measures, the large barbarian rolled his whole body over mightily, with the idea of at once wrenching free from whatever was holding him and getting under the bed where the wine was.

He succeeded in tipping the bed on its side and himself with it. But *that* didn't bother him, it didn't shake up his numb body at all. What *did* bother him was that he couldn't sense any wine nearby – smell it, see it squintily, bump his head into it . . . certainly not the quart or more he remembered having safeguarded for just such an emergency as this.

At about the same time he became dimly aware that he was somehow *attached* to whatever he'd been sleeping on – especially his wrists and shoulders and chest.

However, his legs seemed reasonably free, though somewhat hampered at the knees, and since the bed happened to have fallen partly on the low table and with its head braced against the wall, the blind twist-and-heave he gave now actually brought him to his feet and the bed with him.

He squinted around. The curtained outer doorway was an oblong of lesser darkness. He immediately headed for it. The

55

bed foiled his first efforts to get through, bringing him up short in a most exasperating manner, but by ducking and by turning edgewise he finally managed it, pushing the curtain ahead of him with his face. He wondered muddily if he were paralyzed, the wine he'd drunk all gone into his arms, or if some warlock had put a spell on him. It was certainly degrading to have to go about with one's wrists up about one's ears. Also his head and cheeks and chin felt unaccountably chilly – possibly another evidence of black magic.

The curtain dragged off of his head finally and he saw ahead of him a rather low archway and – vaguely and without being at all impressed by them – crowds of people kneeling and swaying.

Ducking down again, he lumbered through the archway and straightened up. Torchlight almost blinded him. He stopped and stood there blinking. After a bit his vision cleared a little and the first person he saw that meant anything to him was the Gray Mouser.

He remembered now that the last person he had been drinking with was the Mouser. By the same token – in this matter Fafhrd's maggoty mind worked very fast indeed – the Mouser must be the person who had made away with his quart or more of midnight medicine. A great righteous anger flamed in him and he took a very deep breath.

So much for Fafhrd and what *he* saw.

What the *crowd* saw – the god-intoxicated, chanting, weeping crowd – was very different indeed.

They saw a man of divine stature strapped with hands high to a framework of some sort. A mightily muscled man, naked save for a loincloth, with a shorn head and face that, marble white, looked startlingly youthful. Yet with the expression on that marble face of one who is being tortured.

And if anything else were needed (truly, it hardly was) to convince them that here was the god, the divine Issek, they had summoned with their passionately insistent cries, then it was supplied when that nearly seven-foot-tall apparition called out in a deep voice of thunder:

'*Where is the jug*? WHERE IS THE JUG?'

The few people in the crowd who were still standing dropped instantly to their knees at that point or prostrated themselves. Those kneeling in the opposite direction switched around like startled crabs. Two score persons, including Bwadres, fainted, and of these the hearts of five stopped beating forever. At least a dozen individuals went permanently mad, though at the moment they seemed no different from the rest – including (among the twelve) seven philosophers and a niece of Lankhmar's High Overlord. As one, the members of the mob abased themselves in terror and ecstasy – groveling, writhing, beating breasts or temples, clapping hands to eyes and peering fearfully through hardly parted fingers as if at an unbearably bright light.

It may be objected that at least a few of the mob should have recognized the figure before them as that of Bwadres' giant acolyte. After all, the height was right. But consider the differences: The acolyte was full-bearded and shaggy-maned; the apparition was beardless and bald – and strangely so, lacking even eyebrows. The acolyte had always gone robed; the apparition was nearly naked. The acolyte had always used a sweetly high voice; the apparition roared harshly in a voice almost two octaves lower.

Finally, the apparition was bound – to a torture rack, surely – and calling in the voice of one being tortured for his Jug.

As one, the members of the mob abased themselves.

With the exception of the Gray Mouser, Grilli, Wiggin, and Quatch. They knew well enough who faced them. (Pulg knew too, of course, but he, most subtle-brained in some ways and now firmly converted to Issekianity, merely assumed that Issek had chosen to manifest himself in the body of Fafhrd and that he, Pulg, had been divinely guided to prepare that body for the purpose. He humbly swelled with the full realization of the importance of his own position in the scheme of Issek's reincarnation.)

His three henchmen, however, were quite untouched by religious emotions. Grilli for the moment could do nothing as Pulg was still holding his wrist in a grip of fervid strength.

But Wiggin and Quatch were free. Although somewhat dull-brained and little used to acting on their own initiative, they were not long in realizing that the giant had appeared who was supposed to be kept out of the way so that he would not queer the game of their strangely-behaving master and his tricky gray-clad lieutenant. Moreover, they well knew what jug Fafhrd was shouting for so angrily, and since they also knew they had stolen and drunken it empty, they likely also were moved by guilty fears that Fafhrd might soon see them, break loose, and visit vengeance upon them.

They cranked up their crossbows with furious haste, slapped in quarrels, knelt, aimed, and discharged the bolts straight at Fafhrd's naked chest. Several persons in the mob noted their action and shrieked at its wickedness.

The two bolts struck Fafhrd's chest, bounced off, and dropped to the cobbles – quite naturally enough, as they were two of the fowling quarrels (headed merely with little knobs of wood and used for knocking down small birds) with which the Mouser had topped off their quivers.

The crowd gasped at Issek's invulnerability and cried for joy and amazement.

However, although fowling quarrels will hardly break a man's skin, even when discharged at close range, they nevertheless sting mightily even the rather numb body of a man who has recently drunk numerous quarts of wine. Fafhrd roared in agony, punched out his arms convulsively, *and broke the framework to which he was attached.*

The crowd cheered hysterically at this further proper action in the drama of Issek which his acolyte had so often chanted.

Quatch and Wiggin, realizing that their missile weapons had somehow been rendered innocuous, but too dull-witted or wine-fuddled to see anything either occult or suspicious in the manner of that rendering, grabbed at their shortswords and rushed forward at Fafhrd to cut him down before he could finish detaching himself from the fragments of the broken bed which he was now trying to do in a puzzled way.

Yes, Quatch and Wiggin rushed forward, but almost immediately came to a halt – in the very strange posture of men who are trying to lift themselves into the air by heaving at their own belts.

The shortswords would not come out of their scabbards. Mingol glue is indeed a powerful adhesive and the Mouser had been most determined that, however little else he accomplished, Pulg's henchmen should be put in a position where they could harm no one.

However, he had been able to do nothing in the way of pulling Grilli's fangs, as the tiny man was most sharp-witted himself and Pulg had kept him closely at his side. Now almost foaming at the mouth in vulpine rage and disgust, Grilli broke loose from his god-besotted master, whisked out his razor, and sprang at Fafhrd, who at last had clearly realized what was encumbering him and was having a fine time breaking the last pesky fragments of the bed over his knee or by the leverage of foot against cobble – to the accompaniment of the continuing wild cheers of the mob.

But the Mouser sprang rather more swiftly. Grilli saw him coming, shifted his attack to the gray-clad man, feinted twice and loosed one slash that narrowly missed. Thereafter he lost blood too quickly to be interested in attempting any further fencing. Cat's Claw is narrow but it cuts throats as well as any other dagger (though it does not have a sharply curved or barbed tip, as some literal-minded scholars have claimed).

The bout with Grilli left the Mouser standing very close to Fafhrd. The little man realized he still held in his left hand the golden representation of the Jug fashioned by Fafhrd, and that object now touched off in the Mouser's mind a series of inspirations leading to actions that followed one another very much like the successive figures of a dance.

He slapped Fafhrd back-handed on the cheek to attract the giant's attention. Then he sprang to Pulg, sweeping his left hand in a dramatic arc as if conveying something from the naked god to the extortioner, and lightly placed the golden bauble in the supplicating fingers of the latter. (One of those times had come when all ordinary scales of value fail – even

59

for the Mouser – and gold is – however briefly – of no worth.)
Recognizing the holy object, Pulg almost expired in ecstacy.

But the Mouser had already skipped on across the Street.
Reaching Issek's coffer-altar, beside which Bwadres was
stretched unconscious but smiling, he twitched off the garlic
bag and sprang upon the small cask and danced upon it, hooting
to further attract Fafhrd's attention and then pointing at his
own feet.

Fafhrd saw the cask, all right, as the Mouser had intended
he should, and the giant did not see it as anything to do with
Issek's collections (the thought of all such matters was still
wiped from his mind) but simply as a likely source of the liquor
he craved. With a glad cry he hastened toward it across the
Street, his worshipers scuttling out of his way or moaning in
beatific ecstacy when he trod on them with his naked feet. He
caught up the cask and lifted it to his lips.

To the crowd it seemed that Issek was drinking his own
coffer – an unusual yet undeniably picturesque way for a god
to absorb his worshipers' cask offerings.

With a roar of baffled disgust Fafhrd raised the cask to
smash it on the cobbles, whether from pure frustration or with
some idea of getting at the liquor he thought it held is hard to
say, but just then the Mouser caught his attention again. The
small man had snatched two tankards of ale from an abandoned
tray and was pouring the heady liquid back and forth between
them until the high-piled foam trailed down the sides.

Tucking the cask under his left arm – for many drunkards
have a curious prudent habit of absentmindedly hanging onto
things, especially if they may contain liquor – Fafhrd set out
again after the Mouser, who ducked into the darkness of the
nearest portico and then danced out again and led Fafhrd in
a great circle all the way around the roiling congregation.

Literally viewed it was hardly an edifying spectacle – a large
god stumbling after a small gray demon and grasping at a
tankard of beer that just kept eluding him – but the
Lankhmarians were already viewing it under the guise of
two dozen different allegories and symbolisms, several of which
were later written up in learned scrolls.

The second time through the portico Issek and the small gray demon did not come out again. A large chorus of mixed voices kept up expectant and fearful cries for some time, but the two supernatural beings did not reappear.

Lankhmar is full of mazy alleyways and this stretch of the Street of the Gods is particularly rich in them, some of them leading by dark and circuitous routes to localities as distant as the docks.

But the Issekians – old-timers and new converts alike – largely did not even consider such mundane avenues in analyzing their god's disappearance. Gods have their own doorways into and out of space and time and it is their nature to vanish suddenly and inexplicably. Brief reappearances are all we can hope for from a god whose chief life-drama on earth has already been played, and indeed it might prove uncomfortable if he hung around very long, protracting a Second Coming – too great a strain on everybody's nerves for one thing.

The large crowd of those who had been granted the vision of Issek was slow in dispersing, as might well have been expected – they had much to tell each other, much about which to speculate and, inevitably, to argue.

The blasphemous attack of Quatch and Wiggin on the god was belatedly recalled and avenged, though some already viewed the incident as part of a general allegory. The two bullies were lucky to escape with their lives after an extensive mauling.

Grilli's corpse was unceremoniously picked up and tossed in next morning's Death Cart. End of *his* story.

Bwadres came out of his faint with Pulg bending solicitously over him – and it was largely these two persons who shaped the subsequent history of Issekianity.

To make a long or, rather, complex story simple and short, Pulg became what can best be described as Issek's grand vizier and worked tirelessly for Issek's greater glory – always wearing on his chest the god-created golden emblem of the Jug as the sign of his office. He did not upon his conversion to the gentle god give up his old profession, as some moralists might expect, but carried it on with even greater zeal than before, extorting mercilessly from the priests of all gods other than Issek and grinding them down. At the height of its success, Issekianity boasted five large temples in Lankhmar, numerous minor shrines in the same city, and a swelling priesthood under the nominal leadership of Bwadres, who was lapsing once more into general senility.

Issekianity flourished for exactly three years under Pulg's viziership. But when it became known (due to some incautious babblings of Bwadres) that Pulg was not only conducting under the guise of extortion a holy war on all other gods *in* Lankhmar, with the ultimate aim of driving them from the city and if possible from the world, but that he even entertained murky designs of overthrowing the gods *of* Lankhmar or at least forcing them to recognize Issek's overlordship . . . when all this became apparent, the doom of Issekianity was sealed. On the third anniversary of Issek's Second Coming, the night descended ominous and thickly foggy, the sort of night when all wise Lankhmarians hug their indoor fires. About midnight awful screams and piteous howlings were heard throughout the city, along with the rending of thick doors and the breaking of heavy masonry – preceded and followed, some tremulously maintained, by the clicking tread of bones on the march. One youth who peered out through an attic window lived long enough before he expired in gibbering madness to report that he had seen striding through the streets a multitude of black-togaed figures, sooty of hand, foot and feature and skeletally lean.

Next morning the five temples of Issek were empty and defiled and his minor shrines all thrown down, while his numerous clergy, including his ancient high priest and over-weeningly ambitious grand vizier, had vanished to the last member and were gone beyond human ken.

Turning back to a dawn exactly three years earlier we find the Gray Mouser and Fafhrd clambering from a cranky, leaky skiff into the cockpit of a black sloop moored beyond the Great Mole that juts out from Lankhmar and the east bank of the

River Hlal into the Inner Sea. Before coming aboard, Fafhrd first handed up Issek's cask to the impassive and sallow-faced Ourph and then with considerable satisfaction pushed the skiff wholly under water.

The cross-city run the Mouser had led him, followed by a brisk spell of galley-slave work at the oars of the skiff (for which he indeed looked the part in his lean near-nakedness) had quite cleared Fafhrd's head of the fumes of wine, though it now ached villainously. The Mouser still looked a bit sick from his share in the running – he was truly in woefully bad trim from his months of lazy gluttony.

Nevertheless the twain joined with Ourph in the work of upping anchor and making sail. Soon a salty, coldly refreshing wind on their starboard beam was driving them directly away from the land and Lankhmar. Then while Ourph fussed over Fafhrd and bundled a thick cloak about him, the Mouser turned quickly in the morning dusk to Issek's cask, determined to get at the loot before Fafhrd had opportunity to develop any silly religious or Northernly-noble qualms and perhaps toss the cask overboard.

The Mouser's fingers did not find the coin-slit in the top – it was still quite dark – so he upended the pleasantly heavy object, crammed so full it did not even jingle. No coin-slit in that end either, seemingly, though there was what looked like a burned inscription in Lankhmarian hieroglyphs. But it was still too dark for easy reading and Fafhrd was coming up behind him, so the Mouser hurriedly raised the heavy hatchet he had taken from the sloop's tool rack and bashed in a section of wood.

There was a spray of stingingly aromatic fluid of most familiar odor. *The cask was filled with brandy – to the absolute top, so that it had not gurgled.*

A little later they were able to read the burnt inscription. It was most succinct: 'Dear Pulg – Drown your sorrows in this – Basharat.'

It was only too easy to realize how yesterday afternoon the Number Two Extortioner had had a perfect opportunity to effect the substitution – the Street of the Gods deserted, Bwadres almost druggedly asleep from the unaccustomedly large fish dinner, Fafhrd gone from his post to guzzle with the Mouser.

'That explains why Basharat was not on hand last night,' the Mouser said thoughtfully.

Fafhrd was for throwing the cask overboard, not from any disappointment at losing loot, but because of a revulsion at its contents, but the Mouser set aside the cask for Ourph to close and store away – he knew that such revulsions pass. Fafhrd, however, extorted the promise that the fiery fluid only be used in direst emergency – as for burning enemy ships.

The red dome of the sun pushed above the eastern waves. By its ruddy light Fafhrd and the Mouser really looked at each other for the first time in months. The wide sea was around them, Ourph had taken the lines and tiller, and at last nothing pressed. There was an odd shyness in both their gazes – each had the sudden thought that he had taken his friend away from the life-path he had chosen in Lankhmar, perhaps the life-path best suited to his treading.

'Your eyebrows will grow back – I suppose,' the Mouser said at last, quite inanely.

'They will indeed,' Fafhrd rumbled. 'I'll have a fine shock of hair by the time you've worked off that belly.'

'Thank you, Egg-Top,' the Mouser replied. Then he gave a small laugh. 'I have no regrets for Lankhmar,' he said, lying mightily, though not entirely. 'I can see now that if I'd stayed I'd have gone the way of Pulg and all such Great Men – fat, power-racked, lieutenant-plagued, smothered with false-hearted dancing girls, and finally falling into the arms of religion. At least I'm saved that last chronic ailment, which is worse than the dropsy.' He looked at Fafhrd narrowly. 'But how of you, old friend? Will you miss Bwadres and your cobbled bed and your nightly tale-weaving?'

Fafhrd frowned as the sloop plunged on northward and the salt spray dashed him.

'Not I,' he said at last. 'There are always other tales to be woven. I served a god well, I dressed him in new clothes, and then I did a third thing. Who'd go back to being an acolyte after being so much more? You see, old friend, I really *was* Issek.'

The Mouser arched his eyebrows. 'You were?'

Fafhrd nodded twice, most gravely.

III: THEIR MISTRESS, THE SEA

The next few days were not kind to the Mouser and Fafhrd. To begin with, both got seasick from their many months ashore. Between gargantuan groaning retches, Fafhrd monotonously berated the Mouser for having tricked him out of asceticism and stolen from him his religious vocation. While in the intervals of his vomiting, the Gray Mouser cursed Fafhrd back, but chiefly excoriated himself for having been such a fool as to give up the soft life in Lankhmar for sake of a friend.

During this period – brief in reality, an eternity to the sufferers – Ourph the Mingol managed sails and tiller. His impassive, wrinkle-netted face forever threatened to break into a grin, yet never did, though from time to time his jet eyes twinkled.

Fafhrd, first to recover, took back command from Ourph and immediately started ordering an endless series of seaman-like exercises: reefings, furlings, raisings, and changing of sails; shiftings of ballast; inspection of crawl-spaces for rats and roaches; luffings, tackings, jibings, and the like.

The Mouser swore feebly yet bitterly as these exercises sent both Ourph and Fafhrd clumping all over the deck, often across his prone body, and changed the steady pitch and roll of the *Black Treasurer*, to which he'd been getting accustomed, into unpredictable jitterbuggings which awakened nausea anew.

Whenever Fafhrd left off this slave-driving, he would sit cross-legged, deaf to the Mouser's sultry swearing, and silently meditate, his gaze directed at first always toward Lankhmar, but later more and more toward the north.

When the Mouser at last recovered, he forswore all food save watery gruel in small measures, and scorning Fafhrd's nautical exercises, began grimly to put himself through a variety of gymnastical ones until he collapsed sweating and panting – yet only waiting until he had his breath back to begin again.

It was an odd sight to see the Mouser walking about on his hands while Ourph raced forward to change the set of the jib and Fafhrd threw his weight on the tiller and bellowed, 'Hard a-lee!'

Yet at odd moments now and then, chiefly at sunset, when they each sipped a measure of water tinted with sweet wine – the brandy being still under interdict – they began to reminisce and yarn together, only a little at first, then for longer and longer periods.

They spoke of piratings, both inflicted and suffered. They recalled notable storms and calms, sighting of mysterious ships which vanished in fog or distance, never more to be seen. They talked of sea monsters, mermaids, and oceanic devils. They relived the adventure of their crossing of the Outer Sea to the fabled Western Continent, which of all Lankhmarts only Fafhrd, the Mouser, and Ourph knew to be more than legend.

Gradually the Mouser's belly melted and a bristly lawn of hair grew on Fafhrd's pate, cheeks, and chin, and around his mouth. Life became happenings rather than afflictions. They lived as well as saw sunsets and dawns. The stars became friendly. Above all, they began to match their rhythms to those of the sea, as if she were someone they lived and voyaged with, rather than sailed upon.

But their water and stores began to run low, the wine ran out, and they lacked even suitable clothing – Fafhrd in particular.

Their first piratical foray ended in near disaster. The small and lubberly-sailing merchant ship they approached most subtly at dawn suddenly bristled with brown-helmeted pikemen and slingers. It was a Lankhmar bait-ship, designed to trap pirates.

They escaped only because the trap was sprung too soon and the *Black Treasurer* was able to out-sail the bait-ship, transformed into a speedy goer by proper handling. At that,

Ourph was struck senseless by a slung stone and Fafhrd had two ribs cracked by another.

Their next sea-raid was only a most qualified success. The cutter they conquered turned out to be manned by five elderly Mingol witches by profession, they said, and bound on a fortune-telling and trading voyage to the southern settlements around Quarmall.

The Mouser and Fafhrd exacted from them a modest supply of water, food, and wine, and Fafhrd took several silk and fur tunics, some silver-plated jewelry, a longsword and ax which he fancied, and leather to make him boots. However, they left the surly women by no means destitute and forcibly prevented Ourph from raping even one of them, let alone all five as he had boastfully threatened.

They departed then, somewhat ashamed, to the tune of the witchwomen's chanting curses — most venomous ones, calling down on Fafhrd and the Mouser all the worst evils of air and earth, fire and water. Their failure to curse Ourph also, made the Mouser wonder whether the witchwomen were not angriest because Ourph had been prevented in his most lascivious designs.

Now that the *Black Treasurer* was somewhat better provisioned, Fafhrd began to talk airily about voyaging once again across the Outer Sea, or toward the Frozen Sea north of No-Ombrulsk, there to hunt the polar tiger and white-furred giant worm.

That was the last straw to Ourph, who was a most even-tempered, sweet old man — for a Mingol. Overworked, skull-bashed, thwarted of a truly unusual amorous opportunity for one of his age, and now threatened with idiot-far-voyagings, he demanded to be set ashore.

The Mouser and Fafhrd complied. All this while the *Black Treasurer* had been southwesting along Lankhmar's north-western coast. So it was near the small village of Earth's End that they put landside the old Mingol, who was still cursing them grumblingly, despite the gifts with which they had loaded him.

After consultation, the two heroes decided to set course

straight north, which would land them in the forested Land of the Eight Cities at the city of Ool Plerns, whose Mad Duke had once been their patron.

The voyage was uneventful. No ships were sighted. Fafhrd cut, sewed, and nailed himself boots, which he footed with spikes, perhaps from some dream of mountaineering. The Mouser continued his calisthenics and read *The Book of Aarth, The Book of Lesser Gods, the Management of Miracles,* and a scroll titled *Sea Monsters* from the sloop's small but select library.

Nights they would lazily talk for hours, feeling nearest then to the stars, the sea, and each other. They argued as to whether the stars had existed forever or been launched by the gods from Nehwon's highest mountain – or whether, as current metaphysics asserted, the stars were vast firelit gems set in islands at the opposite end of the great bubble (in the waters of eternity) that was Nehwon. They disputed as to who was the world's worst warlock: Fafhrd's Ningauble, the Mouser's Sheelba, or – barely conceivably – some other sorcerer.

But chiefly they talked of their mistress, the sea, whose curving motions they loved again, and to whose moods they now felt preternaturally attuned, particularly in darkness. They spoke of her rages and caressings, her coolths and unending dancings, sometimes lightly footing a minuet, sometimes furiously a-stamp, and her infinitude of secret parts.

The west wind gradually lessened, then shifted to a fluky east wind. Stores were once more depleted. At last they admitted to each other that they couldn't fetch Ool Plerns on this reach and they contented themselves with sailing to intercept the Claws – the narrow but mountainously rocky end of the Eastern Continent's great western-thrusting northern peninsula, comprised of the Land of the Eight Cities, the Cold Waste, and numerous grim and great mountain ranges. The east wind died entire one midnight. The *Black Treasurer* floated in a calm so complete it was as if their aqueous mistress had fallen into a trance. Not a breath stirred. They wondered what the morrow would show, or bring.

IV: WHEN THE SEA-KING'S AWAY

Stripped to his loincloth, underbelt, and with amulet pouch a-dangle under his chin, the Gray Mouser stretched lizard-like along the bowed sprit of the sloop *Black Treasurer* and stared straight down into the hole in the sea. Sunlight un-strained by slightest wisp of cloud beat hotly on his deep-tanned back, but his belly was cold with the magic of the thing.

All around about, the Inner Sea lay calm as a lake of mercury in the cellar of a wizard's castle. No ripple came from the un-bounded horizon to south, east and north, nor rebounded from the endless vertically-fluted curtain of creamy rock that rose a bowshot to the west and was a good three bowshots high, which the Mouser and Fafhrd had only yesterday climbed and atop which they had made a frightening discovery. The Mouser could have thought of those matters, or of the dismal fact that they were becalmed with little food and less water (and a tabooed cask of brandy) a weary sail west from Ool Hrusp, the last civilized port on this coast – or uncivilized either. He could have wondered about the seductive singing that had seemed to come from the sea last night, as of female voices softly im-provising on the themes of waves hissing against sand, gurgling melodiously among rocks, and screaming wind-driven against icy coasts. Or he could perhaps best have pondered on Fafhrd's madness of yesterday afternoon, when the large Northerner had suddenly started to babble dogmatically about finding for himself and the Mouser 'girls under the sea' and had even begun to trim his beard and brush out his brown otterskin tunic and polish his best male costume jewelry so as to be properly attired to receive the submarine girls and arouse their desires. There was an old Simorgyan legend, Fafhrd had insisted, according to which on the seventh day of the seventh moon of the seventh year of the Sevens-Cycle the king of the sea journeyed to the other end of the earth, leaving his opalescently beautiful green wives and faintly silver-scaled slim concubines free to find them lovers if they could . . . and this, Fafhrd had stridently asserted he knew by the spectral calm and other occult tokens, was the place of the sea-king's home and the eve of the day!

In vain had the Mouser pointed out to him that they had not sighted an even faintly feminine-looking fish in days, that there were absolutely no islets or beaches in view suitable for commerce with mermaids or for the sunbathing and primping of loreleis, that there were no black hulks whatever or wrecked pirate ships drifting about that might conceivably have fair captives imprisoned below decks and so technically 'under the sea', that the region beyond the deceptive curtain-wall of creamy rock was the last from which one could expect girls to come, that – to sum it up – the *Black Treasurer* had not fetched the faintest sort of girl-blink either to starboard or larboard for weeks. Fafhrd had simply replied with crushing conviction that the sea-king's girls were there down below, that they were now preparing a magic channel or passageway whereby air-breathers might visit them, and that the Mouser had better be ready like himself to hasten when the summons came.

The Mouser had thought that the heat and dazzle of the un-remitting sun – together with the sudden intense yearnings normal to all sailormen long at sea – must have deranged Fafhrd and he had dug up from the hold and unsuccessfully coaxed the Northerner to wear a wide-brimmed hat and slitted ice-goggles. It had been a great relief to the Mouser when Fafhrd had fallen into a profound sleep with the coming of night, though then the illusion – or reality – of the sweet siren-singing had returned to trouble his own tranquility.

Yes, the Mouser might well have thought of any of these matters, Fafhrd's prophetic utterances in particular, while he lay poised but unsweating in the hot sun along the stout bow-sprit of the *Black Treasurer,* yet the fact is that he had mind only for the jade marvel so close that he could almost reach down a hand and touch the beginning of it.

It is well to approach all miracles and wonders by gradual stages or degrees and we can do this by examining another aspect of the glassy seascape of which the Mouser also might well have been thinking – but wasn't.

Although untroubled by swell, wavelet or faintest ripple or quiver, the Inner Sea around the sloop was not perfectly flat. Here and there, scatteredly, it was dimpled with small depressions about the size and shape of shallow saucers, as if giant invisible featherweight water-beetles were standing about on it – though the dimples were not arranged in any six-legged or four-legged or even tripod patterns. Moreover, a slim stalk of air seemed to go down from the center of each dimple for an indefinite distance into the water, quite like the tiny whirlpool that sometimes forms when the turquoise plug is pulled in the brimful golden bathtub of the Queen of the East (or the drain unstoppered in a bathtub of any humbler material belonging to any lowlier person) – except that there was no whirling of water in this case and the airstalks were not twisted and knotted but straight, as though scores of slim-bladed rapiers with guards like shallow saucers but all as invisible as air had been plunged at random into the motionless waters around the *Black Treasurer*. Or as though a sparse forest of invisible lily pads with straight invisible stems had sprung up around the sloop.

Imagine such an air-stalked dimple magnified so that the saucer was not a palm's breadth but a good spearcast across and the rodlike sword-straight stalk not a fingernail's width but a good four feet, imagine the sloop slid prow-foremost down into that shallow depression but stopping just short of the center and floating motionless there, imagine the bowsprit of the slightly tilted ship projecting over the exact center of the central tube or well of air, imagine a small, stalwart, nut-brown man in a gray loincloth lying along the bowsprit, his feet braced against the foredeck rails, and looking straight down the tube . . . and you have the Gray Mouser's situation exactly!

To be *in* the Mouser's situation and peering down the tube was very fascinating indeed, an experience calculated to drive other thoughts out of any man's mind – or even any woman's!

The water here, a bowshot from the creamy rock-wall, was green, remarkably clear, but too deep to allow a view of the bottom – soundings taken yesterday had shown it to vary between six score and seven score feet. Through this water the well-size tube went down as perfectly circular and as smooth as if it were walled with glass; and indeed the Mouser would have believed that it was so walled – that the water immediately around it had been somehow frozen or hardened without altering in transparency – except that at the slightest noise, such as the Mouser's coughing, little quiverings would run up and down it in the form of series of ring-shaped waves.

What power prevented the tremendous weight of the sea from collapsing the tube in an instant, the Mouser could not begin to imagine.

Yet it was endlessly fascinating to peer down it. Sunlight transmitted through the sea water illuminated it to a considerable depth brightly if greenishly and the circular wall played odd tricks with distance. For instance, at this moment the Mouser, peering down slantwise through the side of the tube, saw a thick fish as long as his arm swimming around it and nosing up to it. The shape of the fish was very familiar yet he could not at once name it. Then thrusting his head out to one side and peering down at the same fish through the clear water alongside the tube, he saw that the fish was three times the length of his body – in fact, a shark. The Mouser shivered and told himself that the curved wall of the tube must act like the reducing lenses used by a few artists in Lankhmar.

On the whole, though, the Mouser might well have decided in the end that the vertical tunnel in the water was an illusion born of sun-glare and suggestion and have put on the ice-goggles and stuffed his ears with wax against any more siren-singing and then perhaps swigged at the forbidden brandy and gone to sleep, except for certain other circumstances footing the whole affair much more firmly in reality. For instance, there was a knotted rope securely tied to the bowsprit and hanging down the center of the tube and this rope creaked from time to time with the weight on it, and also there were threads of black smoke coming out of the watery hole (these were what made the Mouser cough), and last but not least was a torch burning redly far down in the hole – so far down its flame looked no bigger than a candle's – and just beside the flame, somewhat obscured by its smoke and much tinied by distance, was the upward-peering face of Fafhrd!

The Mouser was inclined to take on faith the reality of anything Fafhrd got mixed up with, certainly anything that Fafhrd got physically into – the near-seven-foot Northerner was much too huge a hulk of solid matter to be picturable as strolling arm-in-arm with illusions.

The events leading up to the reality-footing facts of the rope, the smoke, and Fafhrd down the air-well had been quite simple. At dawn the sloop had begun to drift mysteriously among the water dimples, there being no perceptible wind or current. Shortly afterwards it had bumped over the lip of the large saucer-shaped depression and slid to its present position with a a little rush and then frozen there, as though the sloop's bowsprit and the hole were mutually desirous magnetic poles coupled together. Thereafter, while the Mouser had watched with eyes goggling and teeth a-chatter, Fafhrd had sighted down the hole, grunted with stolid satisfaction, slung the knotted rope down it, and then proceeded to array himself, seemingly with both war and love in mind – pomading his bushy hair and beard, perfuming his hairy chest and armpits, putting on a blue silk tunic under the gleaming one of otter-skin and all his silver-plated necklaces, armbands, brooches and rings as well, but also strapping longsword and ax to his sides and lacing on his spiked boots. Then he had lit a long thin torch of resinous pine in the galley firebox and when it was flaming bravely he had, despite the Mouser's solicitous cries and tugging protests, gone out on the bowsprit and lowered himself into the hole, using thumb and forefinger of his right hand to grip the torch and the other three fingers of that hand, along with his left hand, to grip the rope. Only then had he spoken, calling on the Mouser to make ready and follow him if the Mouser were more hot-blooded man than cold-blooded lizard.

The Mouser had made ready to the extent of stripping off most of his clothing – it had occurred to him it would be

74

necessary to dive for Fafhrd when the hole became aware of its own impossibility and collapsed – and he had fetched to the foredeck his own sword Scalpel and dagger Cat's Claw in their case of oiled sealskin with the notion they might be needed against sharks. Thereafter he had simply poised on the bowsprit, as we have seen, observing Fafhrd's slow descent and letting the fascination of it all take hold of him.

At last he dipped his head and called softly down the hole, 'Fafhrd, have you reached bottom yet?' frowning at the ring-shaped ripples even this gentle calling sent traveling down the hole and up again by reflection.

'WHAT DID YOU SAY?'

Fafhrd's answering bellow, concentrated by the tube and coming out of it like a solid projectile, almost blasted the Mouser off the bowsprit. Far more terrifying, the ring-ripples accompanying the bellow were so huge they almost seemed to close off the tube – narrowing it from four to two or three feet at any rate and dashing a spray of drops up into the Mouser's face as they reached the surface, lifting the rim upward as if the water were elastic, and then were reflected down the tube again.

The Mouser closed his eyes in a wince of horror, but when he opened them the hole was still there and the giant ring-ripples were beginning to abate.

Only a shade more loudly than the first time, but much more poignantly, the Mouser called down, 'Fafhrd, don't do that again!'

'WHAT?'

This time the Mouser was prepared for it – just the same it was most horrid to watch those huge rings traveling up and down the tube in an arrow-swift green peristalsis. He firmly resolved to do no more calling, but just then Fafhrd started to speak up the tube in a voice of more rational volume – the rings produced were hardly thicker than a man's wrist.

'COME ON, MOUSER! IT'S EASY! YOU ONLY HAVE TO DROP THE LAST SIX FEET!'

'Don't drop it, Fafhrd!' the Mouser instantly replied. 'Climb back up!'

'I ALREADY HAVE! DROPPED, I MEAN. I'M ON THE BOTTOM. OH, MOUSER...!'

The last part of Fafhrd's call was in a voice so infused with a mingled awe and excitement that the Mouser immediately asked back down, 'What? "Oh, Mouser" – what?'

'IT'S WONDERFUL, IT'S AMAZING, IT'S FANTASTIC!' the reply came back from below – but this time very faintly all of a sudden, as if Fafhrd had somehow gone around an impossible bend or two in the tube.

'*What* is, Fafhrd?' the Mouser demanded – and this time his own voice raised moderate rings. 'Don't go away, Fafhrd. But what *is* down there?'

'EVERYTHING!' the answer came back, not quite so faint this time.

'Are there girls?' the Mouser queried.

'A WHOLE WORLD!'

The Mouser sighed. The moment had come, he knew, as it always did, when outward circumstances and inner urges commanded an act, when curiosity and fascination tipped the scale of caution, when the lure of a vision and an adventure became so great and deep-hooking that he must respond to it or have his inmost self-respect eaten away.

Besides, he knew from long experience that the only way to extricate Fafhrd from the predicament into which he got himself was to go fetch the perfumed and be-sworded lout!

So the Mouser sprang up lightly, clipped to his underbelt his sealskin-cased weapons, hung beside them in loops a short length of knotted line with a slip-noose tied in one end, made sure that the sloop's hatches were securely covered and even that the galley fire was tightly boxed, rattled off a short scornful prayer to the gods *of* Lankhmar, and lowered himself off the bowsprit and down into the green hole.

The hole was chilly and it smelled of fish, smoke, and Fafhrd's pomade. The Mouser's main concern as soon as he got in it, he discovered to his surprise, was not to touch its glassy sides. He had the feeling that if he so much as lightly brushed it, the water's miraculous 'skin' would rupture and he would be engulfed – rather as an oiled needle floating on a bowl of water in its tiny hammock of 'water skin' is engulfed and sinks when one pinks it. He descended rapidly knot by knot, supporting himself by his hands, barely touching his toes to the rope below, praying there would be no sway and that he would be able to check it if it started. It occurred to him that he should have told Fafhrd to guy the rope at the bottom if he possibly could and above all have warned him not to shout up the tube while the Mouser descended – the thought of being squeezed by those dread water-rings was almost too much to bear. Too late now! – any word now would only too surely bring a bellow from the Northerner in reply.

First fears having been thus inspected, though by no means banished, the Mouser began to take some note of his surroundings. The luminous green world was not just one emerald blank as it had seemed at first. There was life in it, though not in the greatest abundance: thin strands of scalloped maroon seaweed, near-invisible jellyfish trailing their opalescent fringes, tiny dark skates hovering like bats, small silvery backboned fish gliding and darting – some of them, a blue-and-yellow-ringed and black-spotted school, even contesting lazily over the *Black Treasurer*'s morning garbage, which the Mouser recognized by a large pallid beef-bone Fafhrd had gnawed briefly before tossing overside.

Looking up, he was hard put not to gasp in horror. The hull of the sloop, pressing down darkly, though pearled with bubbles, looked seven times higher above him than the distance he had descended by his count of the knots. Looking straight up the tube, however, he saw that the circle of deep blue sky had not shrunk correspondingly while the bowsprit bisecting it was still reassuringly thick. The curve of the tube had shrunk the sloop as it had the shark. The illusion was most weird and foreboding, nonetheless.

And now as the Mouser continued his swift descent, the circle overhead did grow smaller and more deeply blue, becoming a cobalt platter, a peacock saucer, and finally no more than a strange ultramarine coin that was the converging point of the tube and rope and in which the Mouser thought he saw a star flash. The Gray One puffed a few rapid kisses toward it,

77

thinking how like they were to a drowning man's last bubbles. The light dimmed. The colours around him faded, the maroon seaweed turned gray, the fish lost their yellow rings, and the Mouser's own hands became blue as those of a corpse. And now he began to make out dimly the sea bottom, at the same extravagant distance below as the sloop was above, though immediately under him the bottom was oddly veiled or blanketed and only far off could he make out rocks and ridged stretches of sand.

His arms and shoulders ached. His palms burned. A monstrously fat grouper swam up to the tube and followed him down it, circling. The Mouser glared at it menacingly and it turned on its side and opened an impossibly large mooncrescent of mouth. The Mouser saw the razor teeth and realized it was the shark he'd seen or another like it, tinied by the lens of the tube. The teeth clashed, some of them inside the tube, only inches from his side. The water's 'skin' did not rupture disastrously, although the Mouser got the eerie impression that the 'bite' was bleeding a little water into the tube. The shark swam off to continue its circling at a moderate distance and the Mouser refrained from any more menacing looks.

Meanwhile the fishy smell had grown stronger and the smoke must have been getting thicker too, for now the Mouser coughed in spite of himself, setting the water rings shooting up and down. He fought to suppress an anguished curse – and at that moment his toes no longer touched rope. He unloosed the extra coil from his belt, went down three more knots, tightened the slip-noose above the second knot from the bottom, and continued on his way.

Five handholds later his feet found a footing in cold muck. He gratefully unclenched his hands, working his cramped fingers, at the same time calling 'Fafhrd!' softly but angrily. Then he looked around.

He was standing in the center of a large low tent of air, which was floored by the velvety sea-muck in which he had sunk to his ankles and roofed by the leadenly gleaming undersurface of the water – not evenly though, but in swells and hollows with ominous downward bulges here and there. The air-tent was about ten feet high at the foot of the tube. Its diameter seemed at least twenty times that, though exactly how far the edges extended it was impossible to judge for several reasons: the great irregularity of the tent's roof, the difficulty of even guessing at the extent of some outer areas where the distance between water-roof and muck-floor was measurable in inches, the fact that the gray light transmitted from above hardly permitted decent vision for more than two dozen yards, and finally the circumstance that there was considerable torch-smoke in the way here and there, writhing in thick coils along the ceiling, collecting in topsy-turvy pockets, though eventually gliding sluggishly up the tube.

What fabulous invisible 'tent-poles' propped up the oceans-heavy roof the Mouser could no more conceive than the force that kept the tube open.

Writhing his nostrils distastefully, both at the smoke and the augmented fishy smell, the Mouser squinted fiercely around the tent's full circumference. Eventually he saw a dull red glow in the black smudge where it was thickest and a little later Fafhrd emerged. The reeking flame of the pine torch, which was still no more than half consumed, showed the Northerner bemired with sea-muck to his thighs and hugging gently to his side with his bent left arm a dripping mess of variously gleaming objects. He was stooped over somewhat, for the roof bulged down where he stood.

'Blubber brain!' the Mouser greeted him. 'Put out that torch before we smother! We can see better without it. Oh, oaf, to blind yourself with smoke for the sake of light!'

To the Mouser there was obviously only one sane way to extinguish the torch – jab it in the wet muck underfoot – but Fafhrd, though evidently most agreeable to the Mouser's suggestion in a vacantly smiling way, had another idea. Despite the Mouser's anguished cry of warning, he casually thrust the flaming stick into the watery roof.

There was a loud hissing and a large downward puff of steam and for a moment the Mouser thought his worst dreads had been realized, for an angry squirt of water from the quenching point struck Fafhrd in the neck. But when the steam cleared it became evident that the rest of the sea was not going to follow the squirt, at least not at once, though now there was an ominous lump, like a rounded tumor, in the roof where Fafhrd had thrust the torch and from it water ran steadily in a stream thick as a quill, digging a tiny crater where it struck the muck below.

'Don't do that!' the Mouser commanded in unwise fury.

'This?' Fafhrd asked gently, poking a finger through the ceiling next to the dripping bulge. Again came the angry squirt, diminishing at once to a trickle, and now there were two bulges closely side by side, quite like breasts.

'Yes, *that* – not again,' the Mouser managed to reply, his voice distant and high because of the self-control it took him not to rage at Fafhrd and so perhaps provoke even more reckless probings.

'Very well, I won't,' the Northerner assured him. 'Though,' he added, gazing thoughtfully at the twin streams, 'it would take those dribblings years to fill up this cavity.'

'Who speaks of years down here?' the Mouser snarled at him. 'Dolt! Iron Skull! What made you lie to me? "Everything" was down here, you said – "a whole world." And what do I find? Nothing! A miserable little cramp-roofed field of stinking mud!' And the Mouser stamped a foot in rage, which only splashed him foully, while a puffed, phosphorescent-whiskered fish expiring on the mire looked up at him reproachfully.

'That rude treading,' Fafhrd said softly, 'may have burst the silver-filigreed skull of a princess. "Nothing," say you? Look you then, Mouser, what treasure I have digged from your stinking field.'

And as he came toward the Mouser, his big feet gliding gently through the top of the muck for all the spikes on his boots, he gently rocked the gleaming things cradled in his left arm and let the fingers of his right hand drift gently among them.

'Aye,' he said, 'jewels and gauds undreamed by those who sail above, yet all teased by me from the ooze while I sought another thing.'

'What other thing, Gristle Dome?' the Mouser demanded harshly, though eyeing the gleaming things hungrily.

'The path,' Fafhrd said a little querulously, as if the Mouser must know what he meant. 'The path that leads from some corner or fold of this tent of air to the sea-king's girls. These things are a sure promise of it. Look you, here, Mouser.' And he opened his bent left arm a little and lifted out most delicately with thumb and fingertips a life-size metallic mask.

Impossible to tell in that drained gray light whether the metal were gold or silver or tin or even bronze and whether the wide wavy streaks down it, like the tracks of blue-green sweat and tears, were verdigris or slime. Yet it was clear that it was female, patrician, all-knowing yet alluring, loving yet cruel, hauntingly beautiful. The Mouser snatched it eagerly yet angrily and the whole lower face crumpled in his hand, leaving only the proud forehead and the eyeholes staring at him more tragically than eyes.

The Mouser flinched back, expecting Fafhrd to strike him, but in the same instant he saw the Northerner turning away and lifting his straight right arm, index finger a-point, like a slow semaphor.

'You were right, oh Mouser!' Fafhrd cried joyously. 'Not only my torch's smoke but its very light blinded me. See! See the path!'

The Mouser's gaze followed Fafhrd's pointing. Now that the smoke was somewhat abated and the torch-flame no longer shot out its orange rays, the patchy phosphorescence of the muck and of the dying sea-things scattered about had become clearly visible despite the muted light filtering from above.

The phosphorescence was not altogether patchy, however. Beginning at the hole from which the knotted rope hung, a path of unbroken greenish-yellow witch-fire a long stride in width led across the muck toward an unpromising-looking corner of the tent of air where it seemed to disappear.

'Don't follow it, Fafhrd,' the Mouser automatically enjoined, but the Northerner was already moving past him, taking long dreamlike strides. By degrees his cradling arm unbent and one

81

by one his ooze-won treasures began to slip from it into the muck. He reached the path and started along it, placing his spike-soled feet in the very center.

'Don't follow it, Fafhrd,' the Mouser repeated – a little hopelessly, almost whiningly, it must be admitted. 'Don't follow it, I say. It leads only to squidgy death. We can still go back up the rope, aye, and take your loot with us . . .'

But meanwhile he himself was following Fafhrd and snatching up, though more cautiously than he had the mask, the objects his comrade let slip. It was not worth the effort, the Mouser told himself as he continued to do it: though they gleamed enticingly, the various necklaces, tiaras, filigreed breast-cups and great-pinned brooches weighed no more and were no thicker than plaitings of dead ferns. He could not equal Fafhrd's delicacy and they fell apart at his touch.

Fafhrd turned back to him a face radiant as one who dreams sleeping of ultimate ecstacies. As the last ghost-gaud slipped from his arm, he said, 'They are nothing – no more than the mask – mere sea-gnawed wraiths of treasure. But oh, the promise of them, Mouser! Oh, the promise!'

And with that he turned forward again and stooped under a large downward bulge in the low leaden-hued roof.

The Mouser took one look back along the glowing path to the small circular patch of sky-light with the knotted rope falling in the center of it. The twin streams of water coming from the two 'wounds' in the ceiling seemed to be running more strongly – where they hit, the muck was splashing. Then he followed Fafhrd.

On the other side of the bulge the ceiling rose again to more than head-height, but the walls of the tent narrowed in sharply. Soon they were treading along a veritable tunnel in the water, a leaden arch-roofed passageway no wider than the phosphorescently yellow-green path that floored it. The tunnel curved just enough now to left, now right, so that there was no seeing any long distance ahead. From time to time the Mouser thought he heard faint whistlings and moanings echoing along it. He stepped over a large crab that was backing feebly and saw beside it a dead man's hand emerging from the glowing

82

muck, one shred-fleshed finger pointing the way they were taking.

Fafhrd half turned his head and muttered gravely, 'Mark me, Mouser, there's magic in this somewhere!'

The Mouser thought he had never in his life heard a less necessary remark. He felt considerably depressed. He had long given up his puerile pleadings with Fafhrd to turn back – he knew there was no way of stopping Fafhrd short of grappling with him, and a tussle that would invariably send them crashing through one of the watery walls of the tunnel was by no means to his liking. Of course, he could always turn back alone. Still . . .

With the monotony of the tunnel and of just putting one foot after the other into the clinging muck and withdrawing it with a soft *plop*, the Mouser found time to become oppressed too with the thought of the weight of the water overhead. It was as though he walked with all the ships of the world on his back. His imagination would picture nothing but the tunnel's instant collapse. He hunched his head into his shoulders and it was all he could do not to drop to his elbows and knees and then stretch himself face down in the muck with the mere anticipation of the event.

The sea seemed to grow a little whiter ahead and the Mouser realized the tunnel was approaching the underreaches of the curtain-wall of creamy rock he and Fafhrd had climbed yesterday. The memory of that climb let his imagination escape at last, perhaps because it fitted with the urge that he and Fafhrd somehow lift themselves out of their present predicament.

It had been a difficult ascent, although the pale rock had proved hard and reliable, for footholds and ledges had been few and they had had to rope up and go by way of a branching chimney, often driving pitons into cracks to create a support where none was – but they had had high hopes of finding fresh water and game, too, likely enough, so far west of Ool Hrusp and its hunters. At last they had reached the top, aching and a little blown from their climb and quite ready to throw themselves down and rest while they surveyed the landscape of grassland and stunted trees that they knew to be characteristic of other parts of this most lonely peninsula stretching south-westward between the Inner and Outer Seas.

Instead they had found . . . nothing. Worse than nothing, in a way, if that were possible. The longed-for top proved to be the merest edge of rock, three feet wide at the most and narrower some places, while on the other side the rock descended even more precipitously than on the side which they had climbed – indeed it was deeply undercut in large areas – and for an equal or rather somewhat greater distance. From the foot of this dizzying drop a wilderness of waves, foam and rocks extended to the horizon.

They had found themselves clinging a-straddle to a veritable rock curtain, paper-thin in respect to its height and horizontal extent, between the Inner and what they realized must be the Outer Sea, which had eaten its way across the unexplored peninsula in this region but not yet quite broken through. As far as eye could see in either direction the same situation obtained, though the Mouser fancied he could make out a thickening of the wall in the direction of Ool Hrusp.

Fafhrd had laughed at the surprise of the thing – gargantuan bellows of mirth that had made the Mouser curse him silently for fear mere vibrations of his voice might shatter and tumble down the knife-edged saddle on which they perched. Indeed the Mouser had grown so angry with Fafhrd's laughter that he had sprung up and nimbly danced a jig of rage on the rock-ribbon, thinking meanwhile of wise Sheelba's saying: 'Know it or not, man treads between twin abysses a tightrope that has neither beginning nor end.'

Having thus expressed their feeling of horrified shock, each in his way, they had surveyed the yeasty sea below more rationally. The amount of surf and the numbers of emergent rocks showed it to be more shallow for some distance out – even likely, Fafhrd had opined, to drain itself at low tide, for his moon-lore told him that tides in this region of the world must at the moment be near high. Of the emergent rocks, one in particular stood out: a thick pillar two bowshots from the curtain wall and as high as a four-story house. The pillar was spiraled by ledges that looked as if they were in part of human cutting, while set in its thicker base and emerging from the foam there appeared an oddly crisscrossed weed-fringed rectangle that looked mightily like a large stout door – though where such a door might lead and who would use it were perplexing questions indeed.

Then, since there was no answering that question or others and since there was clearly no fresh water or game to be had from this literal shell of a coast, they had descended back to the Inner Sea and the *Black Treasurer*, though now each time they had driven a piton it had been with the fear that the whole wall might split and collapse . . .

' 'Ware rocks!'

Fafhrd's warning cry pulled the Mouser out of his waking memory-dream – dropped him in a split instant as if it were from the upper reaches of the creamy curtain-wall to a spot almost an equal distance below its sea-gnarled base. Just ahead of him three thick lumpy daggers of rock thrust down inexplicably through the gray watery ceiling of the tunnel. The Mouser shudderingly wove his head past them, as Fafhrd must have, and then looking beyond his comrade he saw more rocky protuberances encroaching on the tunnel from all sides – saw, in fact, as he strode on, that the tunnel was changing from one of water and muck to one roofed, walled and floored with solid rock. The water-born light faded away behind them, but the increasing phosphorescence natural to the animal life of a sea cavern almost compensated for it, boldly outlining their wet stony way and here and there glowing with especial brilliance and variety of color from the bands, portholes, feelers and eye-rings of many a dying fish and crawler.

The Mouser realized they must be passing far under the curtain-wall he and Fafhrd had climbed yesterday and that the tunnel ahead must be leading under the Outer Sea they had seen tossing with billows. There was no longer that immediate oppressive sense of a crushing weight of ocean overhead or of brushing elbows with magic. Yet the thought that if the tube, tent and tunnel behind them should collapse, then a great gush of solid water would rush into the rock-tunnel and engulf them, was in some ways even worse. Back under the water roof he'd

85

had the feeling that even if it should collapse he might reach the surface alive by bold swimming and conceivably drag the cumbered Fafhrd up with him. But here they'd be hopelessly trapped.

True, the tunnel seemed to be ascending, but not enough or swiftly enough to please the Mouser. Moreover, if it did finally emerge, it would be to that shattering welter of foam they'd peered down at yesterday. Truly, the Mouser found it hard to pick between his druthers, or even to have any druthers at all. His feelings of depression and doom gradually sank to a new and perhaps ultimate nadir, and in a desperate effort to wrench them up he deliberately imagined to himself the zestiest tavern he knew in Lankhmar – a great gray cellar all a-flare with torches, wine streaming and spilling, tankards and coins a-clink, voices braying and roaring, poppy fumes a-twirl, naked girls writhing in lascivious dances ...

'Oh, Mouser ... !'

Fafhrd's deep and feelingful whisper and the Northerner's large hand against his chest halted the Mouser's plodding, but whether it fetched his spirit back below the Outer Sea or simply produced a fantastic alteration in its escapist imagining, the Gray One could not at once be sure.

They were standing in the entrance to a vast submarine grotto that rose in multiple steps and terraces toward an indefinite ceiling from which cascaded down like silver mist a glow about thrice the strength of moonlight. The grotto reeked of the sea like the tunnel behind them; it was likewise scattered with expiring fish and eels and small octopuses; mollusks tiny and huge clustered on its walls and corners between weedy draperies and silver-green veils; while its various niches and dark circular doorways and even the stepped and terraced floor seemed shaped in part at least by the action of rushing waters and grinding sand.

The silver mist did not fall evenly but concentrated itself in swirls and waves of light on three terraces. The first of these was placed centrally and only a level stretch separated it from the tunnel's mouth. Upon this terrace was set a great stone table with weed-fringed sides and mollusk-crusted legs. A great golden basin stood on one end of this table and two golden goblets beside the basin.

Beyond the first terrace rose a second uneven flight of steps with areas of menacing shadow pressing upon it from either side. Behind the areas of darkness were a second and third terrace that the silvery light favored. The one on the right – Fafhrd's side, to call it that, for he stood to the right in the tunnel mouth – was walled and arched with mother-of-pearl, almost as if it were one gigantic shell, and pearly swells rose from its floor like heaped satin pillows. The one on the Mouser's side, slightly below, was backed by an arras of maroon seaweed that fell in wide scalloped strands and billowed on the floor. From between these twin terraces the flight of irregular steps or ledges continued upward into a third area of darkness.

Shifting shadows and dark wavings and odd gleamings hinted that the three areas of darkness might be occupied; there was no doubt that the three bright terraces were. On the upper terrace on Fafhrd's side stood a tall and opulently beautiful woman whose golden hair rose in spiral masses like a shell and whose dress of golden fishnet clung to her pale greenish flesh. Her fingers showed greenish webs between them and on the side of her neck as she turned were faint scorings like a fish's gills.

On the Mouser's side was a slimmer yet exquisitely feminine creature whose silver flesh seemed to merge into silver scales on shoulders, back and flanks under her robe of filmy violet and whose short dark hair was split back from her low forehead's center by a scalloped silver crest a hand's breadth high. She too showed the faint neck-scorings and finger-webs.

The third figure, standing a-crouch behind the table, was sexlessly scrawny, with an effect of wiry old age, and either gowned or clad closely in jet black. A shock of rope-thick hairs dark red as iron rust covered her head while her gills and finger-webs were starkly apparent.

Each of these women wore a metal mask resembling in form and expression the eaten-away one Fafhrd had found in the muck. That of the first figure was gold; of the second, silver; of the third, green-splotched sea-darkened bronze.

The first two women were still, not as if they were part of

a show but as though they were observing one. The scrawny black sea-witch was vibrantly active, although she hardly moved on her black-webbed toes except to shift position abruptly and ever so slightly now and then. She held a short whip in either hand, the webs folded outside her bent knuckles, and with these whips she maintained and directed the swift spinning of a half dozen objects on the polished table top. What these objects were it was impossible to say, except that they were roughly oval. Some by their semi-transparency as they spun might have been large rings or saucers, others actual tops by their opacity. They gleamed silver and green and golden and they spun so swiftly and moved in such swift intersecting orbits as they spun that they seemed to leave gleaming wakes of spin in the misty air behind them. Whenever one would flag in its spinning and its true form begin to blink into visibility, she'd bring it back up to speed again with two or three rapid whip slashes; or should one veer too close to the table's edge or the golden basin, or threaten to collide with another, she'd re-direct its orbit with deft lashings; now and again, with incredible skill, she'd flick one so that it jumped high in the air and then flick it again at landing so that it went on spinning without a break, leaving above it an evanescent loop of silvery air-spin.

These whirring objects made the pulsing moans and whistles the Mouser had heard along the tunnel.

As he watched them now and listened to them, the Gray One became convinced – partly because the silvery curving tubes of spin made him think of the air shaft he'd rope-climbed and the air-tunnel he'd plodded – that these spinning things were a cruel part of the magic that had created and held open the path through the Inner Sea behind them, and that once they should cease whirring then the shaft and tent and tunnel would collapse and the waters of the Inner Sea speed through the rock-tunnel into this grotto.

And indeed the scrawny black sea-witch looked to the Mouser as though she'd been whipping her tops for hours and – more to the point – would be able to keep on whipping them for hours more. She showed no signs of her exertion save the rhythmic rise and fall of her breastless chest and the extra whistle of breath through the mouth-slit of her mask and the gape and close of her gills.

Now she seemed for the first time to see him and Fafhrd, for without leaving off her whipping she thrust her bronze mask toward them, red ropes a-spill across its green-blotched fore-head, and glared at them – hungrily, it seemed. Yet she made them no other menace, but after a searching scrutiny jerked back her head twice, to left and to right, as if for a sign that they should go past her. At the same time the green and silver queens beckoned to them languorously.

This woke the Mouser and Fafhrd from their dazed watching and they complied eagerly enough, though in passing the table the Mouser sniffed wine and paused to take up the two golden goblets, handing one to his comrade. They drained them despite the green hue of the drink, for the stuff smelled right and was fiery sweet yet tart. The black witch took no note of them, but went on whipping her gleaming, mist-waked tops.

As he drank, the Mouser noted that the table top was of purple-splotched, creamy marble polished to an exquisite smoothness. He also saw into the golden bowl. It held no store of green wine, but was filled almost to the brim with a crystal fluid that might or might not have been water. On the fluid floated a model, hardly a finger long of the hull of a black boat. A tiny tube of air seemed to go down from its prow.

But there was no time for closer looking, for Fafhrd was moving on. The Mouser stepped up into his area of shadow to the left as Fafhrd had done to the right . . . and as he so stepped, there sidled from the shadows before him two bluely pallid men armed each with a pair of wave-edged knives. They were sailors, he judged from their pigtails and shuffling gait, although they were both naked, and they were indisputably dead – by token of their unhealthy color, their carelessness of thick slime streaking them, the way their bulging eyes showed only whites and the bottom crescent of the irises, and the fact that their hair, ears and other portions of their anatomies looked somewhat fish-chewed. Behind them waddled a scimitar-wielding dwarf with short spindle legs and monstrous head and gills – a veritable walking embryo. His great saucer eyes too were the upturned ones of a dead thing, which did not make the Mouser feel any easier as he whisked Scalpel and Cat's Claw out of their sealskin case, for the three converged on him confidently where he stood and rapidly shifted to block his way as he sought to circle behind them.

It was probably just as well that the Mouser had at that moment no attention to spare for his comrade's predicament. Fafhrd's area of shadow was black as ink toward the wall, and as the Northerner strode through the margin of it past a ridged and man-sized knob of rock rising from the ledges and between him and the Mouser, there lifted from the further blackness – like eight giant serpents rearing from their lair – the thick, sinuous, crater-studded arms of a monstrous octopus. The sea-beast's movement must have struck internal sparks, for it simultaneously flashed into a yellow-streaked purplish iridescence, showing Fafhrd its baleful eyes large as plates, its cruel beak big as the prow of an overturned skiff, and the rather unlikely circumstance that the end of each mighty tentacle wrapped powerfully around the hilt of a gleaming broadsword.

Snatching at his own sword and ax, Fafhrd backed away from the be-weaponed squid against the rigid knob of rock. Two of the ridges, being the vertical shell-edges of a mollusk four feet across, instantly closed on the slack of his otterskin tunic, firmly holding him there.

Greatly daunted but determined to live nevertheless, the Northerner swung his sword in a great figure eight, the lower loop of which almost nicked the floor while the upper loop rose above his head like a tall arching shield. This double-petaled flower of steel baffled the four blades or so with which the octopus first came chopping at him rather cautiously, and as the sea monster drew back his arms for another volley of slashes, Fafhrd's left arm licked out with his ax and chopped through the nearest tentacle.

His adversary hooted loudly then and struck repeatedly with all his swords, and for a space it looked as though Fafhrd's universal parry must surely be pierced, but then the ax licked out again from the center of the sword-shield, once, twice, and two more tentacle tips fell and the swords they gripped with them. The octopus drew back then out of reach and sprayed a great mist-cloud of stinking black ink from its tube, under cover of which it might work its will unseen on the pinned Northerner, but even as the blinding mist billowed toward him Fafhrd hurled his ax at the huge central head. And although the black fog hid the ax almost as soon as it left his hand, the heavy weapon must have reached a vital spot for immediately the octopus hurled its remaining swords about the grotto at random (fortunately striking no one although they made a fine clatter) as its tentacles thrashed in dying convulsions.

Fafhrd drew a small knife, slashed his otterskin tunic down the front and across the shoulders, stepped out of it with a contemptuous wave to the mollusk as if to say, 'Have it for supper if you will,' and turned to see how his comrade fared. The Mouser, bleeding greenly from two trivial wounds in ribs and shoulder, had just finished severing the major tendons of his three hideous opponents – this having proved the only way to immobilize them when various mortal wounds had slowed them in no way at all nor caused them to bleed one drop of blood of any color.

He smiled sickishly at Fafhrd and turned with him toward the upper terraces. And now it became clear that the Green and Silver Ones were at least in one respect true queens, for they had not fled the prodigious battles as lesser women might, but abided them and now waited with arms lightly outstretched. Their gold and silver masks could not smile, but their bodies did, and as the two adventurers mounted toward them from the shadow into the light (the Mouser's little wounds changing from green to red, but Fafhrd's blue tunic staying pretty inky) it seemed to them that veily finger-webs and light neck-scorings were the highest points of female beauty. The lights faded somewhat on the upper terraces, though not on the lower where the monotonous six-toned music of the tops kept reassuringly on, and the two heroes entered each into the dark lustrous realm where all thoughts of wounds are forgotten and all memories of even the zestiest Lankhmar wine-cellar grow flat, and the Sea, our cruel mother and moving mistress, repays all debts.

A great soundless jar, as of the rock-solid earth moving, recalled the Mouser to his surroundings. Almost simultaneously the whir of one of the tops mounted to a high-pitched whine ending in a tinkly crash. The silver light began to pulse and flicker wildly throughout the grotto. Springing to his feet and looking down the steps, the Mouser saw a memory-etching sight: the rust-topped black sea-witch whipping wildly at her rebellious tops, which leaped and bounded about the table like fierce silver weasels, while through the air around her from all sides but chiefly from the tunnel there converged an arrow-swift flight of flying fish, skates, and ribbon-edged eels, all inky black and with tiny jaws agape.

At that instant Fafhrd seized him by the shoulder and jerked him fully around, pointing up the ledges. A silver lightning flash showed a great cross-beamed, weed-fringed door at the head of the rocky stairs. The Mouser nodded violently – meaning he understood it resembled and must be the door they had yesterday seen from the ribbony cliff-summit – and Fafhrd, satisfied his comrade would follow him, dashed toward it up the ledges.

But the Mouser had a different thought and darted in the opposite direction in the face of an ominous wet reeking wind. Returning a dozen lightning-flashes later, he saw the green and silver queens disappearing into round black tunnel mouths in the rock to either side of the terrace and then they were gone.

As he joined Fafhrd in the work of unsettling the crossbars of the great weedy door and drawing its massive rusty bolts, it quivered under a portentous triple knocking as though someone had smote it thrice with a long-skirted cloak of chain mail. Water squirted under it and through the lower third of the central vertical crack. The Mouser looked behind him then, with the thought that they might yet have to seek another avenue of escape . . . and saw a great white-headed pillar of water jetting more than half the height of the grotto from the mouth of the tunnel connecting with the Inner Sea. Just then the silver cavern-light went out, but almost immediately other light spilled from above. Fafhrd had heaved open half of the great door. Green water foamed about their knees and subsided. They fought their way through and as the great door slammed behind them under a fresh surge of water, they found themselves sloshing about on a wild beach blown with foam, swimming with surf, and floored chiefly with large flat water-worn oval rocks like giants' skipping stones. The Mouser, turned shoreward, squinted desperately at the creamy cliff two bowshots away, wondering if they could possibly reach it through the mounting tide and climb it if they did.

But Fafhrd was looking seaward. The Mouser again felt himself shoulder-grabbed, spun around, and this time dragged up a curving ledge of the great tower-rock in the base of which was set the door through which they had just emerged. He stumbled, cutting his knees, but was jerked ruthlessly on. He decided that Fafhrd must have some very good reason for so rudely enjoining haste and thereafter did his best to hurry without assistance at Fafhrd's heels up the spiraling ramp-like ledge. On the second circling he stole a seaward look, gasped, and increased the speed of his mad dizzy scramble.

The stony beach below was drained and only here and there patched with huge gouts of spume, but roaring toward them from outer ocean was a giant wave that looked almost half as high as the pillar they were mounting – a great white wall of water flecked with green and brown and studded with rocks – a wave such as distant earthquakes send charging across the sea like a massed cavalry of monsters. Behind that wave came a taller one, and behind that a third taller still.

The Mouser and Fafhrd were three gasping circles higher when the stout tower shuddered and shook to the crashing impact of the first giant wave. Simultaneously the landward door at its base burst open from within and the caverntraveling water from the Inner Sea gushed out creamily to be instantly engulfed. The crest of the wave caught at Fafhrd's and the Mouser's ankles without quite tripping them or much slowing their progress. The second and third did likewise, although they had gained another circle before each impact. There was a fourth wave and a fifth, but no higher than the third. The adventurers reached the stumpy summit and cast themselves down on it, clutching at the still-shaking rock and slewing around to watch the shore – Fafhrd noting the astonishing minor circumstance that the Mouser was gripping between his teeth in the corner of his mouth a small black cigar.

The creamy curtain wall shuddered at the impact of the first wave and great cracks ran across it. The second wave shattered it and it fell into the third with an explosion of spray, displacing so much salt water that the return wave almost swamped the tower, its dirty crest tugging at the Mouser's and Fafhrd's fingers and licking along their sides. Again the tower shook and rocked beneath them but did not fall and that was the last of the great waves. Fafhrd and the Mouser circled down the spiraling ledges until they caught up with the declining sea, which still deeply covered the door at the tower's base. Then they looked landward again, where the mist raised by the catastrophe was dissipating.

A full half mile of the curtain wall had collapsed from base to crest, its shards vanishing totally beneath the waves, and through that gap the higher waters of the Inner Sea were pouring in a flat sullen tide that was swiftly obliterating the choppy aftermath of the earthquake waves from the Outer Sea.

On this wide river in the sea the *Black Treasurer* appeared from the mist riding straight toward their refuge rock.

Fafhrd cursed superstitiously. Sorcery working against him he could always accept, but magic operating in his favor he invariably found disturbing.

As the sloop drew near, they dove together into the sea, reached it with a few brisk strokes, scrambled aboard, steered it past the rock, and then lost no time in toweling and dressing their nakedness and preparing hot drinks. Soon they were looking at each over steaming mugs of grog. The brandy keg had been broached at last.

'Now that we've changed oceans,' Fafhrd said, 'we'll raise No-Ombrulsk in a day with this wet wind.'

The Mouser nodded and then smiled steadily at his comrade

for a space. Finally he said, 'Well, old friend, are you sure that is all you have to say?'

Fafhrd frowned. 'Well, there's one thing,' he replied somewhat uncomfortably after a bit. 'Tell me, Mouser, did your girl ever take off her mask?'

'Did yours?' the Mouser asked back, eyeing him quizzically.

Fafhrd frowned. 'Well, more to the point,' he said gruffly, 'did any of it really happen? We lost our swords and duds but we have nothing to show for it.'

The Mouser grinned and took the black cigar from the corner of his mouth and handed it to Fafhrd.

'This is what I went back for,' he said, sipping his grog. 'I thought we needed it to get our ship back, and perhaps we did.'

It was a tiny replica, carved in jet with the Mouser's teeth marks deeply indenting it near the stern, of the *Black Treasurer*.

V: THE WRONG BRANCH

It is rumored by the wise-brained rats which burrow the cited earth and by the knowledgeable cats that stalk its shadows and by the sagacious bats that wing its night and by the sapient zats which soar through airless space, slanting their metal wings to winds of light, that those two swordsmen and blood-brothers, Fafhrd and the Gray Mouser, have adventured not only in the World of Nehwon with its great empire of Lankhmar, but also in many other worlds and times and dimensions, arriving at these through certain secret doors far inside the mazy caverns of Ningauble of the Seven Eyes — whose great cave, in this sense, exists simultaneously in many worlds and times. It is a Door, while Ningauble glibly speaks the languages of many worlds and universes, loving the gossip of all times and places.

In each new world, the rumor goes, the Mouser and Fafhrd awaken with knowledge and speaking skills and personal memories suitable to it, and Lankhmar then seems to them only a dream and they know not its languages, though it is ever their primal homeland.

It is even whispered that on one occasion they lived a life in the strangest of worlds variously called Gaia, Midgard, Terra, and Earth, swashbuckling there along the eastern shore of an inner sea in kingdoms that were great fragments of a vasty empire carved out a century before by one called Alexander the Great.

So much Srith of the Scrolls has to tell us. What we know from informants closer to the source is as follows:

After Fafhrd and the Gray Mouser escaped from the sea-king's wrath, they set a course for chilly No-Ombrulsk, but by midnight the favoring west wind had shifted around into a blustering northeaster. It was Fafhrd's judgment, at which the Mouser sneered, that this thwarting was the beginning of the sea-king's revenge on them. They perforce turned tail (or stern, as finicky sailormen would have us say) and ran south under jib alone, always keeping the grim mountainous coast in view to larboard, so they would not be driven into the trackless Outer Sea, which they had crossed only once in their lives before, and then in dire circumstance, much farther south.

Next day they reentered the Inner Sea by way of the new strait that had been created by the fall of the curtain rocks. That they were able to make this perilous and uncharted passage without holing the *Black Treasurer*, or even scraping her keel, was cited by the Mouser as proof that they had been forgiven or forgotten by the sea-king, if such a formidable being indeed existed. Fafhrd, contrariwise, murkily asserted that the sea-queen's weedy and polygynous husband was only playing cat and mouse with them, letting them escape one danger so as to raise their hopes and then dash them even more devilishly at some unknown future time.

Their adventurings in the Inner Sea, which they knew almost as well as a queen of the east her turquoise and golden bathing pool, tended more and more to substantiate Fafhrd's pessimistic hypothesis. They were becalmed a score of times and hit by three-score sudden squalls. They had thrice to out-sail pirates and once best them in bloody hand-to-hand encounter. Seeking to reprovision in Ool Hrusp, they were themselves accused of piracy by the Mad Duke's harbor patrol, and only the moonless night and some very clever tacking – and a generous measure of luck – allowed the *Black Treasurer* to escape, its side bepricked and its sails transfixed with arrows enough to make it resemble a slim aquatic ebon hedge-hog, or a black needlefish.

Near Kvarch Nar they did manage to reprovision, though only with coarse food and muddy river water. Shortly there-after the seams of the *Black Treasurer* were badly strained and two opened by glancing collision with an underwater reef which never should have been where it was. The only possible point where they could careen and mend their ship was the tiny beach on the southwest side of the Dragon Rocks, and it took them two days of nip-and-tuck sailing and bailing to get them there with deck above water. Whereupon while one patched or napped, the other must stand guard against inquisitive two- and three-headed dragons and even an occasional mono-cephalic. When they got a cauldron of pitch seething for final repairs, the dragons all deserted them, put off by the black stuff's stink – a circumstance which irked rather than pleased the two adventurers, since they hadn't had the wit to keep a pot of pitch a-boil from the start. (They were most touchy and thin-skinned now from their long run of ill fortune.)

A-sail once more, the Mouser at long last agreed with Fafhrd that they truly had the sea-king's curse on them and must seek sorcerous aid in getting it removed – because if they merely forsook sea for land, the sea-king might well pursue them through his allies the Rivers and the Rainstorms, and they would still be under the full curse whenever they again took to ocean.

It was a close question as to whether they should consult Sheelba of the Eyeless Face, or Ningauble of the Seven Eyes. But since Sheelba laired in the Salt Marsh next to the city of Lankhmar, where their recent close connection with Pulg and Issekianity might get them into more trouble, they decided to consult Ningauble in his caverns in the low mountains behind Ilthmar.

Even the sail to Ilthmar was not without dangers. They were attacked by giant squids and by flying fish of the poison-spined variety. They also had to use all their sailor skill and expend all the arrows which the Ool Hruspians had given them, in order to stand off yet one more pirate attack. The brandy was all drunk.

As they were anchoring in Ilthmar harbor, the *Black Treasurer* literally fell apart like a joke-box, starboard side parting from larboard like two quarters of a split melon, while the mast and cabin, weighted by the keel, sank speedily as a rock.

Fafhrd and Mouser saved only the clothes they were in, their swords, dirk, and ax. And it was well they hung onto the latter, for while swimming ashore they were attacked by a school of sharks, and each man had to defend self and comrade while swimming encumbered. Ilthmarts lining the quays and moles cheered the heroes and the sharks impartially, or rather as to how they had laid their money, the odds being mostly three-to-one against both heroes surviving, with various shorter odds on the big man, the little man, or one or the other turning the trick.

Ilthmarts are a somewhat heartless people and much given to gambling. Besides, they welcome sharks into their harbor, since it makes for an easy way of disposing of common criminals, robbed and drunken strangers, slaves grown senile or otherwise useless, and also assures that the shark-god's chosen victims will always be spectacularly received.

When Fafhrd and the Mouser finally staggered ashore panting, they were cheered by such Ilthmarts as had won money on them. A larger number were busy booing the sharks.

The cash they got by selling the wreckage of the *Black Treasurer* was not enough to buy or hire them horses, though sufficient to provide food, wine, and water for one drunk and a few subsequent days of living.

During the drunk they more than once toasted the *Black Treasurer*, a faithful ship which had literally given its all for them, worked to death by storms, pirate attacks, the gnawing of sea-things, and other sacraments of the sea-king's rage. The Mouser drank curses on the sea-king, while Fafhrd crossed his fingers. They also had more or less courteously to fight off the attentions of numerous dancing girls, most of them fat and retired.

It was a poor drunk, on the whole. Ilthmar is a city in which even a minimally prudent man dare not sleep soused, while the endless repetitions of its rat-god, more powerful even than its shark-god, in sculptures, murals, and smaller decor (and in large live rats silent in the shadows or a-dance in the alleys) make for a certain nervousness in newcomers after a few hours.

Thereafter it was a dusty two-day trudge to the caverns of Ningauble, especially for men untrained to tramping by many months a-sea and with the land becoming sandy desert toward the end.

The coolth of the hidden-mouthed rocky tunnel leading to Ningauble's deep abode was most welcome to men weary, dry, and powdered with fine sand. Fafhrd, being the more knowledgeable of Ningauble and his mazy lair, led the way, hands groping above and before him for stalactites and sharp rock edges which might inflict grievous head-bashings and other wounds. Ningauble did not approve the use by others of torch or candle in his realm.

After avoiding numerous side passages they came to a Y-shaped branching. Here the Mouser, pressing ahead, made out a pale glow far along the left-hand branch and insisted they explore that tunnel.

'After all,' he said, 'if we find we've chosen wrong, we can always come back.'

'But the right-hand branch is the one leading to Ningauble's auditorium,' Fafhrd protested. 'That is, I'm almost certain it is. That desert sun curdled my brain.'

'A plague on you for a pudding-head and a know-not-know,' the Mouser snapped, himself irritable still from the heat and dryness of their tramping, and strode confidently a-crouch down the left-hand branch. After two heartbeats, Fafhrd shrugged and followed.

The light grew ever more cooly bright ahead. Each experienced a brief spell of dizziness and a momentary unsettling of the rock underfoot, as if there were a very slight earthquake.

'Let's go back,' Fafhrd said.

'Let's at least *see*,' the Mouser retorted. 'We're already there.'

A few steps more and they were looking down another slope of desert. Just outside the entrance arch there stood with preternatural calm a richly-caparisoned white horse, a smaller black one with silver harness buckles and rings, and a sturdy mule laden with water-bags, pots, and parcels looking as though they contained provender for man and four-foot beast. By each of the saddles hung a bow and quiver of arrows, while to the white horse's saddle was affixed a most succinct note on a scrap of parchment:

The sea-king's curse is lifted. Ning.

There was something very strange about the writing, though neither could wholly define wherein the strangeness lay. Perhaps it was that Ningauble had written down the sea-king as Poseidon, but that seemed a most acceptable alternate. And yet...

'It is most peculiar of Ningauble,' Fafhrd said, his voice sounding subtly odd to the Mouser and to himself too, '—most peculiar to do favors without demanding much information and even service in return.'

'Let us not look gift-steeds in the mouth,' the Mouser advised. 'Nor even a gift mule, for that matter.'

The wind had changed while they had been in the tunnels, so that it was not now blowing sultry from the east, but cool from the west. Both men felt greatly refreshed, and when they discovered that one of the mule's bags contained not branch water, but delicious strong water, their minds were made up. They mounted, Fafhrd the white, the Mouser the black, and single-footed confidently west, the mule tramping after.

A day told them that something unusual had happened, for they did not fetch Ilthmar or even the Inner Sea.

Also, they continued to be bothered by something strange about the words they were using, though each understood the other clearly enough.

In addition, both realized that something was happening to his memories and even common knowledge, though they did not at first reveal to each other this fear. Desert game was plentiful, and delicious when broiled, enough to quiet wonderings about an indefinable difference in the shape and coloration of the animals. And they found a rarely sweet desert spring.

It took a week, and also encounter with a peaceful caravan of silk-and-spice merchants, before they realized that they were speaking to each other not in Lankhmarese, pidgin Mingol, and Forest Tongue, but in Phoenician, Aramaic, and

Greek; and that Fafhrd's childhood memories were not of the Cold Waste, but of lands around a sea called Baltic; the Mouser's not of Tovilyis, but Tyre; and that here the greatest city was not called Lankhmar, but Alexandria.

And even with those thoughts, the memory of Lankhmar and the whole world of Nehwon began to fade in their minds, become a remembered dream or series of dreams.

Only the memory of Ningauble and his caverns stayed sharp and clear. But the exact nature of the trick he had played on them became cloudy.

No matter, the air here was sharp and clean, the food good, the wine sweet and addling, the men built nicely enough to promise interesting women. What if the names and the new words seemed initially weird? Such feelings diminished even as one thought about them.

Here was a new world, promising unheard-of adventures. Though even as one thought 'new', it became a world more familiar.

They cantered down the white sandy track of their new, yet foreordained, destiny.

VI: ADEPT'S GAMBIT

1. *Tyre*

It happened that while Fafhrd and the Gray Mouser were dallying in a wine shop near the Sidonian Harbor of Tyre, where all wine shops are of doubtful repute, a long-limbed yellow-haired Galatian girl lolling in Fafhrd's lap turned suddenly into a wallopingly large sow. It was a singular occurrence, even in Tyre. The Mouser's eyebrows arched as the Galatian's breasts, exposed by the Cretan dress that was the style revival of the hour, became the uppermost pair of slack white dugs, and he watched the whole proceeding with unfeigned interest.

The next day four camel traders, who drank only water disinfected with sour wine, and two purple-armed dyers, who were cousins of the host, swore that no transformation took place and that they saw nothing, or very little out of the ordinary. But three drunken soldiers of King Antiochus and four women with them, as well as a completely sober Armenian juggler, attested the event in all its details. An Egyptian mummy-smuggler won brief attention with the claim that the oddly garbed sow was only a semblance, or phantom, and made dark references to visions vouchsafed men by the animal gods of his native land, but since it was hardly a year since the Selucids had beaten the Ptolomies out of Tyre, he was quickly shouted down. An impecunious traveling lecturer from Jerusalem took up an even more attenuated position, maintaining that the sow was not a sow, or even a semblance, but only the semblance of a semblance of a sow.

Fafhrd, however, had no time for such metaphysical niceties. When, with a roar of disgust not unmingled with terror, he had shoved the squealing monstrosity halfway across the room so that it fell with a great splash into the water tank, it turned back again into a long-limbed Galatian girl and a very angry one, for the stale water in which the sow had floundered drenched her garments and plastered down her yellow hair (the Mouser murmured, 'Aphrodite!') and the sow's uncorsetable bulk had split the tight Cretan waist. The stars of midnight were peeping through the skylight above the tank, and the wine cups had been many times refilled, before her anger was dissipated. Then, just as Fafhrd was impressing a reintroductory kiss upon her melting lips, he felt them once again become slobbering and tusky. This time she picked herself up from between two wine casks and, ignoring the shrieks, excited comments, and befuddled stares as merely part of a rude mystification that had been carried much too far, she walked with Amazonian dignity from the room. She paused only once, on the dark and deep-worn threshold, and then but to hurl at Fafhrd a small dagger, which he absentmindedly deflected upward with his copper goblet, so that it struck full in the mouth a wooden satyr on the wall, giving that deity the appearance of introspectively picking his teeth.

Fafhrd's sea-green eyes became likewise thoughtful as he wondered what magician had tampered with his love life. He slowly scanned the wine shop patrons, face by sly-eyed face, pausing doubtfully when he came to a tall, dark-haired girl beyond the water tank, finally returning to the Mouser. There he stopped, and a certain suspiciousness became apparent in his gaze.

The Mouser folded his arms, flared his snub nose, and returned the stare with all the sneering suavity of a Parthian ambassador. Abruptly he turned, embraced and kissed the cross-eyed Greek girl sitting beside him, grinned wordlessly at Fafhrd, dusted from his coarse-woven gray silk robe the antimony that had fallen from her eyelids, and folded his arms again.

Fafhrd began softly to beat the base of his goblet against the butt of his palm. His wide, tight-laced leather belt, wet with the sweat that stained his white linen tunic, creaked faintly.

Meanwhile murmured speculation as to the person responsible for casting a spell on Fafhrd's Galatian eddied around the tables and settled uncertainly on the tall, dark-haired girl, probably because she was sitting alone and therefore could not join in the suspicious whispering.

'She's an odd one,' Chloe, the cross-eyed Greek, confided to the Mouser. 'Silent Salmacis they call her, but I happen to know that her real name is Ahura.'

'A Persian?' asked the Mouser.

Chloe shrugged. 'She's been around for years, though no one knows exactly where she lives or what she does. She used to be a gay, gossipy little thing, though she never would go with men. Once she gave me an amulet, to protect me from someone, she said – I still wear it. But then she was away for a while,' Chloe continued garrulously, 'and when she came back she was just like you see her now – shy, and tight-mouthed as a clam, with a look in her eyes of someone peering through a crack in a brothel wall.'

'Ah,' said the Mouser. He looked at the dark-haired girl, and continued to look, appreciatively, even when Chloe tugged at his sleeve. Chloe gave herself a mental bastinado for having been so foolish as to call a man's attention to another girl.

Fafhrd was not distracted by this byplay. He continued to stare at the Mouser with the stony intentness of a whole avenue of Egyptian colossi. The cauldron of his anger came to a boil.

'Scum of wit-weighted culture,' he said, 'I consider it the nadir of base perfidy that you should try out on me your puking sorcery.'

'Softly, man of strange loves,' purred the Mouser. 'This unfortunate mishap has befallen several others besides yourself, among them an ardent Assyrian warlord whose paramour was changed into a spider between the sheets, and an impetuous Ethiop who found himself hoisted several yards into the air and kissing a giraffe. Truly, to one who knows the literature, there is nothing new in the annals of magic and thaumaturgy.'

'Moreover,' continued Fafhrd, his low-pitched voice loud in the silence, 'I regard it an additional treachery that you should practice your pig-trickery on me in an unsuspecting moment of pleasure.'

'And even if I should choose sorcerously to discommode your lechery,' hypothesized the Mouser, 'I do not think it would be the woman that I would metamorphose.'

'Furthermore,' pursed Fafhrd, leaning forward and laying his hand on the large sheathed dirk beside him on the bench, 'I judge it an intolerable and direct affront to myself that you should pick a Galatian girl, member of a race that is cousin to my own.'

'It would not be the first time,' observed the Mouser portentously, slipping his fingers inside his robe, 'that I have had to fight you over a woman.'

'But it would be the first time,' asserted Fafhrd, with an even greater portentousness, 'that you had to fight me over a pig!'

For a moment he maintained his belligerent posture, head lowered, jaw outthrust, eyes slitted. Then he began to laugh.

It was something, Fafhrd's laughter. It began with windy snickers through the nostrils, next spewed out between clenched teeth, then became a series of jolting chortles, swiftly grew into a roar against which the barbarian had to brace himself, legs spread wide, head thrown back, as if against a gale. It was a laughter of the storm-lashed forest or the sea, a laughter that conjured up wide visions, that seemed to blow from a more primeval, heartier, lusher time. It was the laughter of the Elder Gods observing their creature man and noting their omissions, miscalculations and mistakes.

The Mouser's lips began to twitch. He grimaced wryly, seeking to avoid the infection. Then he joined in.

Fafhrd paused, panted, snatched up the wine pitcher, drained it.

'Pig-trickery!' he bellowed, and began to laugh all over again.

The Tyrian riffraff gawked at them in wonder – astounded, awestruck, their imagination cloudily stirred.

Among them, however, was one whose response was noteworthy. The dark-haired girl was staring at Fafhrd avidly, drinking in the sound, the oddest sort of hunger and baffled curiosity – and calculation – in her eyes.

The Mouser noticed her and stopped his laughter to watch. Mentally Chloe gave herself an especially heavy swipe on the soles of her bound, naked feet.

Fafhrd's laughter trailed off. He blew out the last of it soundlessly, sucked in a normal breath, hooked his thumbs in his belt.

'The dawn stars are peeping,' he commented to the Mouser, ducking his head for a look through the skylight. 'It's time we were about the business.'

And without more ado he and Mouser left the shop, pushing out of their way a newly arrived and very drunken merchant of Pergamum, who looked after them bewilderedly, as if he were trying to decide whether they were a tall god and his dwarfish servitor, or a small sorceror and the great-thewed automaton who did his bidding.

Had it ended there, two weeks would have seen Fafhrd claiming that the incident of the wine shop was merely a drunken dream that had been dreamed by more than one – a kind of coincidence with which he was by no means unfamiliar. But it did not. After 'the business' (which turned out to be much more complicated than had been anticipated, evolving from a fairly simple affair of Sidonian smugglers into a glittering intrigue studded with Cilician pirates, a kidnapped Cappadocian princess, a forged letter of credit on a Syracusan financier, a bargain with a female Cyprian slave-dealer, rendezvous that turned into an ambush, some priceless tomb-filched Egyptian jewels that no one ever saw, and a band of Idumean brigands who came galloping out of the desert to upset everyone's calculations) and after Fafhrd and the Gray Mouser had returned to the soft embraces and sweet polyglot of the seaport ladies, pig-trickery befell Fafhrd once more, this time ending in a dagger brawl with some men who thought they were rescuing a pretty Bithynian girl from death by salty and odorous drowning at the hands of a murderous red-haired giant – Fafhrd had insisted on dipping the girl, while still meta-morphosed, into a hogshead of brine remaining from pickled pork. This incident suggested to the Mouser a scheme he never told Fafhrd: namely, to engage an amiable girl, have Fafhrd turn her into a pig, immediately sell her to a butcher, next sell her to an amorous merchant when she had escaped the bewildered butcher as a furious girl, have Fafhrd sneak after the merchant and turn her back into a pig (by this time he ought to be able to do it merely by making eyes at her), then sell her to another butcher and begin all over again. Low prices, quick profits.

For a while Fafhrd stubbornly continued to suspect the Mouser, who was forever dabbling in black magic and carried a gray leather case of bizarre instruments picked from the pockets of wizards and recondite books looted from Chaldean libraries – even though long experience had taught Fafhrd that the Mouser seldom read systematically beyond the prefaces in the majority of his books (though he often unrolled the latter portions to the accompaniment of penetrating glances and trenchant criticisms) and that he was never able to evoke the same results two times running with his enchantments. That he could manage to transform two of Fafhrd's lights of love was barely possible; that he should get a sow each time was unthinkable. Besides, the thing happened more than twice; in fact, there never was a time when it did not happen. Moreover, Fafhrd did not really believe in magic, least of all the Mouser's. And if there was any doubt left in his mind, it was dispelled when a dark and satiny-skinned Egyptian beauty in the Mouser's close embrace was transformed into a giant snail. The Gray One's disgust at the slimy tracks on his silken garments was not to be mistaken, and was not lessened when two witnesses, traveling horse doctors, claimed that they had seen no snail, giant or ordinary, and agreed that the Mouser was suffering from an obscure kind of wet rot that induced hallucinations in its victim, and for which they were prepared to offer a rare Median remedy at the bargain price of nineteen drachmas a jar.

Fafhrd's glee at his friend's discomfiture was short-lived, for after a night of desperate and far-flung experimentation, which, some said, blazed from the Sidonian harbor to the

Temple of Melkarth a trail of snail tracks that next morning baffled all the madams and half the husbands in Tyre, the Mouser discovered something he had suspected all the time, but had hoped was not the whole truth: namely, that Chloe alone was immune to the strange plague his kisses carried.

Needless to say, this pleased Chloe immensely. An arrogant self-esteem gleamed like two clashing swords from her crossed eyes and she applied nothing but costly scented oil to her poor, mentally bruised feet – and not only mental oil, for she quickly made capital of her position by extorting enough gold from the Mouser to buy a slave whose duty it was to do very little else. She no longer sought to avoid calling the Mouser's attention to other women, in fact she rather enjoyed doing so, and the next time they encountered the dark-haired girl variously called Ahura and Silent Salmacis, as they were entering a tavern known as the Murex Shell, she volunteered more information.

'Ahura's not so innocent, you know, in spite of the way she sticks to herself. Once she went off with some old man – that was before she gave me the charm – and once I heard a primped-up Persian lady scream at her, "What have you done with your brother?" Ahura didn't answer, just looked at the woman coldly as a snake, and after a while the woman ran out. Brr! You should have seen her eyes!'

But the Mouser pretended not to be interested.

Fafhrd could undoubtedly have had Chloe for the polite asking, and Chloe was more than eager to extend and cement in this fashion her control over the twain. But Fafhrd's pride would not allow him to accept such a favor from his friend, and he had frequently in past days, moreover, railed against Chloe as a decadent and unappetizing contemplater of her own nose.

So he perforce led a monastic life and endured contemptuous feminine glares across the drinking table and fended off painted boys who misinterpreted his misogyny and was much irritated by a growing rumor to the effect that he had become a secret eunuch priest of Cybele. Gossip and speculation had already fantastically distorted the truer accounts of what had happened, and it did not help when the girls who had been transformed denied it for fear of hurting their business. Some people got the idea that Fafhrd had committed the nasty sin of bestiality and they urged his prosecution in the public courts. Others accounted him a fortunate man who had been visited by an amorous goddess in the guise of a swine, and who thereafter scorned all earthly girls. While still others whispered that he was a brother of Circe and that he customarily dwelt on a floating island in the Tyrrhenian Sea, where he kept cruelly transformed into pigs a whole herd of beautiful shipwrecked maidens. His laughter was heard no more and dark circles appeared in the white skin around his eyes and he began to make guarded inquiries among magicians in hopes of finding some remedial charm.

'I think I've hit on a cure for your embarrassing ailment,' said the Mouser carelessly one night, laying aside a raggedy brown papyrus. 'Came across it in this obscure treatise, "The Demonology of Isaiah ben Elshaz." It seems that whatever change takes place in the form of the woman you love, you should continue to make love to her, trusting to the power of your passion to transform her back to her original shape.'

Fafhrd left off honing his great sword and asked, 'Then why don't you try kissing snails?'

'It would be disagreeable and, for one free of barbarian prejudices, there is always Chloe.'

'Pah! You're just going with her to keep your self-respect. I know you. For seven days now you'd had thoughts for no one but that Ahura wench.'

'A pretty chit, but not to my liking,' said the Mouser icily. 'It must be your eye she's the apple of. However, you really should try my remedy; I'm sure you'd prove so good at it that the shes of all the swine in the world would come squealing after you.'

Whereupon Fafhrd did go so far as to hold firmly at arm's length the next sow his pent passion created, and feed it slops in the hope of accomplishing something by kindness. But in the end he had once again to admit defeat and assuage with owl-stamped Athenian silver didrachmas an hysterically angry Scythian girl who was sick at the stomach. It was then that an ill-advised curious young Greek philosopher suggested to the Northman that the soul or inward form of the thing loved is alone of importance, the outward form having no ultimate significance.

'You belong to the Socratic school?' Fafhrd questioned gently.

The Greek nodded.

'Socrates was the philosopher who was able to drink unlimited quantities of wine without blinking?'

Again the quick nod.

'That was because his rational soul dominated his animal soul?'

'You are learned,' replied the Greek, with a more respectful but equally quick nod.

'I am not through. Do you consider yourself in all ways a true follower of your master?'

This time the Greek's quickness undid him. He nodded, and two days later he was carried out of the wine shop by friends, who found him cradled in a broken wine barrel, as if new-born in no common manner. For days he remained drunk, time enough for a small sect to spring up who believed him a reincarnation of Dionysus and as such worshiped him. The sect was dissolved when he became half sober and delivered his first oracular address, which had as its subject the evils of drunkenness.

The morning after the deification of the rash philosopher, Fafhrd awoke when the first sunbeams struck the flat roof on which he and the Mouser had chosen to pass the night. Without sound or movement, suppressing the urge to groan out for someone to buy him a bag of snow from the white-capped Lebanons (over which the sun was even now peeping) to cool his aching head, he opened an eye on the sight that he in his wisdom had expected: the Mouser sitting on his heels and looking at the sea.

'Son of a wizard and a witch,' he said, 'it seems that once again we must fall back upon our last resource.'

The Mouser did not turn his head, but he nodded it once, deliberately.

'The first time we did not come away with our lives,' Fafhrd went on.

'The second time we lost our souls to the Other Creatures,' the Mouser chimed in, as if they were singing a dawn chant to Isis.

'And the last time we were snatched away from the bright dream of Lankhmar.'

'He may trick us into drinking the drink, and we not awake for another five hundred years.'

'He may send us to our deaths and we not to be reincarnated for another two thousand,' Fafhrd continued.

'He may show us Pan, or offer us to the Elder Gods, or whisk us beyond the stars, or send us into the underworld of Quarmall,' the Mouser concluded.

There was a pause of several moments.

Then the Gray Mouser whispered, 'Nevertheless, we must visit Ningauble of the Seven Eyes.'

And he spoke truly, for as Fafhrd had guessed, his soul was hovering over the sea dreaming of dark-haired Ahura.

2. Ningauble

So they crossed the snowy Lebanons and stole three camels, virtuously choosing to rob a rich landlord who made his tenants milk rocks and sow the shores of the Dead Sea, for it was unwise to approach the Gossiper of the Gods with an overly dirty conscience. After seven days of pitching and tossing across the desert, furnace days that made Fafhrd curse Muspelheim's fire gods, in whom he did not believe, they reached the Sand Combers and the Great Sand Whirlpools, and warily slipping past them while they were only lazily twirling, climbed the Rocky Islet. The city-loving Mouser ranted at Ningauble's preference for 'a godforsaken hole in the desert', although he suspected that the Newsmonger and his agents came and went by a more hospitable road than the one provided for visitors, and although he knew as well as Fafhrd that the Snarer of Rumors (especially the false, which are the more valuable) must live as close to India and the infinite garden lands of the Yellow Men as to barbaric Britain and marching Rome, as close to the heaven-steaming trans-Ethiopian jungle as to the mystery of lonely tablelands and star-scraping mountains beyond the Caspian Sea.

With high expectations they tethered their camels, took torches, and fearlessly entered the Bottomless Caves, for it was not so much in the visiting of Ningauble that danger lay as in the tantalizing charm of his advice, which was so great that one had to follow wherever it led.

Nevertheless Fafhrd said, 'An earthquake swallowed Ningauble's house and it stuck in his throat. May he not hiccup.'

As they were passing over the Trembling Bridge spanning the Pit of Ultimate Truth, which could have devoured the light of ten thousand torches without becoming any less black, they met and edged wordlessly past a helmeted, impassive fellow whom they recognized as a far-journeying Mongol. They speculated as to whether he too were a visitor of the Gossiper, or a spy – Fafhrd had no faith in the clairvoyant power of the seven eyes, averring that they were merely a sham to awe fools and that Ningauble's information was gathered by a corps of peddlers, panders, slaves, urchins, eunuchs, and midwives, which outnumbered the grand armies of a dozen kings.

They reached the other side with relief and passed a score of tunnel mouths, which the Mouser eyed most wistfully.

'Mayhap we should choose one at random,' he muttered, 'and seek yet another world. Ahura's not Aphrodite, nor yet Astarte – quite.'

'Without Ning's guidance?' Fafhrd retorted. 'And carrying our curses with us? Press on!'

Presently they saw a faint light flickering on the stalactited roof, reflected from a level above them. Soon they were struggling toward it up the Staircase of Error, an agglomeration of great rough rocks. Fafhrd stretched his long legs; the Mouser leaped catlike. The little creatures that scurried about their feet, brushed their shoulders in slow flight, or merely showed their yellow, insatiably curious eyes from crevice and rocky perch, multiplied in number; for they were nearing the Arch-eavesdropper.

A little later, having wasted no time in reconnoitering, they stood before the Great Gate, whose iron-studded upper reaches disdained the illumination of the tiny fire. It was not the gate, however, that interested them, but its keeper, a monstrously paunched creature sitting on the floor beside a vast heap of potsherds, and whose only movement was a rubbing of what seemed to be his hands. He kept them under the shabby but voluminous cloak which also completely hooded his head. A third of the way down the cloak, two large bats clung.

Fafhrd cleared his throat.

The movement ceased under the cloak.

Then out of the top of it sinuously writhed something that seemed to be a serpent, only in place of a head it bore an opalescent jewel with a dark central speck. Nevertheless, one might finally have judged it a serpent, were it not that it also resembled a thick-stalked exotic bloom. It restlessly turned this way and that until it pointed at the two strangers. Then it went rigid and the bulbous extremity seemed to glow more brightly. There came a low purring and five similar stalks twisted rapidly from under the hood and aligned themselves with their companion. Then the six black pupils dilated.

'Fat-bellied rumor monger!' hailed the Mouser nervously. 'Must you forever play at peep show?'

For one could never quite get over the faint initial uneasiness that came with meeting Ningauble of the Seven Eyes.

'That is an incivility, Mouser,' a voice from under the hood quavered thinly. 'It is not well for men who come seeking sage counsel to cast fleers before them. Nevertheless, I am today in a merry humor and will give ear to your problem. Let me see, now, what world do you and Fafhrd come from?'

'Earth, as you very well know, you king of shreds of lies and patches of hypocrisy,' the Mouser retorted thinly, stepping nearer. Three of the eyes closely followed his advance, while a fourth kept watch on Fafhrd.

At the same time, 'Further incivilities,' Ningauble murmured sadly, shaking his head so that his eye-stalks jogged. 'You think it easy to keep track of the times and spaces and of the worlds manifold? And speaking of time, is it not time indeed that you ceased to impose on me, because you once got me an unborn ghoul that I might question it of its parentage? The service to me was slight, accepted only to humor you; and I, by the name of the Spoorless God, have repaid it twenty times over.'

'Nonsense, Midwife of Secrets,' retorted the Mouser, stepping forward familiarly, his gay impudence almost restored. 'You know as well as I that deep in your great paunch you are trembling with delight at having a chance to mouth your knowledge to two such appreciative listeners as we.'

'That is as far from the truth as I am from the Secret of the Sphinx,' commented Ningauble, four of his eyes following the Mouser's advance, one keeping watch on Fafhrd, while the sixth looped back around the hood to reappear on the other side and gaze suspiciously behind them.

'But, Ancient Tale-bearer, I am sure you have been closer to the Sphinx than any of her stony lovers. Very likely she first received her paltry riddle from your great store.'

Ningauble quivered like jelly at this tickling flattery.

'Nevertheless,' he piped, 'today I am in a merry humor and will give ear to your question. But remember that it will almost certainly be too difficult for me.'

'We know your great ingenuity in the face of insurmountable obstacles,' rejoined the Mouser in the properly soothing tones.

'Why doesn't your friend come forward?' asked Ningauble, suddenly querulous again.

Fafhrd had been waiting for that question. It always went against his grain to have to behave congenially toward one who called himself the Mightiest Magician as well as the Gossiper of the Gods. But that Ningauble should let hang from his shoulders two bats whom he called Hugin and Munin in open burlesque of Odin's ravens, was too much for him. It was more a patriotic than religious matter with Fafhrd. He believed in Odin only during moments of sentimental weakness.

'Slay the bats or send them slithering and I'll come, but not before,' he dogmatized.

'Now I'll tell you nothing,' said Ningauble pettishly, 'for, as all know, my health will not permit bickering.'

'But, Schoolmaster of Falsehood,' purred the Mouser, darting a murderous glance at Fafhrd, 'that is indeed to be regretted, especially since I was looking forward to regaling you with the intricate scandal that the Friday concubine of the satrap Philip withheld even from her body slave.'

'Ah well,' conceded the Many-Eyed One, 'it is time for Hugin and Munin to feed.'

The bats reluctantly unfurled their wings and flew lazily into the darkness.

Fafhrd stirred himself and moved forward, sustaining the scrutiny of the majority of the eyes, all six of which the Northman considered artfully manipulated puppet-orbs. The seventh no man had seen, or boasted of having seen, save the Mouser, who claimed it was Odin's other eye, stolen from sagacious Mimer – this not because he believed it, but to irk his Northern comrade.

'Greetings, Snake Eyes,' Fafhrd boomed.

'Oh, is it you, Hulk?' said Ningauble carelessly. 'Sit down, both, and share my humble fire.'

'Are we not to be invited beyond the Great Gate and share your fabulous comforts too?'

'Do not mock me, Gray One. As all know, I am poor, penurious Ningauble.'

So with a sigh the Mouser settled himself on his heels, for he well knew that the Gossiper prized above all else a reputation for poverty, chastity, humility, and thrift, therefore playing his own doorkeeper, except on certain days when the Great Gate muted the tinkle of impious sistrum and the lascivious wail of flute and the giggles of those who postured in the shadow shows.

But now Ningauble coughed piteously and seemed to shiver and warmed his cloaked members at the fire. And the shadows flickered weakly against iron and stone, and the little creatures crept rustling in, making their eyes wide to see and their ears cupped to hear; and upon their rhythmically swinging, weaving stalks pulsated the six eyes. At intervals, too, Ningauble would pick up, seemingly at random, a potsherd from the great pile and rapidly scan the memorandum scribbled on it, without breaking the rhythm of the eyestalks or, apparently, the thread of his attention.

The Mouser and Fafhrd crouched on their hams.

As Fafhrd started to speak, Ningauble questioned rapidly, 'And now, my children, you had something to tell me concerning the Friday concubine—'

'Ah, yes, Artist of Untruth,' the Mouser cut in hastily. 'Concerning not so much the concubine as three eunuch priests of Cybele and a slave-girl from Samos – a tasty affair of wondrous complexity, which you must give me leave to let simmer in my mind so that I may serve it up to you skimmed of the slightest fat of exaggeration and with all the spice of true detail.'

'And while we wait for the Mouser's mind-pot to boil,' said Fafhrd casually, at last catching the spirit of the thing, 'you may the more merrily pass the time by advising us as to a trifling difficulty,' And he gave a succinct account of their tantalizing bedevilment by sow- and snail-changed maidens.

'And you say that Chloe alone proved immune to the spell?' queried Ningauble thoughtfully, tossing a potsherd to the far side of the pile. 'Now that brings to my mind—'

'The exceedingly peculiar remark at the end of Diotima's fourth epistle to Socrates?' interrupted the Mouser brightly. 'Am I not right, Father?'

'You are not,' replied Ningauble coldly. 'As I was about to observe, when this tick of the intellect sought to burrow the skin of my mind, there must be something that throws a protective influence around Chloe. Do you know of any god or demon in whose special favor she stands, or any incantation or rune she habitually mumbles, or any notable talisman, charm, or amulet she customarily wears or inscribes on her body?'

'She did mention one thing,' the Mouser admitted diffidently after a moment. 'An amulet given her years ago by some

Persian, or Greco-Persian girl. Doubtless a trifle of no consequence.'

'Doubtless. Now, when the first sow-change occurred, did Fafhrd laugh the laugh? He did? That was unwise, as I have many times warned you. Advertise often enough your connection with the Elder Gods and you may be sure that some greedy searcher from the pit ...'

'But what *is* our connection with the Elder Gods?' asked the Mouser, eagerly, though not hopefully. Fafhrd grunted derisively.

'Those are matters best not spoken of,' Ningauble ordained. 'Was there anyone who showed a particular interest in Fafhrd's laughter?'

The Mouser hesitated. Fafhrd coughed. Thus prodded, the Mouser confessed, 'Oh, there was a girl who was perhaps a trifle more attentive than the others to his bellowing. A Persian girl. In fact, as I recall, the same one who gave Chloe the amulet.'

'Her name is Ahura,' said Fafhrd. 'The Mouser's in love with her.'

'A fable!' the Mouser denied laughingly, double-daggering Fafhrd with a superstitious glare. 'I can assure you, Father, that she is a very shy, stupid girl, who cannot possibly be concerned in any way with our troubles.'

'Of course, since you say so,' Ningauble observed, his voice icily rebuking. 'However, I can tell you this much: the one who has placed the ignominious spell upon you is, insofar as he partakes of humanity, a man ...'

(The Mouser was relieved. It was unpleasant to think of dark-haired, lithe Ahura being subjected to certain methods of questioning which Ningauble was reputed to employ. He was irked at his own clumsiness in trying to lead Ningauble's attention away from Ahura. Where she was concerned, his wit failed him.)

'... and an adept,' Ningauble concluded. 'Yes, my sons, an adept – a master practitioner of blackest magic without faintest blink of light.'

The Mouser started. Fafhrd groaned, 'Again?'

'Again,' Ningauble affirmed. 'Though why, save for your connection with the Elder Gods, you should interest those most recondite of creatures, I cannot guess. They are not men who wittingly will stand in the glaringly illuminated foreground of history. They seek—'

'But who is it?' Fafhrd interjected.

'Be quiet, Mutilator of Rhetoric. They seek the shadows, and surely for good reason. They are the glorious amateurs of high magic, disdaining practical ends, caring only for the satisfaction of their insatiable curiosities, and therefore doubly dangerous. They are . . .'

'But what's his name?'

'Silence, Trampler of Beautiful Phrases. They are in their fashion fearless, irreligiously considering themselves the co-equals of destiny and having only contempt for the Demigod-dess of Chance, the Imp of Luck, and the Demon of Improbability. In short, they are adversaries before whom you should certainly tremble and to whose will you should unquestionably bow.'

'But his name, Father, his name!' Fafhrd burst out, and the Mouser, his impudence again in the ascendant, remarked, 'It is he of the Sabihoon, is it not, Father?'

'It is not. The Sabihoon are an ignorant fisher folk who inhabit the hither shore of the far lake and worship the beast god Wheen, denying all others,' a reply that tickled the Mouser, for to the best of his knowledge he had just invented the Sabihoon.

'No, his name is . . .' Ningauble paused and began to chuckle. 'I was forgetting that I must under no circumstances tell you his name.'

Fafhrd jumped up angrily. 'What?'

'Yes, children,' said Ningauble, suddenly making his eye-stalks staringly rigid, stern and uncompromising. 'And I must furthermore tell you that I can in no way help you in this matter . . .' (Fafhrd clenched his fists) '. . . and I am very glad of it too . . .' (Fafhrd swore) '. . . for it seems to me that no more fitting punishment could have been devised for your abominable lecheries, which I have so often bemoaned . . .'

(Fafhrd's hand went to his sword hilt) '. . . in fact, if it had been up to me to chastise you for your manifold vices, I would have chosen the very same enchantment . . .' (But now he had gone too far; Fafhrd growled, 'Oh, so it is you who are behind it!' ripped out his sword and began to advance slowly on the hooded figure) '. . . Yes, my children, you must accept your lot without rebellion or bitterness . . .' (Fafhrd continued to advance) '. . . Far better that you should retire from the world as I have and give yourselves to meditation and repentance . . .' (The sword, flickering with firelight, was only a yard away) '. . . Far better that you should live out the rest of this incarnation in solitude, each surrounded by his faithful band of sows or snails . . .' (The sword touched the ragged robe) '. . . devoting your remaining years to the promotion of a better understanding between mankind and the lower animals. However—' (Ningauble sighed and the sword hesitated) '. . . if it is still your firm and foolhardy intention to challenge this adept, I suppose I must aid you with what little advice I can give, though warning you that it will plunge you into maelstroms of trouble and lay upon you geases you will grow gray in fulfilling, and incidentally be the means of your deaths.'

Fafhrd lowered his sword. The silence in the black cave grew heavy and ominous. Then, in a voice that was distant yet resonant, like the sound that came from the statue of Memnon at Thebes when the first rays of the morning sun fell upon it, Ningauble began to speak.

'It comes to me, confusedly, like a scene in a rusted mirror; nevertheless, it comes, and thus: You must first possess yourselves of certain trifles. The shroud of Ahriman, from the secret shrine near Persepolis—'

'But what about the accursed swordsmen of Ahriman, Father?' put in the Mouser. 'There are twelve of them. Twelve, Father, and all very accursed and hard to persuade.'

'Do you think I am setting toss-and-fetch problems for puppy dogs?' wheezed Ningauble angrily. 'To proceed: You must secondly obtain powdered mummy from the Demon Pharaoh, who reigned for three horrid and unhistoried midnights after the death of Ikhnaton—'

'But, Father,' Fafhrd protested, blushing a little, 'you know who owns that powdered mummy, and what she demands of any two men who visit her.'

'Shh! I'm your elder, Fafhrd, by eons. Thirdly, you must get the cup from which Socrates drank the hemlock; fourthly, a sprig from the original Tree of Life, and lastly . . .' He hesitated as if his memory had failed him, dipped up a potsherd from the pile, and read from it: 'And lastly, you must procure the woman who will come when she is ready.'

'What woman?'

'The woman who will come when she is ready.' Ningauble tossed back the fragment, starting a small landslide of shards.

'Corrode Loki's bones!' cursed Fafhrd, and the Mouser said, 'But, Father, no woman comes when she's ready. She always waits.'

Ningauble sighed merrily and said, 'Do not be downcast, children. Is it ever the custom of your good friend the Gossiper to give simple advice?'

'It is not,' said Fafhrd.

'Well, having all these things, you must go to the Lost City of Ahriman that lies east of Armenia — whisper not its name—'

'Is it Khatti?' whispered the Mouser.

'No, Blowfly. And furthermore, why are you interrupting me when you are supposed to be hard at work recalling all the details of the scandal of the Friday concubine, the three eunuch priests, and the slave girl from Samos?'

'Oh truly, Spy of the Unmentionable, I labor at that until my mind becomes a weariness and a wandering, and all for love of you.' The Mouser was glad of Ningauble's question, for he had forgotten the three eunuch priests, which would have been most unwise, as no one in his senses sought to cheat the Gossiper of even a pinch of misinformation promised.

Ningauble continued, 'Arriving at the Lost City, you must seek out the ruined black shrine, and place the woman before the great tomb, and wrap the shroud of Ahriman around her, and let her drink the powdered mummy from the hemlock cup, diluting it with a wine you will find where you find the mummy, and place in her hand the sprig from the Tree of Life, and wait for the dawn.'

'And then?' rumbled Fafhrd.

'And then the mirror becomes all red with rust. I can see no further, except that someone will return from a place which it is unlawful to leave, and that you must be wary of the woman.'

'But, Father, all this scavenging of magical trumpery is a great bother,' Fafhrd objected. 'Why shouldn't we go at once to the Lost City?'

'Without the map on the shroud of Ahriman?' murmured Ningauble.

'And you still can't tell us the name of the adept we seek?' the Mouser ventured. 'Or even the name of the woman? Puppy dog problems indeed! We give you bitch, Father, and by the time you return her, she's dropped a litter.'

Ningauble shook his head ever so slightly, the six eyes retreated under the hood to become an ominous multiple gleam, and the Mouser felt a shiver crawl on his spine.

'Why is it, Riddle-Vendor, that you always give us half knowledge?' Fafhrd pressed angrily. 'Is it that at the last moment our blades may strike with half force?'

Ningauble chuckled.

'It is because I know you too well, children. If I said one word more, Hulk, you could be cleaving with your great sword – at the wrong person. And your cat-comrade would be brewing his child's magic – the wrong child's magic. It is no simple creature you foolhardily seek, but a mystery, no single identity but a mirage, a stony thing that has stolen the blood and substance of life, a nightmare crept out of dream.'

For a moment it was as if, in the far reaches of that nighted cavern, something that waited stirred. Then it was gone.

Ningauble purred complacently, 'And now I have an idle moment, which, to please you, I will pass in giving ear to the story that the Mouser has been impatiently waiting to tell me.'

So, there being no escape, the Mouser began, first explaining that only the surface of the story had to do with the concubine, the three priests, and the slave girl; the deeper portion touching mostly, though not entirely, on four infamous hand-maidens of Ishtar and a dwarf who was richly compensated for his deformity. The fire grew low and a little, lemurlike creature came edging in to replenish it, and the hours stretched on, for the Mouser always warmed to his own tales. There came a place where Fafhrd's eyes bugged with astonishment, and another where Ningauble's paunch shook like a small mountain in earthquake, but eventually the tale came to an end, suddenly and seemingly in the middle, like a piece of foreign music.

Then farewells were said and final questions refused answer, and the two seekers started back the way they had come. And Ningauble began to sort in his mind the details of the Mouser's story, treasuring it the more because he knew it was an im-provisation, his favorite proverb being, 'He who lies artistically, treads closer to the truth than ever he knows.'

Fafhrd and the Mouser had almost reached the bottom of the boulder stair when they heard a faint tapping and turned to see Ningauble peering down from the verge, supporting himself with what looked like a cane and rapping with another.

'Children,' he called, and his voice was tiny as the note of the lone flute in the Temple of Baal, 'it comes to me that something in the distant spaces lusts for something in you. You must guard closely what commonly needs no guarding.'

'Yes, Godfather of Mystification.'

'You will take care?' came the elfin note. 'Your beings depend on it.'

'Yes, Father.'

And Ningauble waved once and hobbled out of sight. The little creatures of his great darkness followed him, but whether to report and receive orders or only to pleasure him with their gentle antics, no man could be sure. Some said that Ningauble had been created by the Elder Gods for men to guess about and so sharpen their imaginations for even tougher riddles. None knew whether he had the gift of foresight, or whether he merely set the stage for future events with such a bewildering cunning that only an efreet or an adept could evade acting the part given him.

3. *The Woman Who Came*

After Fafhrd and the Gray Mouser emerged from the Bottom-less Caves into the blinding upper sunlight, their trail for a space becomes dim. Material relating to them has, on the whole, been scanted by annalists, since they were heroes too disreputable for classic myth, too cryptically independent ever to let themselves be tied to a folk, too shifty and improbable in their adventurings to please the historian, too often involved with a riffraff of dubious demons, unfrocked sorcerors, and discredited deities – a veritable underworld of the supernatural. And it becomes doubly difficult to piece together their actions during a period when they were engaged in thefts requiring stealth, secrecy, and bold misdirection. Occasionally, however, one comes across the marks they left upon the year.

For instance, a century later the priests of Ahriman were chanting, although they were too intelligent to believe it them-selves, the miracle of Ahriman's snatching of his own hallowed shroud. One night the twelve accursed swordsmen saw the blackly scribbled shroud rise like a pillar of cobwebs from the altar, rise higher than mortal man, although the form within seemed anthropoid. Then Ahriman spoke from the shroud, and they worshiped him, and he replied with obscure parables and finally strode giantlike from the secret shrine.

The shrewdest of the century-later priests remarked, 'I'd say a man on stilts, or else—' (happy surmise!) '—one man on the shoulders of another.'

Then there were things that Nikri, body slave to the in-famous False Laodice, told the cook while she anointed the bruises of her latest beating. Things concerning two strangers who visited her mistress, and the carousal her mistress proposed to them, and how they escaped the black eunuch scimitarmen she had set to slay them when the carousal was done.

'They were magicians, both of them,' Nikri averred, for at the peak of the doings they transformed my lady into a hideous, wiggly-horned sow, a horrid chimera of snail and swine. But that wasn't the worst, for they stole her chest of aphrodisiac wines. When she discovered that the demon mummia was gone with which she'd hoped to stir the lusts of Ptolemy, she screamed in rage and took her back-scratcher to me. Ow, but that hurts!'

The cook chuckled.

But as to who visited Hieronymus, the greedy tax farmer and connoisseur of Antioch, or in what guise, we cannot be sure. One morning he was found in his treasure room with his limbs stiff and chill, as if from hemlock, and there was a look of terror on his fat face, and the famous cup from which he had often caroused was missing, although there were circular stains on the table before him. He recovered, but would never tell what had happened.

The priests who tended the Tree of Life in Babylon were a little more communicative. One evening just after sunset they saw the topmost branches shake in the gloaming and heard the snick of a pruning knife. All around them, without other sound or movement, stretched the desolate city, from which the inhabitants had been herded to nearby Seleucia three-quarters of a century before and to which the priests crept back only in a great fear to fulfill their sacred duties. They instantly prepared, some of them to climb the Tree armed with tempered golden sickles, others to shoot down with gold-tipped arrows whatever blasphemer was driven forth, when suddenly a large gray batlike shape swooped from the Tree and vanished behind a jagged wall. Of course, it might conceivably have been a gray-cloaked man swinging on a thin, tough, rope, but there were too many things whispered about the creatures that flapped by night through the ruins of Babylon for the priests to dare pursuit.

Finally Fafhrd and the Gray Mouser reappeared in Tyre, and a week later they were ready to depart on the ultimate stage of their quest. Indeed, they were already outside the gates, lingering at the landward end of Alexander's mole, spine of an ever-growing isthmus. Gazing at it, Fafhrd remembered how once an unintroduced stranger had told him a tale about two fabulous adventurers who had aided mightily in the fore-doomed defense of Tyre against Alexander the Great more than a hundred years ago. The larger had heaved heavy stone blocks on the attacking ships, the smaller had dove to file through the chains with which they were anchored. Their names, the stranger had said, were Fafhrd and the Gray Mouser. Fafhrd had made no comment.

It was near evening, a good time to pause in adventurings, to recall past escapades, to hazard misty, wild, rosy speculations concerning what lay ahead.

'I think any woman would do,' insisted the Mouser bickering. 'Ningauble was just trying to be obscure. Let's take Chloe.'

'If only she'll come when she's ready,' said Fafhrd, half smiling.

The sun was dipping ruddy-golden into the rippling sea. The merchants who had pitched shop on the landward side in order to get first crack at the farmers and inland traders on market day were packing up wares and taking down canopies.

'Any woman will eventually come when she's ready, even Chloe,' retorted the Mouser. 'We'd only have to take along a silk tent for her and a few pretty conveniences. No trouble at all.'

'Yes,' said Fafhrd. 'We could probably manage it without more than one elephant.'

Most of Tyre was darkly silhouetted against the sunset, although there were gleams from the roofs here and there, and the gilded peak of the Temple of Melkarth sent a little water-borne glitter track angling in toward the greater one of the sun. The fading Phoenician port seemed entranced, dreaming of past glories, only half listening to today's news of Rome's implacable eastward advance, and Philip of Macedon's loss of the first round at the Battle of the Dogs' Heads, and now Antiochus preparing for the second, with Hannibal come to help him from Tyre's great fallen sister Carthage across the sea.

'I'm sure Chloe will come if we wait until tomorrow,' the Mouser continued. 'We'll have to wait in any case, because Ningauble said the woman wouldn't come until she was ready.'

A cool little wind came out of the wasteland that was Old Tyre. The merchants hurried; a few of them were already going home along the mole, their slaves looking like hunchbacks and otherwise misshapen monsters because of the packs on their shoulders and heads.

'No,' said Fafhrd, 'we'll start. And if the woman doesn't come when she's ready, then she isn't the woman who will come when she's ready, or if she is, she'll have to hump herself to catch up.'

The three horses of the adventurers moved restlessly and the Mouser's whinnied. Only the great camel, on which were slung the wine-sacks, various small chests, and snugly-wrapped weapons, stood sullenly still. Fafhrd and the Mouser casually watched the one figure on the mole that moved against the homing stream; they were not exactly suspicious, but after the year's doings they could not overlook the possibility of death-dealing pursuers, taking the form either of accursed swordsmen, black eunuch scimitarmen, gold-weaponed Babylonian priests, or such agents as Hieronymus of Antioch might favor.

'Chloe would have come on time, if only you'd helped me persuade her,' argued the Mouser. 'She likes you, and I'm sure she must have been the one Ningauble meant, because she has that amulet which works against the adept.'

The sun was a blinding sliver on the sea's rim, then went under. All the little glares and glitters on the roofs of Tyre winked out. The Temple of Melkarth loomed black against the fading sky. The last canopy was being taken down and most of the merchants were more than halfway across the mole. There was still only one figure moving shoreward.

'Weren't seven nights with Chloe enough for you?' asked Fafhrd. 'Besides, it isn't she you'll be wanting when we kill the adept and get this spell off us.'

'That's as it may be,' retorted the Mouser. 'But remember we have to catch our adept first. And it's not only I whom Chloe's company could benefit.'

A faint shout drew their attention across the darkling water to where a lateen-rigged trader was edging into the Egyptian

Harbor. For a moment they thought the landward end of the mole had been emptied. Then the figure moving away from the city came out sharp and black against the sea, a slight figure, not burdened like the slaves.

'Another fool leaves sweet Tyre at the wrong time,' observed the Mouser. 'Just think what a woman will mean in those cold mountains we're going to, Fafhrd, a woman to prepare dainties and stroke your forehead.'

Fafhrd said, 'It isn't your forehead, little man, you're thinking of.'

The cool wind came again and the packed sand moaned at its passing. Tyre seemed to crouch like a beast against the threats of darkness. A last merchant searched the ground hurriedly for some lost article.

Fafhrd put his hand on his horse's shoulder and said, 'Come on.'

The Mouser made a last point. 'I don't think Chloe would insist on taking the slave girl to oil her feet, that is, if we handled it properly.'

Then they saw that the other fool leaving sweet Tyre was coming toward them, and that it was a woman, tall and slender, dressed in stuffs that seemed to melt into the waning light, so that Fafhrd found himself wondering whether she truly came from Tyre or from some aerial realm whose inhabitants may venture to earth only at sunset. Then, as she continued to approach at an easy, swinging stride, they saw that her face was fair and that her hair was raven; and the Mouser's heart gave a great leap and he felt that this was the perfect consummation of their waiting, that he was witnessing the birth of an Aphrodite, not from the foam but the dusk; for it was indeed his dark-haired Ahura of the wine shops, no longer staring with cold, shy curiosity, but eagerly smiling.

Fafhrd, not altogether untouched by similar feelings, said slowly, 'So you are the woman who came when she was ready?'

'Yes,' added the Mouser gaily, 'and did you know that in a minute more you'd have been too late?'

4. *The Lost City*

During the next week, one of steady northward journeying along the fringe of the desert, they learned little more of the motives or history of their mysterious companion than the dubious scraps of information Chloe had provided. When asked why she had come, Ahura replied that Ningauble had sent her, that Ningauble had nothing to do with it and that it was all an accident, that certain dead Elder Gods had dreamed her a vision, that she sought a brother lost in a search for the Lost City of Ahriman; and often her only answer was silence, a silence that seemed sometimes sly and sometimes mystical. However, she stood up well to hardship, proved a tireless rider, and did not complain at sleeping on the ground with only a large cloak snuggled around her. Like some especially sensitive migratory bird, she seemed possessed of an even greater urge than their own to get on with the journey.

Whenever opportunity offered, the Mouser paid assiduous court to her, limited only by the fear of working a snail-change. But after a few days of this tantalizing pleasure, he noticed that Fafhrd was vying for it. Very swiftly the two comrades became rivals, contesting as to who should be the first to offer Ahura assistance on those rare occasions when she needed it, striving to top each other's brazenly boastful accounts of incredible adventures, constantly on the alert lest the other steal a moment alone. Such a spate of gallantry had never before been known on their adventurings. They remained good friends – and they were aware of that – but very surly friends – and they were aware of that too. And Ahura's shy, or sly, silence encouraged them both.

They forded the Euphrates south of the ruins of Carchemish, and struck out for the headwaters of the Tigris, intersecting but swinging east away from the route of Xenophon and the Ten Thousand. It was then that their surliness came to a head. Ahura had roamed off a little, letting her horse crop the dry herbage, while the two sat on a boulder, and expostulated in whispers, Fafhrd proposing that they both agree to cease paying court to the girl until their quest was over, the Mouser doggedly advancing his prior claim. Their whispers became so heated that they did not notice a white pigeon swooping toward them until it landed with a downward beat of wings on an arm Fafhrd had flung wide to emphasize his willingness to renounce the girl temporarily – if only the Mouser would.

Fafhrd blinked, then detached a scrap of parchment from the pigeon's leg, and read, 'There is danger in the girl. You must both forgo her.'

The tiny seal was an impression of seven tangled eyes.

'Just *seven* eyes!' remarked the Mouser. 'Pah, he is modest!' And for a moment he was silent, trying to picture the gigantic web of unknown strands by which the Gossiper gathered his information and conducted his business.

But this unsuspected seconding of Fafhrd's argument finally won from him a sulky consent, and they solemnly pledged not to lay hand on the girl, or each in any way to further his cause, until they had found and dealt with the adept.

They were now in townless land that caravans avoided, a land like Xenophon's, full of chill misty mornings, dazzling noons, and treacherous twilights, with hints of shy, murderous, mountain-dwelling tribes recalling the omnipresent legends of 'little people' as unlike men as cats are unlike dogs. Ahura seemed unaware of the sudden cessation of the attentions paid her, remaining as provocatively shy and indefinite as ever.

The Mouser's attitude toward Ahura, however, began to undergo a gradual but profound change. Whether it was the souring of his inhibited passion, or the shrewder insight of a mind no longer a-bubble with the fashioning of compliments and witticisms, he began to feel more and more that the Ahura he loved was only a faint spark almost lost in the darkness of a stranger who daily became more riddlesome, dubious, and even, in the end, repellent. He remembered the other name Chloe had given Ahura, and found himself brooding oddly over the legend of Hermaphroditus bathing in the Carian fountain and becoming joined in one body with the nymph Salmacis. Now when he looked at Ahura he could see only avid eyes that peered secretly at the world through a crevice. He began to think of her chuckling soundlessly at night at the mortifying spell that had been laid upon himself and Fafhrd. He became obsessed with Ahura in a very different way, and took to spying on her and studying her expression when she was not looking, as if hoping in that way to penetrate her mystery.

Fafhrd noticed it and instantly suspected that the Mouser was contemplating going back on his pledge. He restrained his indignation with difficulty and took to watching the Mouser as closely as the Mouser watched Ahura. No longer when it became necessary to procure provisions was either willing to hunt alone. The easy amicability of their friendship deteriorated. Then, late one afternoon while they were traversing a shadowy ravine east of Armenia, a hawk dove suddenly and sank its talons in Fafhrd's shoulder. The Northerner killed the creature in a flurry of reddish feathers before he noticed that it too carried a message.

'Watch out for the Mouser,' was all it said, but coupled with the smart of the talon-pricks, that was quite enough for Fafhrd. Drawing up beside the Mouser while Ahura's horse pranced skittishly away from the disturbance, he told the Mouser his full suspicions and warned him that any violation of their agreement would at once end their friendship and bring them into deadly collision.

The Mouser listened like a man in a dream, still moodily watching Ahura. He would have liked to have told Fafhrd his real motives, but was doubtful whether he could make them intelligible. Moreover, he was piqued at being misjudged. So when Fafhrd's direful outburst was finished he made no comment. Fafhrd interpreted this as an admission of guilt and cantered on in a rage.

They were now nearing that rugged vantage-land from which the Medes and the Persians had swooped down on Assyria and Chaldea, and where, if they could believe Ningauble's geography, they would find the forgotten lair of the Lord of Eternal Evil. At first the archaic map on the shroud of Ahriman proved more maddening than helpful, but after a while, clarified in part by a curiously erudite suggestion of Ahura, it began to make disturbing sense, showing them a deep gorge where the foregoing terrain led one to expect a saddle-backed crest, and a valley where there ought to have been a mountain. If the map held true, they would reach the Lost City in a very few days.

All the while, the Mouser's obsession deepened, and at last took definite and startling form. He believed that Ahura was a man.

It was very strange that the intimacy of camp life and the Mouser's own zealous spying should not long ago have turned up concrete proof or disproof of this clear-cut supposition. Nevertheless, as the Mouser wonderingly realized on reviewing events, they had not. Granted, Ahura's form and movements, all her least little actions were those of a woman, but he re-called painted and padded minions, sweet not simpering, who had aped femininity almost as well. Preposterous – but there it was. From that moment his obsessive curiosity became a com-pulsive sweat and he redoubled his moody peering, much to the anger of Fafhrd, who took to slapping his sword hilt at unexpected intervals, though without ever startling the Mouser into looking away. Each in his way stayed as surly sullen as the camel that displayed a more and more dour balkiness at this preposterous excursion from the healthy desert.

Those were nightmare days for the Gray One, as they advanced ever closer through gloomy gorges and over craggy crests toward Ahriman's primeval shrine. Fafhrd seemed an ominous, white-faced giant reminding him of someone he had known in waking life, and their whole quest a blind treading of the more subterranean routes of dream. He still wanted to tell the giant his suspicions, but could not bring himself to it, because of their monstrousness and because the giant loved Ahura. And all the while Ahura eluded him, a phantom fluttering just beyond reach; though, when he forced his mind to make the comparison, he realized that her behaviour had in no way altered, except for an intensification of the urge to press onward, like a vessel nearing its home port.

Finally there came a night when he could bear his torturing curiosity no longer. He writhed from under a mountain of oppressive unremembered dreams and, propped on an elbow, looked around him, quiet as the creature for which he was named.

It would have been cold if it had not been so still. The fire had burned to embers. It was rather the moonlight that showed him Fafhrd's tousled head and elbow outthrust from shaggy bearskin cloak. And it was the moonlight that struck full on Ahura stretched beyond the embers, her lidded, tranquil face fixed on the zenith, seeming hardly to breathe.

He waited a long time. Then, without making a sound, he laid back his gray cloak, picked up his sword, went around the fire, and kneeled beside her. Then, for another space, he dispassionately scrutinized her face. But it remained the hermaphroditic mask that had tormented his waking hours – if he were still sure of the distinction between waking and dream. Suddenly his hands grasped at her – and as abruptly checked. Again he stayed motionless for a long time. Then, with movements as deliberate and rehearsed-seeming as a sleep-walker's, but more silent, he drew back her woollen cloak, took a small knife from his pouch, lifted her gown at the neck, careful not to touch her skin, slit it to her knee, treating her chiton the same.

The breasts, white as ivory, that he had known would not be there, were there. And yet, instead of his nightmare lifting, it deepened.

It was something too profound for surprise, this wholly unexpected further insight. For as he knelt there, somberly studying, he knew for a certainty that this ivory flesh too was a mask, as cunningly fashioned as the face and for as frighteningly incomprehensible a purpose.

The ivory eyelids did not flicker, but the edges of the teeth showed in what he fancied was a deliberate, flickery smile.

He was never more certain than at this moment that Ahura was a man.

The embers crunched behind him.

Turning, the Mouser saw only the streak of gleaming steel poised above Fafhrd's head, motionless for a moment, as if with superhuman forbearance a god should give his creature a chance before loosing the thunderbolt.

The Mouser ripped out his own slim sword in time to ward the titan blow. From hilt to point, the two blades screamed.

And in answer to the scream, melting into, continuing, and augmenting it, there came from the absolute calm of the west a gargantuan gust of wind that sent the Mouser staggering forward and Fafhrd reeling back, and rolled Ahura across the place where the embers had been.

Almost as suddenly the gale died. As it died, something whipped batlike toward the Mouser's face and he grabbed at it. But it was not a bat, or even a large leaf. It felt like papyrus.

The embers, blown into a clump of dry grass, had perversely started a blaze. To its flaring light he held the thin scrap that had fluttered out of the infinite west.

He motioned frantically to Fafhrd, who was clawing his way out of a scrub pine.

There was squid-black writing on the scrap, in large characters, above the tangled seal.

'By whatever gods you revere, give up this quarrel. Press onward at once. Follow the woman.'

They became aware that Ahura was peering over their abutting shoulders. The moon came gleamingly from behind the small black tatter of cloud that had briefly obscured it. She looked at them, pulled together chiton and gown, belted them with her cloak. They collected their horses, extricated the fallen camel from the cluster of thorn bushes in which it was satisfiedly tormenting itself, and set out.

After that the Lost City was found almost too quickly; it seemed like a trap or the work of an illusionist. One moment Ahura was pointing out to them a boulder-studded crag; the next, they were looking down a narrow valley choked with crazily-leaning, moonsilvered monoliths and their accomplice shadows.

From the first it was obvious that 'city' was a misnomer. Surely men had never dwelt in those massive stone tents and huts, though they may have worshipped there. It was a habitation for Egyptian colossi, for stone automata. But Fafhrd and the Mouser had little time to survey its entirety, for without warning Ahura sent her horse clattering and sliding down the slope.

Thereafter it was a harebrained, drunken gallop, their horses plunging shadows, the camel a lurching ghost, through forests of crude-hewn pillars, past teetering single slabs big enough for palace walls, under lintels for elephants, always following the elusive hoofbeat, never catching it, until they suddenly emerged into clear moonlight and drew up in an open space between a great sarcophagus-like block or box with steps leading up to it, and a huge, crudely man-shaped monolith.

But they had hardly begun to puzzle out the things around them before they became aware that Ahura was gesturing impatiently. They recalled Ningauble's instructions, and realized that it was almost dawn. So they unloaded various bundles and boxes from the shivering, snapping camel, and Fafhrd unfolded the dark, cobwebby shroud of Ahriman and wrapped it around Ahura as she stood wordlessly facing the tomb, her face a marble portrait of eagerness, as if she sprang from the stone around her.

While Fafhrd busied himself with other things, the Mouser opened the ebony chest they had stolen from the False Laodice. A fey mood came upon him and, dancing cumbrously in imitation of a eunuch serving man, he tastefully arrayed a flat stone with all the little jugs and jars and tiny amphorae that the chest contained. And in an appropriate falsetto he sang:

> 'I laid a board for the Great Seleuce,
> I decked it pretty and abstruse;
> And he must have been pleased,
> For when stuffed, he wheezed,
> "As punishment castrate the man."'

'You thee, Fafhwd,' he lisped, 'the man had been cath-twated ath a boy, and tho it wath no punithment at all. Becauthe of pweviouth cathtwathion—'

'I'll castrate your wit-engorged top end,' Fafhrd cried, raising the next implement of magic, but thought better of it.

Then Fafhrd handed him Socrates' cup and, still prancing

and piping, the Mouser measured into it the mummy powder and added the wine and stirred them together and, dancing fantastically toward Ahura, offered it to her. When she made no movement, he held it to her lips and she greedily gulped it without taking her eyes from the tomb.

Then Fafhrd came with the sprig from the Babylonian Tree of Life, which still felt marvelously fresh and firm-leafed to his touch, as if the Mouser had only snipped it a moment ago. And he gently pried open her clenched fingers and placed the sprig inside them and folded them again.

Thus ready, they waited. The sky reddened at the edge and seemed for a moment to grow darker, the stars fading and the moon turning dull. The outspread aphrodisiacs chilled, refusing the night breeze their savor. And the woman continued to watch the tomb, and behind her, seeming to watch the tomb too, as if it were her fantastic shadow, loomed the man-shaped monolith, which the Mouser now and then scrutinized uneasily over his shoulder, being unable to tell whether it were of primevally crude workmanship or something that men had laboriously defaced because of its evil.

The sky paled until the Mouser could begin to make out some monstrous carvings on the side of the sarcophagus – of men like stone pillars and animals like mountains – and until Fafhrd could see the green of the leaves in Ahura's hand.

Then he saw something astounding. In an instant the leaves withered and the sprig became a curled and blackened stick. In the same instant Ahura trembled and grew paler still, snow pale, and to the Mouser it seemed that there was a tenuous black cloud forming around her head, that the riddlesome stranger he hated was pouring upward like a smoky jinni from her body, the bottle.

The thick stone cover of the sarcophagus groaned and began to rise.

Ahura began to move toward the sarcophagus. To the Mouser it seemed that the cloud was drawing her along like a black sail.

The cover was moving more swiftly, as if it were the upper jaw of a stone crocodile. The black cloud seemed to the Mouser to strain triumphantly toward the widening slit, dragging the white wisp behind it. The cover opened wide. Ahura reached the top and then either peered down inside or, as the Mouser saw it, was almost sucked in along with the black cloud. She shook violently. Then her body collapsed like an empty dress.

Fafhrd gritted his teeth, a joint cracked in the Mouser's wrist. The hilts of their swords, unconsciously drawn, bruised their palms.

Then, like an idler from a day of bowered rest, an Indian prince from the tedium of the court, a philosopher from quizzical discourse, a slim figure rose from the tomb. His limbs were clad in black, his body in silver metal, his hair and beard raven and silky. But what first claimed the sight, like an ensign on a masked man's shield, was a chatoyant quality of his youthful olive skin, a silvery gleaming that turned one's thoughts to fishes' bellies and leprosy – that, and a certain familiarity.

For the face of this black and silver stranger bore an unmistakable resemblance to Ahura.

5. *Anra Devadoris*

Resting his long hands on the edge of the tomb, the newcomer surveyed them pleasantly and nodded as if they were intimates. Then he vaulted lightly over and came striding down the steps, treading on the shroud of Ahriman without so much as a glance at Ahura.

He eyed their swords. 'You anticipate danger?' he asked, politely stroking the beard which, it seemed to the Mouser, could never have grown so bushily silky except in a tomb.

'You are an adept?' Fafhrd retorted, stumbling over the words a little.

The stranger disregarded the question and stooped to study amusedly the zany array of aphrodisiacs.

'Dear Ningauble,' he murmured, 'is surely the father of all seven-eyed Lechers. I suppose you know him well enough to guess that he had you fetch these toys because he wants them for himself. Even in his duel with me, he cannot resist the temptation of a profit on the side. But perhaps this time the old pander had curtsied to destiny unwittingly. At least, let us hope so.'

And with that he unbuckled his sword belt and carelessly laid it by, along with the wondrously slim, silver-hilted sword. The Mouser shrugged and sheathed his own weapon, but Fafhrd only grunted.

'I do not like you,' he said. 'Are you the one who put the swine-curse on us?'

The stranger regarded him quizzically.

'You are looking for a cause,' he said. 'You wish to know the name of an agent you feel has injured you. You plan to unleash your rage as soon as you know. But behind every cause is another cause, and behind the last agent is yet another agent. An immortal could not slay a fraction of them. Believe me, who have followed that trail further than most and who have had some experience of the special obstacles that are placed in the way of one who seeks to live beyond the confines of his skull and the meager present – the traps that are set for him, the titanic enmities he awakens. I beseech you to wait a while before warring, as I shall wait before answering your second question. That I am an adept I freely admit.'

At this last statement the Mouser felt another light-headed impulse to behave fantastically, this time in mimicry of a magician. Here was the rare creature on whom he could test the rune against adepts in his pouch! He wanted to hum a death spell between his teeth, to flap his arms in an incantational gesture, to spit at the adept and spin widdershins on his left heel thrice. But he too chose to wait.

'There is always a simple way of saying things,' said Fafhrd ominously.

'But there is where I differ with you,' returned the adept, almost animatedly. 'There are no ways of saying certain things, and others are so difficult that a man pines and dies before the right words are found. One must borrow phrases from the sky, words from beyond the stars. Else were all an ignorant, imprisoning mockery.'

The Mouser stared at the adept, suddenly conscious of a monstrous incongruity about him – as if one should glimpse a hint of double-dealing in the curl of Solon's lips, or cowardice in the eyes of Alexander, or imbecility in the face of Aristotle. For although the adept was obviously erudite, confident, and powerful, the Mouser could not help thinking of a child morbidly avid for experience, a timid, painfully curious small boy. And the Mouser had the further bewildering feeling that this was the secret for which he had spied so long on Ahura.

Fafhrd's sword-arm bulged and he seemed about to make an even pithier rejoinder. But instead he sheathed his sword, walked over to the woman, held his fingers to her wrists for a moment, then tucked his bearskin cloak around her.

'Her ghost has gone only a little way,' he said. 'It will soon return. What did you do to her, you black and silver popinjay?'

'What matters what I've done to her or you, or me?' retorted the adept, almost peevishly. 'You are here, and I have business with you.' He paused. 'This, in brief, is my proposal: that I make you adepts like myself, sharing with you all knowledge of which your minds are capable, on condition only that you continue to submit to such spells as I have put upon you and may put upon you in future, to further our knowledge. What do you say to that?'

'Wait, Fafhrd!' implored the Mouser, grabbing his comrade's arm. 'Don't strike yet. Let's look at the statue from all sides. Why, magnanimous magician, have you chosen to make this offer to us, and why have you brought us out here to make it, instead of getting your yes or no in Tyre?'

'An adept,' roared Fafhrd, dragging the Mouser along. 'Offers to make me an adept! And for that I should go on kissing swine! Go spit down Fenris' throat!'

'As to why I have brought you here,' said the adept coolly, 'there are certain limitations on my powers of movement, or at least on my powers of satisfactory communication. There is, moreover, a special reason, which I will reveal to you as soon as we have concluded our agreement – though I may tell you that, unknown to yourselves, you have already aided me.'

'But why pick on *us*? Why?' persisted the Mouser, bracing himself against Fafhrd's tugging.

'Some whys, if you follow them far enough, lead over the rim of reality,' replied the black and silver one. 'I have sought knowledge beyond the dreams of ordinary men; I have ventured far into the darkness that encircles minds and stars. But now, midmost of the pitchy windings of that fearsome labyrinth, I find myself suddenly at my skein's end. The tyrant powers who ignorantly guard the secret of the universe without knowing what it is, have scented me. Those vile wardens of whom Ningauble is the merest agent and even Ormadz a cloudy symbol, have laid their traps and built their barricades. And my best torches have snuffed out, or proved too flickery-feeble. I need new avenues of knowledge.'

He turned upon them eyes that seemed to be changing to twin holes in a curtain. 'There is something in the inmost core of you, something that you, or others before you, have close-guarded down the ages. Something that lets you laugh in a way that only the Elder Gods ever laughed. Something that makes you see a kind of jest in horror and disillusionment and death. There is much wisdom to be gained by the unraveling of that something.'

'Do you think us pretty woven scarves for your slick fingers to fray,' snarled Fafhrd. 'So you can piece out that rope you're at the end of, and climb all the way down to Niflheim?'

'Each adept must fray himself, before he may fray others,' the stranger intoned unsmilingly. 'You do not know the treasure you keep virgin and useless within you, or spill in senseless laughter. There is much richness in it, many complexities, destiny-threads that lead beyond the sky to realms undreamt.' His voice became swift and invoking.

'Have you no itch to understand, no urge for greater adventuring than schoolboy rambles? I'll give you gods for foes, stars for your treasure-trove, if only you will do as I command. All men will be your animals; the best, your hunting pack. Kiss snails and swine? That's but an overture. Greater than Pan, you'll frighten nations, rape the world. The universe will tremble at your lust, but you will master it and force it down. That ancient laughter will give you the might—'

'Filth-spewing pimp! Scabby-lipped pander! Cease!' bellowed Fafhrd.

'Only submit to me and to my will,' the adept continued rapturously, his lips working so that his black beard twitched rhythmically. 'All things we'll twist and torture, know their cause. The lechery of gods will pave the way we'll tramp through windy darkness 'til we find the one who lurks in senseless Odin's skull twitching the strings that move your lives and mine. All knowledge will be ours, all for us three. Only give up your wills, submit to me!'

For a moment the Mouser was hypnotized by the glint of ghastly wonders. Then he felt Fafhrd's biceps, which had slackened under his grasp – as if the Northerner were yielding too – suddenly tighten, and from his own lips he heard words projected coldly into the echoing silence.

'Do you think a rhyme is enough to win us over to your nauseous titillations? Do you think we care a jot for your high-flown muck-peering? Fafhrd, this slobberer offends me, past ills that he has done us aside. It only remains to determine which one of us disposes of him. I long to unravel him, beginning with the ribs.'

'Do you not understand what I have offered you, the magnitude of the boon? Have we no common ground?'

'Only to fight on. Call up your demons, sorceror, or else look to your weapon.'

An unearthly lust receded, rippling from the adept's eyes, leaving behind only a deadliness. Fafhrd snatched up the cup of Socrates and dropped it for a lot, swore as it rolled toward the Mouser, whose cat-quick hand went softly to the hilt of the slim sword called Scalpel. Stooping, the adept groped blindly behind him and regained his belt and scabbard, drawing from it a blade that looked as delicate and responsive as a needle. He stood, a lank and icy indolence, in the red of the risen sun, the black anthropomorphic monolith looming behind him for his second.

The Mouser drew Scalpel silently from its sheath, ran a

finger caressingly down the side of the blade, and in so doing noticed an inscription in black crayon which read, 'I do not approve of this step you are taking. Ningauble.' With a hiss of annoyance the Mouser wiped it off on his thigh and concentrated his gaze on the adept – so preoccupiedly that he did not observe the eyes of the fallen Ahura quiver open.

'And now, Dead Sorceror,' said the Gray One lightly, 'my name is the Gray Mouser.'

'And mine is Anra Devadoris.'

Instantly the Mouser put into action his carefully weighed plan: to take two rapid skips forward and launch his blade-tipped body at the adept's sword, which was to be deflected, and at the adept's throat, which was to be sliced. He was already seeing the blood spurt when, in the middle of the second skip, he saw, whirring like an arrow toward his eyes, the adept's blade. With a belly-contorted effort he twisted to one side and parried blindly. The adept's blade whipped in greedily around Scalpel, but only far enough to snag and tear the skin at the side of the Mouser's neck. The Mouser recovered balance crouching, his guard wide open, and only a backward leap saved him from Anra Devadoris' second serpentlike strike. As he gathered himself to meet the next attack, he gaped amazedly, for never before in his life had he been faced by superior speed. Fafhrd's face was white. Ahura, however, her head raised a little from the furry cloak, smiled with a weak and incredulous, but evil joy – a frankly vicious joy wholly unlike her former sly, intangible intimations of cruelty.

But Anra Devadoris smiled wider and nodded with a patronizing gratefulness at the Mouser, before gliding in. And now it was the blade Needle that darted in unhurried lightning attack, and Scalpel that whirred in frenzied defense. The Mouser retreated in jerky, circling stages, his face sweaty, his throat hot, but his heart exulting, for never before had he fought this well – not even on that stifling morning when, his head in a sack, he had disposed of a whimsically cruel Egyptian kidnapper.

Inexplicably, he had the feeling that his days spent in spying on Ahura were now paying off.

Needle came slipping in and for the moment the Mouser could not tell upon which side of Scalpel it skirred and so sprang backward, but not swiftly enough to escape a prick in the side. He cut viciously at the adept's withdrawing arm – and barely managed to jerk his own arm out of the way of a stop thrust.

In a nasty voice so low that Fafhrd hardly heard her, and the Mouser heard not at all, Ahura called, 'The spiders tickled your flesh ever so lightly as they ran, Anra.'

Perhaps the adept hesitated almost imperceptibly, or perhaps it was only that his eyes grew a shade emptier. At all events, the Mouser was not given that opportunity, for which he was desperately searching, to initiate a counterattack and escape the deadly whirligig of his circling retreat. No matter how intently he peered, he could spy no gap in the sword-woven steel net his adversary was tirelessly casting toward him, nor could he discern in the face behind the net any betraying grimace, any flicker of eye hinting at the next point of attack, any flaring of nostrils or distension of lips telling of gasping fatigue similar to his own. It was inhuman, unalive, the mask of a machine built by some Daedalus, or of a leprously silver automaton stepped out of myth. And like a machine, Devadoris seemed to be gaining strength and speed from the very rhythm that was sapping his own.

The Mouser realized that he must interrupt that rhythm by a counterattack, any counterattack, or fall victim to a swiftness become blinding.

And then he further realized that the proper opportunity for that counterattack would never come, that he would wait in vain for any faltering in his adversary's attack, that he must risk everything on a guess.

His throat burned, his heart pounded on his ribs for air, a stinging, numbing poison seeped through his limbs.

Devadoris started a feint, or a deadly thrust, at his face.

Simultaneously, the Mouser heard Ahura jeer, 'They hung their webs on your beard and the worms knew your secret parts, Anra.'

He guessed – and cut at the adept's knee.

143

Either he guessed right, or else something halted the adept's deadly thrust.

The adept easily parried the Mouser's cut, but the rhythm was broken and his speed slackened.

Again he developed speed, again at the last possible moment the Mouser guessed. Again Ahura eerily jeered, 'The maggots made you a necklace, and each marching beetle paused to peer into your eye, Anra.'

Over and over it happened, speed, guess, macabre jeer, but each time the Mouser gained only momentary respite, never the opportunity to start an extended counterattack. His circling retreat continued so uninterruptedly that he felt as if he had been caught in a whirlpool. With each revolution, certain fixed landmarks swept into view: Fafhrd's blanched agonized face; the hulking tomb; Ahura's hate-contorted, mocking visage; the red stab of the risen sun; the gouged black, somber monolith, with its attendant stony soldiers and their gigantic stone tents; Fafhrd again . . .

And now the Mouser knew his strength was failing for good and all. Each guessed counterattack brought him less respite, was less of a check to the adept's speed. The landmarks whirled dizzily, darkened. It was as if he had been sucked to the maelstrom's center, as if the black cloud which he had fancied pouring from Ahura were enveloping him vampirously, choking off his breath.

He knew that he would be able to make only one more counter-cut, and must therefore stake all on a thrust at the heart.

He readied himself.

But he had waited too long. He could not gather the necessary strength, summon the speed.

He saw the adept preparing the lightning death-stroke.

His own thrust was like the gesture of a paralyzed man seeking to rise from his bed.

Then Ahura began to laugh.

It was a horrible, hysterical laugh; a giggling, snickering laugh; a laugh that made him dully wonder why she should find such joy in his death; and yet, for all the difference, a laugh that sounded like a shrill, distorted echo of Fafhrd's or his own.

Puzzledly, he noted that Needle had not yet transfixed him, that Devadoris' lightning thrust was slowing, slowing, as if the hateful laughter were falling in cumbering swathes around the adept, as if each horrid peal dropped a chain around his limbs.

The Mouser leaned on his own sword and collapsed, rather than lunged, forward.

He heard Fafhrd's shuddering sigh.

Then he realized that he was trying to pull Scalpel from the adept's chest and that it was an almost insuperably difficult task, although the blade had gone in as easily as if Anra Devadoris had been a hollow man. Again he tugged, and Scalpel came clear, fell from his nerveless fingers. His knees shook, his head sagged, and darkness flooded everything.

Fafhrd, sweat-drenched, watched the adept. Anra Devadoris' rigid body teetered like a stone pillar, slim cousin to the monolith behind him. His lips were fixed in a frozen, foreknowing smile. The teetering increased, yet for a while, as if he were an incarnation of death's ghastly pendulum, he did not fall. Then he swayed too far forward and fell like a pillar, without collapse. There was a horrid, hollow crash as his head struck the black pavement.

Ahura's hysterical laughter burst out afresh.

Fafhrd ran forward calling to the Mouser, anxiously shook the slumped form. Snores answered him. Like some spent Theban phalanx-man drowsing over his pike in the twilight of the battle, the Mouser was sleeping the sleep of complete exhaustion. Fafhrd found the Mouser's gray cloak, wrapped it around him, and gently laid him down.

Ahura was shaking convulsively.

Fafhrd looked at the fallen adept, lying there so formally outstretched, like a tomb-statue rolled over. Devadoris' lankness was skeletal. He had bled hardly at all from the wound given him by Scalpel, but his forehead was crushed like an eggshell. Fafhrd touched him. The skin was cold, the muscles hard as stone.

Fafhrd had seen men go rigid immediately upon death —

Macedonians who had fought too desperately and too long. But they had become weak and staggering toward the end. Anra Devadoris had maintained the appearance of ease and perfect control up to the last moment, despite the poisons that must have been coursing through his veins almost to the exclusion of blood. All through the duel, his chest had hardly heaved.

'By Odin crucified!' Fafhrd muttered. 'He was something of a man, even though he was an adept.'

A hand was laid on his arm. He jerked around. It was Ahura come behind him. The whites showed around her eyes. She smiled at him crookedly, then lifted a knowing eyebrow, put her finger to her lips, and dropped suddenly to her knees beside the adept's corpse. Gingerly she touched the satin smooth surface of the tiny blood-clot on the adept's breast. Fafhrd, noting afresh the resemblance between the dead and the crazy face, sucked in his breath. Ahura scurried off like a startled cat.

Suddenly she froze like a dancer and looked back at him, and a gloating, transcendent vindictiveness came into her face. She beckoned to Fafhrd. Then she ran lightly up the steps to the tomb and pointed into it and beckoned again. Doubtfully the Northerner approached, his eyes on her strained and unearthly face, beautiful as an efreet's. Slowly he mounted the steps.

Then he looked down.

Looked down to feel that the wholesome world was only a film on primary abominations. He realized that what Ahura was showing him had somehow been her ultimate degradation and the ultimate degradation of the thing that had named itself Anra Devadoris. He remembered the bizarre taunts that Ahura had thrown at the adept during the duel. He remembered her laughter, and his mind eddied along the edge of suspicions of pit-spawned improprieties and obscene intimacies. He hardly noticed that Ahura had slumped over the wall of the tomb, her white arms hanging down as if pointing all ten slender fingers in limp horror. He did not know that the blackly puzzled eyes of the suddenly awakened Mouser were peering up at him.

Thinking back, he realized that Devadoris' fastidiousness

and exquisitely groomed appearance had made him think of the tomb as an eccentric entrance to some luxurious underground palace.

But now he saw that there were no doors in that cramping cell into which he peered, nor cracks indicating where hidden doors might be. Whatever had come from there, had lived there, where the dry corners were thick with webs and the floor swarmed with maggots, dung beetles, and furry black spiders.

6. *The Mountain*

Perhaps some chuckling demon, or Ningauble himself, planned it that way. At all events, as Fafhrd stepped down from the tomb, he got his feet tangled in the shroud of Ahriman and bellowed wildly (the Mouser called it 'bleating') before he noticed the cause, which was by that time ripped to tatters.

Next Ahura, aroused by the tumult, set them into a brief panic by screaming that the black monolith and its soldiery were marching toward them to grind them under stony feet.

Almost immediately afterwards the cup of Socrates momentarily froze their blood by rolling around in a semicircle, as if its learned owner were invisibly pawing for it, perhaps to wet his throat after a spell of dusty disputation in the underworld. Of the withered sprig from the Tree of Life there was no sign, although the Mouser jumped as far and as skittishly as one of his namesakes when he saw a large black walking-stick insect crawling away from where the sprig might have fallen.

But it was the camel that caused the biggest commotion, by suddenly beginning to prance about clumsily in a most uncharacteristically ecstatic fashion, finally cavorting up eagerly on two legs to the mare, which fled in squealing dismay. Afterwards it became apparent that the camel must have gotten into the aphrodisiacs, for one of the bottles was pashed as if by a hoof, with only a scummy licked patch showing where its leaked contents had been, and two of the small clay jars were vanished entirely. Fafhrd set out after the two beasts on one of the remaining horses, hallooing crazily.

The Mouser, left alone with Ahura, found his glibness put to the test in saving her sanity by a barrage of small talk, mostly well-spiced Tyrian gossip, but including a wholly apocryphal tale of how he and Fafhrd and five small Ethiopian boys once played Maypole with the eye-stalks of a drunken Ningauble, leaving him peering about in the oddest directions. (The Mouser was wondering why they had not heard from their seven-eyed mentor. After victories Ningauble was always particularly prompt in getting in his demands for payment; and very exacting too – he would insist on a strict accounting for the three missing aphrodisiac containers.)

The Mouser might have been expected to take advantage of this opportunity to press his suit with Ahura, and if possible assure himself that he was now wholly free of the snail-curse. But, her hysterical condition aside, he felt strangely shy with her, as if, although this was the Ahura he loved, he were now meeting her for the first time. Certainly this was a wholly different Ahura from the one with whom they had journeyed to the Lost City, and the memory of how he had treated that other Ahura put a restraint on him. So he cajoled and comforted her as he might have some lonely Tyrian waif, finally bringing two funny little hand-puppets from his pouch and letting them amuse her for him.

And Ahura sobbed and stared and shivered, and hardly seemed to hear what nonsense the Mouser was saying, yet grew quiet and sane-eyed and appeared to be comforted.

When Fafhrd eventually returned with the still giddy camel and the outraged mare, he did not interrupt, but listened gravely, his gaze occasionally straying to the dead adept, the black monolith, the stone city, or the valley's downward slope to the north. High over their heads a flock of birds was flying in the same direction. Suddenly they scattered wildly, as if an eagle had dropped among them. Fafhrd frowned. A moment later he heard a whirring in the air. The Mouser and Ahura looked up too, momentarily glimpsed something slim hurtling downward. They cringed. There was a thud as a long whitish arrow buried itself in a crack in the pavement hardly a foot from Fafhrd and stuck there vibrating.

After a moment Fafhrd touched it with shaking hand. The shaft was crusted with ice, the feathers stiff, as if, incredibly, it had sped for a long time through frigid supramundane air. There was something tied snugly around the shaft. He detached and unrolled an ice-brittle sheet of papyrus, which softened under his touch, and read, 'You must go farther. Your quest is not ended. Trust in omens. Ningauble.'

Still trembling, Fafhrd began to curse thunderously. He crumpled the papyrus, jerked up the arrow, broke it in two, threw the parts blindly away. 'Misbegotten spawn of a eunuch, an owl, and an octopus!' he finished. 'First he tries to skewer us from the skies, then he tells us our quest is not ended – when we've just ended it!'

The Mouser, well-knowing these rages into which Fafhrd was apt to fall after battle, especially a battle in which he had not been able to participate, started to comment coolly. Then he saw the anger abruptly drain from Fafhrd's eyes, leaving a wild twinkle which he did not like.

'Mouser!' said Fafhrd eagerly. 'Which way did I throw the arrow?'

'Why, north,' said the Mouser without thinking.

'Yes, and the birds were flying north, and the arrow was coated with ice!' The wild twinkle in Fafhrd's eyes became a berserk brilliance. 'Omens, he said? We'll trust in omens all right! We'll go north, north, and still north!'

The Mouser's heart sank. Now would be a particularly difficult time to combat Fafhrd's long-standing desire to take him to 'that wonderously cold land where only brawny, hot-blooded men may live and they but by the killing of fierce, furry animals' – a prospect poignantly disheartening to a lover of hot baths, the sun, and southern nights.

'This is the chance of all chances,' Fafhrd continued, intoning like a skald. 'Ah, to rub one's naked hide with snow, to plunge like walrus into ice-garnished water. Around the Caspian and over greater mountains than these goes a way that men of my race have taken. Thor's gut, but you will love it! No wine, only hot mead and savory smoking carcasses, skin-toughening furs to wear, cold air at night to keep dreams clear

149

and sharp, and great strong-hipped women. Then to raise sail on a winter ship and laugh at the frozen spray. Why have we so long delayed? Come! By the icy member that begot Odin, we must start at once!'

The Mouser stifled a groan. 'Ah, blood-brother,' he intoned, not a whit less brazen-voiced, 'my heart leaps even more than yours at the thought of nerve-quickening snow and all the other niceties of the manly life I have long yearned to taste. But' – here his voice broke sadly – 'we forget this good woman, whom in any case, even if we disregard Ningauble's injunction, we must take safely back to Tyre.'

He smiled inwardly.

'But I don't want to go back to Tyre,' interrupted Ahura, looking up from the puppets with an impishness so like a child's that the Mouser cursed himself for ever having treated her as one. 'This lonely spot seems equally far from all builded places. North is as good a way as any.'

'Flesh of Freya!' bellowed Fafhrd, throwing his arms wide. 'Do you hear what she says, Mouser? By Idun, that was spoken like a true snow-land woman! Not one moment must be wasted now. We shall smell mead before a year is out. By Frigg, a woman! Mouser, you good for one so small, did you not notice the pretty way she put it?'

So it was bustle about and pack and (for the present, at least, the Mouser conceded) no way out of it. The chest of aphro-disiacs, the cup, and the tattered shroud were bundled back onto the camel, which was still busy ogling the mare and smack-ing its great leathery lips. And Fafhrd leaped and shouted and clapped the Mouser's back as if there were not an eon-old dead stone city around them and a lifeless adept warming in the sun.

In a matter of moments they were jogging off down the valley, with Fafhrd singing tales of snowstorms and hunting and monsters big as icebergs and giants as tall as frost moun-tains, and the Mouser dourly amusing himself by picturing his own death at the hands of some overly affectionate 'great strong-hipped' woman.

Soon the way became less barren. Scrub trees and the

valley's downward trend hid the city behind them. A surge of relief which the Mouser hardly noticed went through him as the last stony sentinel dipped out of sight, particularly the black monolith left to brood over the adept. He turned his attention to what lay ahead – a conical mountain barring the valley's mouth and wearing a high cap of mist, a lonely thunderhead which his imagination shaped into incredible towers and spires.

Suddenly his sleepy thoughts snapped awake. Fafhrd and Ahura had stopped and were staring at something wholly unexpected – a low wooden windowless house pressed back among the scrubby trees, with a couple of tilled fields behind it. The rudely carved guardian spirits at the four corners of the roof and topping the kingposts seemed Persian, but Persian purged of all southern influence – ancient Persian.

And ancient Persian too appeared the thin features, straight nose, and black-streaked beard of the aged man watching them circumspectly from the low doorway. It seemed to be Ahura's face he scanned most intently – or tried to scan, since Fafhrd mostly hid her.

'Greetings, Father,' called the Mouser. 'Is this not a merry day for riding, and yours good lands to pass?'

'Yes,' replied the aged man dubiously, using a rusty dialect. 'Though there are none, or few, who pass.'

'Just as well to be far from the evil stinking cities,' Fafhrd interjected heartily. 'Do you know the mountain ahead, Father? Is there an easy way past it that leads north?'

At the word 'mountain' the aged man cringed. He did not answer.

'Is there something wrong about the path we are taking?' the Mouser asked quickly. 'Or something evil about that misty mountain?'

The aged man started to shrug his shoulders, held them contracted, looked again at the travelers. Friendliness seemed to fight with fear in his face, and to win, for he leaned forward and said hurriedly, 'I warn you, sons, not to venture farther. What is the steel of your swords, the speed of your steeds, against – but remember' – he raised his voice – 'I accuse no one.' He looked quickly from side to side. 'I have nothing at all to complain of. To me the mountain is a great benefit. My fathers returned here because the land is shunned by thief and honest men alike. There are no taxes on this land – no money taxes. I question nothing.'

'Oh, well, Father, I don't think we'll go farther,' sighed the Mouser wilily. 'We're but idle fellows who follow our noses across the world. And sometimes we smell a strange tale. And that reminds me of a matter in which you may be able to give us generous lads some help.' He chinked the coins in his pouch. 'We have heard a tale of a demon that inhabits here – a young demon dressed in black and silver, pale, with a black beard.'

As the Mouser was saying these things the aged man was edging backward and at the finish he dodged inside and slammed the door, though not before they saw someone pluck at his sleeve. Instantly there came muffled angry expostulation in a girl's voice.

The door burst open. They heard the aged man say ' . . . bring it down upon us all.' Then a girl of about fifteen came running toward them. Her face was flushed, her eyes anxious and scared.

'You must turn back!' she called to them as she ran. 'None but wicked things go to the mountain – or the doomed. And the mist hides a great horrible castle. And powerful, lonely demons live there. And one of them—'

She clutched at Fafhrd's stirrup. But just as her fingers were about to close on it, she looked beyond him straight at Ahura. An expression of abysmal terror came into her face. She screamed, 'He! The black beard!' and crumpled to the ground.

The door slammed and they heard a bar drop into place.

They dismounted. Ahura quickly knelt by the girl, signed to them after a moment that she had only fainted. Fafhrd approached the barred door, but it would not open to any knocking, pleas, or threats. He finally solved the riddle by kicking it down. Inside he saw: the aged man cowering in a dark corner; a woman attempting to conceal a young child in a pile of straw; a very old woman sitting on a stool, obviously blind, but frightenedly peering about just the same; and a young man holding an ax in trembling hands. The family resemblance was very marked.

Fafhrd stepped out of the way of the young man's feeble ax-blow and gently took the weapon from him.

The Mouser and Ahura brought the girl inside. At sight of Ahura there were further horrified shrinkings.

They laid the girl on the straw, and Ahura fetched water and began to bathe her head.

Meanwhile, the Mouser, by playing on her family's terror and practically identifying himself as a mountain demon, got them to answer his questions. First he asked about the stone city. It was a place of ancient devil-worship, they said, a place to be shunned. Yes, they had seen the black monolith of Ahriman, but only from a distance. No, they did not worship Ahriman – see the fire-shrine they kept for his adversary Ormadz? But they dreaded Ahriman, and the stones of the devil-city had a life of their own.

Then he asked about the misty mountain, and found it harder to get satisfactory answers. The cloud always shrouded its peak, they insisted. Though once toward sunset, the young man admitted, he thought he had glimpsed crazily leaning green towers and twisted minarets. But there was danger up there, horrible danger. What danger? He could not say.

The Mouser turned to the aged man. 'You told me,' he said harshly, 'that my brother demons exact no money tax from you for this land. What kind of tax, then, do they exact?'

'Lives,' whispered the aged man, his eyes showing more white.

'Lives eh? How many? And when do they come for them?'

'They never come. We go. Maybe every ten years, maybe every five, there comes a yellow-green light on the mountain-top at night, and a powerful calling in the air. Sometimes after such a night one of us is gone – who was too far from the house when the green light came. To be in the house with others helps resist the calling. I never saw the light except from our door, with a fire burning bright at my back and someone holding me. My brother went when I was a boy. Then for many years

153

afterwards the light never came, so that even I began to wonder whether it was not a boyhood legend or illusion.

'But seven years ago,' he continued quaveringly, staring at the Mouser, 'there came riding late one afternoon, on two gaunt and death-wearied horses, a young man and an old – or rather the semblances of a young man and an old, for I knew without being told, knew as I crouched trembling inside the door, peering through the crack, that the masters were returning to the Castle Called Mist. The old man was bald as a vulture and had no beard. The young man had the beginnings of a silky black one. He was dressed in black and silver, and his face was very pale. His features were like—' Here his gaze flickered fearfully toward Ahura. 'He rode stiffly, his lanky body rocking from side to side. He looked as if he were dead.

'They rode on toward the mountain without a sideward glance. But ever since that time the greenish-yellow light has glowed almost nightly from the mountaintop, and many of our animals have answered the call – and the wild ones too, to judge from their diminishing numbers. We have been careful, always staying near the house. It was not until three years ago that my eldest son went. He strayed too far in hunting and let darkness overtake him.

'And we have seen the black-bearded young man many times, usually at a distance, treading along the skyline or standing with head bowed upon some crag. Though once when my daughter was washing at the stream she looked up from her clothes-pounding and saw his dead eyes peering through the reeds. And once my eldest son, chasing a wounded snow-leopard into a thicket, found him talking with the beast. And once, rising early on a harvest morning, I saw him sitting by the well, staring at our doorway, although he did not seem to see me emerge. The old man we have seen too, though not so often. And for the last two years we have seen little or nothing of either, until—' And once again his gaze flickered helplessly toward Ahura.

Meanwhile the girl had come to her senses. This time her terror of Ahura was not so extreme. She could add nothing to the aged man's tale.

They prepared to depart. The Mouser noted a certain veiled vindictiveness toward the girl, especially in the eyes of the woman with the child, for having tried to warn them. So turning in the doorway he said, 'If you harm one hair of the girl's head, we will return, and the black-bearded one with us, and the green light to guide us by and wreak terrible vengeance.'

He tossed a few gold coins on the floor and departed.

(And so, although, or rather because her family looked upon her as an ally of demons, the girl from then on led a pampered life, and came to consider her blood as superior to theirs, and played shamelessly on their fear of the Mouser and Fafhrd and Black-beard, and finally made them give her all the golden coins, and with them purchased seductive garments after fortunate passage to a faraway city, where by clever stratagem she became the wife of a satrap and lived sumptuously ever afterwards – something that is often the fate of romantic people, if only they are romantic enough.)

Emerging from the house, the Mouser found Fafhrd making a brave attempt to recapture his former berserk mood. 'Hurry up, you little apprentice-demon!' he welcomed. 'We've a tryst with the good land of snow and cannot lag on the way!'

As they rode off, the Mouser rejoined good-naturedly, 'But what about the camel, Fafhrd? You can't very well take it to the ice country. It'll die of the phlegm.'

'There's no reason why snow shouldn't be as good for camels as it is for men,' Fafhrd retorted. Then, rising in his saddle and turning back, he waved toward the house and shouted, 'Lad! You that held the ax! When in years to come your bones feel a strange yearning, turn your face to the north. There you will find a land where you can become a man indeed.'

But in their hearts both knew that this talk was a pretense, that other planets now loomed in their horoscopes – in particular one that shone with a greenish-yellow light. As they pressed on up the valley, its silence and the absence of animal and insect life now made sinister, they felt mysteries hovering all around. Some, they knew, were locked in Ahura, but both refrained from questioning her, moved by vague apprehensions of terrifying upheavals her mind had undergone.

Finally the Mouser voiced what was in the thoughts of both of them. 'Yes, I am much afraid that Anra Devadoris, who sought to make us his apprentices, was only an apprentice himself and apt, apprentice-wise, to take credit for his master's work. Black-beard is gone, but the beardless one remains. What was it Ningauble said? . . . no simple creature, but a mystery? . . . no single identity, but a mirage?'

'Well, by all the fleas that bite the Great Antiochus, and all the lice that tickle his wife!' remarked a shrill, insolent voice behind them. 'You doomed gentlemen already know what's in this letter I have for you.'

They whirled around. Standing beside the camel – he might conceivably have been hidden, it is true, behind a nearby boulder – was a pertly grinning brown urchin, so typically Alexandrian that he might have stepped this minute out of Rakotis with a skinny mongrel sniffing at his heels. (The Mouser half expected such a dog to appear at the next moment.)

'Who sent you, boy?' Fafhrd demanded. 'How did you get here?'

'Now who and how would you expect?' replied the urchin. 'Catch.' He tossed the Mouser a wax tablet. 'Say, you two, take my advice and get out while the getting's good. I think so far as your expedition's concerned, Ningauble's pulling up his tent pegs and scuttling home. Always a friend in need, my dear employer.'

The Mouser ripped the cords, unfolded the tablet, and read:

'Greetings, my brave adventurers. You have done well, but the best remains to be done. Hark to the calling. Follow the green light. But be very cautious afterwards. I wish I could be of more assistance. Send the shroud, the cup, and the chest back with the boy as first payment.'

'Loki-brat! Regin-spawn!' burst out Fafhrd. The Mouser looked up to see the urchin lurching and bobbing back toward the Lost City on the back of the eagerly fugitive camel. His impudent laughter returned shrill and faint.

'There,' said the Mouser, 'rides off the generosity of poor, penurious Ningauble. Now we know what to do with the camel.'

'Zutt!' said Fafhrd. 'Let him have the brute and the toys. Good riddance to his gossiping!'

'Not a very high mountain,' said the Mouser an hour later, 'but high enough. I wonder who carved this neat little path and who keeps it clear?'

As he spoke, he was winding loosely over his shoulder a long thin rope of the sort used by mountain climbers, ending in a hook.

It was sunset, with twilight creeping at their heels. The little path, which had grown out of nothing, only gradually revealing itself, now led them sinuously around great boulders and along the crests of ever steeper rock-strewn slopes. Conversation, which was only a film on wariness, had played with the methods of Ningauble and his agents – whether they communicated with one another directly, from mind to mind, or by tiny whistles that emitted a note too high for human ears to hear, but capable of producing a tremor in any brother whistle or in the ear of the bat.

It was a moment when the whole universe seemed to pause. A spectral greenish light gleamed from the cloudy top ahead – but that was surely only the sun's sky-reflected afterglow. There was a hint of all-pervading sound in the air, a mighty susurrus just below the threshold of hearing, as if an army of unseen insects were tuning up their instruments. These sensations were as intangible as the force that drew them onward, a force so feeble that they knew they could break it like a single spider-strand, yet did not choose to try.

As if in response to some unspoken word, both Fafhrd and the Mouser turned toward Ahura. Under their gaze she seemed to be changing momently, opening like a night flower, becoming ever more childlike, as if some master hypnotist were stripping away the outer, later petals of her mind, leaving only a small limpid pool, from whose unknown depths, however, dark bubbles were dimly rising.

They felt their infatuation pulse anew, but with a shy restraint on it. And their hearts fell silent as the hooded

157

heights above, as she said, 'Anra Devadoris was my twin brother.'

7. *Ahura Devadoris*

'I never knew my father. He died before we were born. In one of her rare fits of communicativeness my mother told me, "Your father was a Greek, Ahura. A very kind and learned man. He laughed a great deal." I remember how stern she looked as she said that, rather than how beautiful, the sunlight glinting from her ringleted, black-dyed hair.

'But it seemed to me that she had slightly emphasized the word "Your". You see, even then I wondered about Anra. So I asked Old Berenice the housekeeper about it. She told me she had seen Mother bear us, both on the same night.

'Old Berenice went on to tell me how my father had died. Almost nine months before we were born, he was found one morning beaten to death in the street just outside the door. A gang of Egyptian longshoremen who were raping and robbing by night were supposed to have done it, although they were never brought to justice – that was back when the Ptolemies had Tyre. It was a horrible death. He was almost pashed to a pulp against the cobbles.

'At another time Old Berenice told me something about my mother, after making me swear by Athena and by Set and by Moloch, who would eat me if I did, never to tell. She said that Mother came from a Persian family whose five daughters in the old times were all priestesses, dedicated from birth to be the wives of an evil Persian god, forbidden the embraces of mortals, doomed to spend their nights alone with the stone image of the god in a lonely temple "halfway across the world", she said. Mother was away that day and Old Berenice dragged me down into a little basement under Mother's bedroom and pointed out three ragged gray stones set among the bricks and told me they came from the temple. Old Berenice liked to frighten me, although she was deathly afraid of Mother.

'Of course I instantly went and told Anra, as I always did.'

The little path was leading sharply upward now, along the

spine of a crest. Their horses went at a walk, first Fafhrd's, then Ahura's, last the Mouser's. The lines were smoothed in Fafhrd's face, although he was still very watchful, and the Mouser looked almost like a quaint child.

Ahura continued, 'It is hard to make you understand my relationship with Anra, because it was so close that even the word "relationship" spoils it. There was a game we would play in the garden. He would close his eyes and guess what I was looking at. In other games we would change sides, but never in this one.

'He invented all sorts of versions of the game and didn't want to play any others. Sometimes I would climb up by the olive tree onto the tiled roof – Anra couldn't make it – and watch for an hour. Then I'd come down and tell him what I'd seen – some dyers spreading out wet green cloth for the sun to turn it purple, a procession of priests around the Temple of Melkarth, a galley from Pergamum setting sail, a Greek official impatiently explaining something to his Egyptian scribe, two henna-handed ladies giggling at some kilted sailors, a mysterious and lonely Jew – and he would tell me what kind of people they were and what they had been thinking and what they were planning to do. It was a very special kind of imagination, for afterwards when I began to go outside I found out that he was usually right. At the time I remember thinking that it was as if he were looking at the pictures in my mind and seeing more than I could. I liked it. It was such a gentle feeling.

'Of course our closeness was partly because Mother, especially after she changed her way of life, wouldn't let us go out at all or mix with other children. There was more reason for that than just her strictness. Anra was very delicate. He once broke his wrist and it was a long time healing. Mother had a slave come in who was skilled in such things, and he told Mother he was afraid that Anra's bones were becoming too brittle. He told about children whose muscles and sinews gradually turned to stone, so that they became living statues. Mother struck him in the face and drove him from the house – an action that cost her a dear friend, because he was an important slave.

159

'And even if Anra had been allowed to go out, he couldn't have. Once after I had begun to go outside I persuaded him to come with me. He didn't want to, but I laughed at him, and he could never stand laughter. As soon as we climbed over the garden wall he fell down in a faint and I couldn't rouse him from it, though I tried and tried. Finally I climbed back so I could open the door and drag him in, and Old Berenice spotted me and I had to tell her what had happened. She helped me carry him in, but afterwards she whipped me because she knew I'd never dare tell Mother I'd taken him outside. Anra came to his senses while she was whipping me, but was sick for a week afterwards. I don't think I ever laughed at him after that, until today.

'Cooped up in the house, Anra spent most of his time studying. While I watched from the roof or wheedled stories from Old Berenice and the other slaves, or later on went out to gather information for him, he would stay in Father's library, reading, or learning some new language from Father's grammars and translations. Mother taught both of us to read Greek, and I picked up speaking knowledge of Aramaic and scraps of other tongues from the slaves and passed them on to him. But Anra was far cleverer than I at reading. He loved letters as passionately as I did the outside. For him, they were alive. I remember him showing me some Egyptian hieroglyphs and telling me that they were all animals and insects. And then he showed me some Egyptian hieratics and demotics and told me those were the same animals in disguise. But Hebrew, he said, was best of all, for each letter was a magic charm. That was before he learned Old Persian. Sometimes it was years before we found out how to pronounce the languages he learned. That was one of my most important jobs when I started to go outside for him.

'Father's library had been kept just as it was when he died. Neatly stacked in cannisters were all the renowned philosophers, historians, poets, rhetoricians, and grammarians. But tossed in a corner along with postsherds and papyrus scraps like so much trash, were rolls of a very different sort. Across the back of one of them my father had scribbled, derisively

I'm sure, in his big impulsive hand, "Secret Wisdom!" It was those that from the first captured Anra's curiosity. He would read the respectable books in the cannisters, but chiefly so he could go back and take a brittle roll from the corner, blow off the dust, and puzzle out a little more.

'They were very strange books that frightened and disgusted me and made me want to giggle all at once. Many of them were written in a cheap and ignorant style. Some of them told what dreams meant and gave directions for working magic – all sorts of nasty things to be cooked together. Others – Jewish rolls in Aramaic – were about the end of the world and wild adventures of evil spirits and mixed-up, messy monsters – things with ten heads and jeweled cartwheels for feet, things like that. Then there were Chaldean star-books that told how all the lights in the sky were alive and their names and what they did to you. And one jerky, half illiterate roll in Greek told about something horrible, which for a long while I couldn't understand, connected with an ear of corn and six pomegranate seeds. It was in another of those sensational Greek rolls that Anra first found out about Ahriman and his eternal empire of evil, and after that he couldn't wait until he'd mastered Old Persian. But none of the few Old Persian rolls in Father's library were about Ahriman, so he had to wait until I could steal such things for him outside.

'My going outside was after Mother changed her way of life. That happened when I was seven. She was always a very moody and frightening woman, though sometimes she'd be very affectionate toward me for a little while, and she always spoiled and pampered Anra, though from a distance, through the slaves, almost as if she were afraid of him.

'Now her moods became blacker and blacker. Sometimes I'd surprise her looking in horror at nothing, or beating her forehead while her eyes were closed and her beautiful face was all taut, as if she were going mad. I had the feeling she'd been backed up to the end of some underground tunnel and must find a door leading out, or lose her mind.

'Then one afternoon I peeked into her bedroom and saw her looking into her silver mirror. For a long, long while she studied her face in it and I watched her without making a sound. I knew that something important was happening. Finally she seemed to make some sort of difficult inward effort and the lines of anxiety and sternness and fear disappeared from her face, leaving it smooth and beautiful as a mask. Then she unlocked a drawer I'd never seen into before and took out all sorts of little pots and vials and brushes. With these she colored and whitened her face and carefully smeared a dark, shining powder around her eyes and painted her lips reddish-orange. All this time my heart was pounding and my throat was choking up, I didn't know why. Then she laid down her brushes and dropped her chiton and felt of her throat and breasts in a thoughtful way and took up the mirror and looked at herself with a cold satisfaction. She was very beautiful, but it was a beauty that terrified me. Until now I'd always thought of her as hard and stern outside, but soft and loving within, if only you could manage to creep into that core. But now she was all turned inside out. Strangling my sobs, I ran to tell Anra and find out what it meant. But this time his cleverness failed him. He was as puzzled and disturbed as I.

'It was right afterwards that she became even stricter with me, and although she continued to spoil Anra from a distance, kept us shut up from the world more than ever. I wasn't even allowed to speak to the new slave she'd bought, an ugly, smirking, skinny-legged girl named Phryne who used to massage her and sometimes play the flute. There were all sorts of visitors coming to the house now at night, but Anra and I were always locked in our little bedroom high up by the garden. We'd hear them yelling through the wall and sometimes screaming and bumping around the inner court to the sound of Phryne's flute. Sometimes I'd lie staring at the darkness in an inexplicable sick terror all night long. I tried every way to get Old Berenice to tell me what was happening, but for once her fear of Mother's anger was too great. She'd only leer at me.

'Finally Anra worked out a plan for finding out. When he first told me about it, I refused. It terrified me. That was when I discovered the power he had over me. Up until that time the things I had done for him had been part of a game I enjoyed as much as he. I had never thought of myself as a slave obeying commands. But now when I rebelled, I found out not only that my twin had an obscure power over my limbs, so that I could hardly move them at all, or imagined I couldn't, if he were unwilling, but also that I couldn't bear the thought of him being unhappy or frustrated.

'I realize now that he had reached the first of those crises in his life when his way was blocked and he pitilessly sacrificed his dearest helper to the urgings of his insatiable curiosity.

'Night came. As soon as we were locked in I let a knotted cord out the little high window and wriggled out and climbed down. Then I climbed the olive tree to the roof. I crept over the tiles down to the square skylight of the inner court and managed to squirm over the edge – I almost fell – into a narrow, cobwebby space between the ceiling and the tiles. There was a faint murmur of talk from the dining room, but the court was empty. I lay still as a mouse and waited.'

Fafhrd uttered a smothered exclamation and stopped his horse. The others did likewise. A pebble rattled down the slope, but they hardly heard it. Seeming to come from the heights above them and yet to fill the whole darkening sky was something that was not entirely a sound, something that tugged at them like the Sirens' voices at fettered Odysseus. For a while they listened incredulously, then Fafhrd shrugged and started forward again, the others following.

Ahura continued, 'For a long time nothing happened, except occasionally slaves hurried in and out with full and empty dishes, and there was some laughter, and I heard Phryne's flute. Then suddenly the laughter grew louder and changed to singing, and there was the sound of couches pushed back and the patter of footsteps, and there swept into the court a Dionysiac rout.

'Phryne, naked, piped the way. My mother followed, laughing, her arms linked with those of two dancing young men, but clutching to her bosom a large silver wine-bowl. The wine sloshed over and stained purple her white silk chiton around her breasts, but she only laughed and reeled more wildly. After those came many others, men and women, young and old, all singing and dancing. One limber young man skipped high, clapping his heels, and one fat old grinning fellow panted and had to be pulled by girls, but they kept it up three times around the court before they threw themselves down on the couches and cushions. Then while they chattered and laughed and kissed and embraced and played pranks and watched a naked girl prettier than Phryne dance, my mother offered the bowl around for them to dip their wine cups.

'I was astounded – and entranced. I had been almost dead with fear, expecting I don't know what cruelties and horrors. Instead, what I saw was wholly lovely and natural. The revelation burst on me, "So this is the wonderful and important thing that people do." My mother no longer frightened me. Though she still wore her new face, there was no longer any hardness about her, inside or out, only joy and beauty. The young men were so witty and gay I had to put my fist in my mouth to keep from screaming with laughter. Even Phryne, squatting on her heels like a skinny boy as she piped, seemed for once unmalicious and likeable. I couldn't wait to tell Anra.

'There was only one disturbing note, and that was so slight I hardly noticed it. Two of the men who took the lead in the joking, a young red-haired fellow and an older chap with a face like a lean satyr, seemed to have something up their sleeves. I saw them whisper to some of the others. And once the younger grinned at Mother and shouted, "I know something about you from way back!" And once the older called at her mockingly, "I know something about your great-grandmother, you old Persian you!" Each time Mother laughed and waved her hand derisively, but I could see that she was bothered underneath. And each time some of the others paused momentarily, as if they had an inkling of something, but didn't want to let on. Eventually the two men drifted out, and from then on there was nothing to mar the fun.

'The dancing became wilder and staggering, the laughter louder, more wine was spilled than drank. Then Phryne threw away her flute and ran and landed in the fat man's lap with a jounce that almost knocked the wind out of him. Four or five of the others tumbled down.

'Just at that moment there came a crashing and a loud rending of wood, as if a door were being broken in. Instantly everyone was as still as death. Someone jerked around and a lamp snuffed out, throwing half the court into shadow.

'Then loud, shaking footsteps, like two paving blocks walking, sounded through the house, coming nearer and nearer.

'Everyone was frozen, staring at the doorway. Phryne still had her arm around the fat man's neck. But it was in Mother's face that the truly unbearable terror showed. She had retreated to the remaining lamp and dropped to her knees there. The whites showed around her eyes. She began to utter short, rapid screams, like a trapped dog.

'Then through the doorway clomped a great ragged-edged, square-limbed, naked stone man fully seven feet high. His face was just expressionless black gashes in a flat surface, and before him was thrust a mortary stone member. I couldn't bear to look at him, but I had to. He tramped echoingly across the room to Mother, jerked her up, still screaming, by the hair, and with the other hand ripped down her wine-stained chiton. I fainted.

'But it must have ended about there, for when I came to, sick with terror, it was to hear everyone laughing uproariously. Several of them were bending over Mother, at once reassuring and mocking her, the two men who had gone out among them, and to one side was a jumbled heap of cloth and thin boards, both crusted with mortar. From what they said I understood that the red-haired one had worn the horrible disguise, while satyr-face had made the footsteps by rhythmically clomping on the floor with a brick, and had simulated the breaking door by jumping on a propped-up board.

' "Now tell us your great-grandmother wasn't married to a stupid old stone demon back in Persia!" he jeered pleasantly, wagging his finger.

'Then came something that tortured me like a rusty dagger and terrified me, in a very quiet way, as much as the image. Although she was white as milk and barely able to totter, Mother did her best to pretend that the loathsome trick they'd played on her was just a clever joke. I knew why. She was horribly afraid of losing their friendship and would have done anything rather than be left alone.

'Her pretense worked. Although some of them left, the rest yielded to her laughing entreaties. They drank until they sprawled out snoring. I waited until almost dawn, then summoned all my courage, made my stiff muscles pull me onto the tiles, cold and slippery with dew, and with what seemed the last of my strength, dragged myself back to our room.

'But not to sleep. Anra was awake and avid to hear what had happened. I begged him not to make me, but he insisted. I had to tell him everything. The pictures of what I'd seen kept bobbing up in my wretchedly tired mind so vividly that it seemed to be happening all over again. He asked all sorts of questions, wouldn't let me miss a single detail. I had to relive that first thrilling revelation of joy, tainted now by the knowledge that the people were mostly sly and cruel.

'When I got to the part about the stone image, Anra became terribly excited. But when I told him about it all being a nasty joke, he seemed disappointed. He became angry, as if he suspected me of lying.

'Finally he let me sleep.

'The next night I went back to my cubbyhole under the tiles.'

Again Fafhrd stopped his horse. The mist masking the mountaintop had suddenly begun to glow, as if a green moon were rising, or as if it were a volcano spouting green flames. The hue tinged their upturned faces. It lured like some vast cloudy jewel. Fafhrd and the Mouser exchanged a glance of fatalistic wonder. Then all three proceeded up the narrowing ridge.

Ahura continued, 'I'd sworn by all the gods I'd never do it. I'd told myself I'd rather die. But . . . Anra made me.

'Daytimes I wandered around like a stupefied little ghostslave. Old Berenice was puzzled and suspicious and once or twice I thought Phryne grimaced knowingly. Finally even Mother noticed and questioned me and had a physician in.

'I think I would have gotten really sick and died, or gone

mad, except that then, in desperation at first, I started to go outside, and a whole new world opened to me.'

As she spoke on, her voice rising in hushed excitement at the memory of it, there was painted in the minds of Fafhrd and the Mouser a picture of the magic city that Tyre must have seemed to the child – the waterfront, the riches, the bustle of trade, the hum of gossip and laughter, the ships and strangers from foreign lands.

'Those people I had watched from the roof – I could touch almost anywhere. Every person I met seemed a wonderful mystery, something to be smiled and chattered at. I dressed as a slave-child, and all sorts of folk got to know me and expect my coming – other slaves, tavern wenches and sellers of sweet-meats, street merchants and scribes, errand boys and boatmen, seamstresses and cooks. I made myself useful, ran errands my-self, listened delightedly to their endless talk, passed on gossip I'd heard, gave away bits of food I'd stolen at home, became a favorite. It seemed to me I could never get enough of Tyre. I scampered from morning to night. It was generally twilight before I climbed back over the garden wall.

'I couldn't fool Old Berenice, but after a while I found a way to escape her whippings. I threatened to tell Mother it was she who had told red-hair and satyr-face about the stone image. I don't know if I guessed right or not, but the threat worked. After that, she would only mumble venomously when-ever I sneaked in after sunset. As for Mother, she was getting farther away from us all the time, alive only by night, lost by day in frightened brooding.

'Then, each evening, came another delight. I would tell Anra everything I had heard and seen, each new adventure, each little triumph. Like a magpie I repeated for him all the bright colors, sounds, and odors. Like a magpie I repeated for him the babble of strange languages I'd heard, the scraps of learned talk I'd caught from priests and scholars. I forgot what he'd done to me. We were playing the game again, the most wonderful version of all. Often he helped me, suggesting new places to go, new things to watch for, and once he even saved me from being kidnapped by a couple of ingratiating

Alexandrian slave-dealers whom anyone but I would have suspected.

'It was odd how that happened. The two had made much of me, were promising me sweetmeats if I would go somewhere nearby with them, when I thought I heard Anra's voice whisper "Don't." I became cold with terror and darted down an alley.

'It seemed as though Anra were now able sometimes to see the pictures in my mind even when I was away from him. I felt ever so close to him.

'I was wild for him to come out with me, but I've told you what happened the one time he tried. And as the years passed, he seemed to become tied even tighter to the house. Once when Mother vaguely talked of moving to Antioch, he fell ill and and did not recover until she had promised we would never, never go.

'Meanwhile he was growing up into a slim and darkly handsome youth. Phryne began to make eyes at him and sought excuses to go to his room. But he was frightened and rebuffed her. However, he coaxed me to make friends with her, to be near her, even share her bed those nights when Mother did not want her. He seemed to like that.

'You know the restlessness that comes to a maturing child, when he seeks love, or adventure, or the gods, or all three. That restlessness had come to Anra, but his only gods were in those dusty, dubious rolls my father had labeled "Secret Wisdom!" I hardly knew what he did by day any more except that there were odd ceremonies and experiments mixed with his studies. Some of them he conducted in the little basement where the three gray stones were. At such times he had me keep watch. He no longer told me what he was reading or thinking, and I was so busy in my new world that I hardly noticed the difference.

'And yet I could see the restlessness growing. He sent me on longer and more difficult missions, had me inquire after books the scribes had never heard of, seek out all manner of astrologers and wise-women, required me to steal or buy stranger and stranger ingredients from the herb doctors. And when I did win such treasures for him, he would only snatch them from me unjoyfully and be twice as gloomy the evening after. Gone were such days of rejoicing as when I had brought him the first Persian rolls about Ahriman, the first lodestone, or repeated every syllable I had overheard of the words of a famous philosopher from Athens. He was beyond all that now. He sometimes hardly listened to my detailed reports, as if he had already glanced through them and knew they contained nothing to interest him.

'He grew haggard and sick. His restlessness took the form of a frantic pacing. I was reminded of my mother trapped in that blocked-off, underground corridor. It made my heart hurt to watch him. I longed to help him, to share with him my new exciting life, to give him the thing he so desperately wanted.

'But it was not my help he needed. He had embarked on a dark, mysterious quest I did not understand, and he had reached a bitter, corroding impasse where of his own experience he could go no farther.

'He needed a teacher.'

8. *The Old Man Without a Beard*

'I was fifteen when I met the Old Man Without a Beard. I called him that and I still call him that, for there is no other distinguishing characteristic my mind can seize and hold. Whenever I think of him, even whenever I look at him, his face melts into the mob. It is as if a master actor, after portraying every sort of character in the world, should have hit on the simplest and most perfect of disguises.

'As to what lies behind that too-ordinary face – the something you can sometimes sense but hardly grasp – all I can say is a satiety and an emptiness that are not of this world.'

Fafhrd caught his breath. They had reached the end of the ridge. The leftward slope had suddenly tilted upward, become the core of the mountain. While the rightward slope had swung downward and out of sight, leaving an unfathomable black abyss. Between, the path continued upward, a stony strip only a few feet wide. The Mouser touched reassuringly the coil of rope over his shoulder. For a moment their horses hung back. Then, as if the faint green glow and the ceaseless murmuring that bathed them were an intangible net, they were drawn on.

'I was in a wine shop. I had just carried a message to one of the men-friends of the Greek girl Chloe, hardly older than myself, when I noticed him sitting in a corner. I asked Chloe about him. She said he was a Greek chorister and commercial poet down on his luck, or no, that he was an Egyptian fortune-teller, changed her mind again, tried to remember what a Samian pander had told her about him, gave him a quick puzzled look, decided that she didn't really know him at all and that it didn't matter.

'But his very emptiness intrigued me. Here was a new kind of mystery. After I had been watching him for some time, he turned around and looked at me. I had the impression that he had been aware of my inquiring gaze from the beginning, but had ignored it as a sleepy man a buzzing fly.

'After that one glance he slumped back into his former position, but when I left the shop he walked at my side.

' "You're not the only one who looks through your eyes, are you?" he said quietly.

'I was so startled by his question that I didn't know how to reply, but he didn't require me to. His face brightened without becoming any more individualized and he immediately began to talk to me in the most charming and humorous way, though his words gave no clue as to who he was or what he did.

'However, I gathered from hints he let fall that he possessed some knowledge of those odd sorts of things that always interested Anra and so I followed him willingly, my hand in his.

'But not for long. Our way led up a narrow twisting alley, and I saw a sideways glint in his eye, and felt his hand tighten on mine in a way I did not like. I became somewhat frightened and expected at any minute the danger warning from Anra.

'We passed a lowering tenement and stopped at a rickety

three-story shack leaning against it. He said his dwelling was at the top. He was drawing me toward the ladder that served for stairs, and still the danger warning did not come.

'Then his hand crept toward my wrist and I did not wait any longer, but jerked away and ran, my fear growing greater with every step.

'When I reached home, Anra was pacing like a leopard. I was eager to tell him all about my narrow escape, but he kept interrupting me to demand details of the Old Man and angrily flirting his head because I could tell him so little. Then, when I came to the part about my running away, an astounding look of tortured betrayal contorted his features, he raised his hands as if to strike me, then threw himself down on the couch, sobbing.

'But as I leaned over him anxiously, his sobs stopped. He looked around at me, over his shoulder, his face white but composed, and said, "Ahura, I must know everything about him."

'In that one moment I realized all that I had overlooked for years – that my delightful airy freedom was a sham – that it was not Anra, but I, that was tethered – that the game was not a game, but a bondage – that while I had gone about so open and eager, intent only on sound and color, form and movement, he had been developing the side I had no time for, the intellect, the purpose, the will – that I was only a tool to him, a slave to be sent on errands, an unfeeling extension of his own body, a tentacle he could lose and grow again, like an octopus – that even my misery at his frantic disappointment, my willingness to do anything to please him, was only another lever to be coldly used against me – that our very closeness, so that we were only two halves of one mind, was to him only another tactical advantage.

'He had reached the second great crisis of his life, and again he unhesitatingly sacrificed his nearest.

'There was something uglier to it even than that, as I could see in his eyes as soon as he was sure he had me. We were like brother and sister kings in Alexandria or Antioch, play-mates from infancy, destined for each other, but unknowingly, and the boy crippled and impotent – and now, too soon and horridly had come the bridal night.

'The end was that I went back to the narrow alley, the lowering tenement, the rickety shack, the ladder, the third story, and the Old Man Without a Beard.

'I didn't give in without a struggle. Once I was out of the house I fought every inch of the way. Up until now, even in the cubbyhole under the tiles, I had only to spy and observe for Anra. I had not to do things.

'But in the end it was the same. I dragged myself up the last rung and knocked on the warped door. It swung open at my touch. Inside, across a fumy room, behind a large empty table, by the light of a single ill-burning lamp, his eyes as unwinking as a fish's, and upon me, sat the Old Man Without a Beard.'

Ahura paused, and Fafhrd and the Mouser felt a clamminess descend upon their skins. Looking up, they saw uncoiling downward from dizzy heights, like the ghosts of constrictive snakes or jungle vines, thin tendrils of green mist.

'Yes,' said Ahura, 'there is always mist or smokiness of some sort where he is.

'Three days later I returned to Anra and told him everything – a corpse giving testimony as to its murderer. But in this instance the judge relished the testimony, and when I told him of a certain plan the Old Man had in mind, an unearthly joy shimmered on his face.

'The Old Man was to be hired as a tutor and physician for Anra. This was easily arranged, as Mother always acceded to Anra's wishes and perhaps still had some hope of seeing him stirred from his seclusion. Moreover, the Old Man had a mixture of unobtrusiveness and power that I am sure would have won him entry everywhere. Within a matter of weeks he had quietly established a mastery over everyone in the house – some, like Mother, merely to be ignored; others, like Phryne ultimately to be used.

'I will always remember Anra on the day the Old Man came. This was to be his first contact with the reality beyond the garden wall, and I could see that he was terribly frightened. As the hours of waiting passed, he retreated to his room, and think it was mainly pride that kept him from calling the whole thing off. We did not hear the Old Man coming – only Old Berenice, who was counting the silver outside, stopped her muttering. Anra threw himself back on the couch in the farthest corner of the room, his hands gripping its edge, his eyes fixed on the doorway. A shadow lurched into sight there, grew darker and more definite. Then the Old Man put down on the threshold the two bags he was carrying and looked beyond me at Anra. A moment later my twin's painful gasps died in a faint hiss of expired breath. He had fainted.

'That evening his new education began. Everything that had happened was, as it were, repeated on a deeper, stranger level. There were languages to be learned, but not any languages to be found in human books; rituals to be intoned, but not to any gods that ordinary men have worshiped; magic to be brewed, but not with herbs that I could buy or steal. Daily Anra was instructed in the ways of inner darkness, the sicknesses and unknown powers of the mind, the eon-buried emotions that must be due to insidious impurities the gods overlooked in the earth from which they made man. By silent stages our home became a temple of the abominable, a monastery of the unclean.

'Yet there was nothing of tainted orgy, of vicious excess about their actions. Whatever they did, was done with strict self-discipline and mystic concentration. There was no looseness anywhere about them. They aimed at a knowledge and a power, born of darkness, true, but one which they were willing to make any self-sacrifice to obtain. They were religious, with this difference: their ritual was degradation, their aim a world chaos played upon like a broken lyre by their master minds, their god the quintessence of evil, Ahriman, the ultimate pit.

'As if performed by sleepwalkers, the ordinary routine of our home went on. Indeed, I sometimes felt that we were all of us, except Anra, merely dreams behind the Old Man's empty eyes – actors in a deliberate nightmare where men portrayed beasts; beasts, worms; worms, slime.

'Each morning I went out and made my customary way through Tyre, chattering and laughing as before, but emptily, knowing that I was no more free than if visible chains leashed me to the house, a puppet dangled over the garden wall. Only at the periphery of my masters' intentions did I dare oppose them even passively – once I smuggled the girl Chloe a protective amulet because I fancied they were considering her as a subject for such experiments as they had tried on Phryne. And daily the periphery of their intentions widened – indeed, they would long since have left the house themselves, except for Anra's bondage to it.

'It was to the problem of breaking that bondage that they now devoted themselves. I was not told how they hoped to manage it, but I soon realized that I was to play a part.

'They would shine glittering lights into my eyes and Anra would chant until I slept. Hours or even days later I would awake to find that I had gone unconsciously about my daily business, my body a slave to Anra's commands. At other times Anra would wear a thin leather mask which covered all his features, so that he could only see, if at all, through my eyes. My sense of oneness with my twin grew steadily with my fear of him.

'Then came a period in which I was kept closely pent up, as if in some savage prelude to maturity or death or birth, or all three. The Old Man said something about "not to see the sun or touch the earth." Again I crouched for hours in the cubbyhole under the tiles or on reed mats in the little basement. And now it was my eyes and ears that were covered rather than Anra's. For hours I, whom sights and sounds had nourished more than food, could see nothing but fragmentary memories of the child-Anra sick, or the Old Man across the fumy room, or Phryne writhing on her belly and hissing like a snake. But worst of all was my separation from Anra. For the first time since our birth I could not see his face, hear his voice, feel his mind. I withered like a tree from which the sap is withdrawn, an animal in which the nerves have been killed.

'Finally came a day or night, I know not which, when the Old Man loosened the mask from my face. There could hardly have been more than a glimmer of light, but my long-blindfolded eyes made out every detail of the little basement with a painful clarity. The three gray stones had been dug out of the pavement. Supine beside them lay Anra, emaciated, pale, hardly breathing, looking as though he were about to die.'

The three climbers stopped, confronted by a ghostly green wall. The narrow path had emerged onto what must be the mountain's tablelike top. Ahead stretched a level expanse of dark rock, mist-masked after the first few yards. Without a word they dismounted and led their trembling horses forward into a moist realm which, save that the water was weightless, most resembled a faintly phosphorescent sea bottom.

'My heart leaped out toward my twin in pity and horror. I realized that despite all tyranny and torment I still loved him more than anything in the world, loved him as a slave loves the weak, cruel master who depends for everything on that slave, loved him as the ill-used body loves the despot mind. And I felt more closely linked to him, our lives and deaths interdependent, than if we had been linked by bonds of flesh and blood, as some rare twins are.

'The Old Man told me I could save him from death if I chose. For the present I must merely talk to him in my usual fashion. This I did, with an eagerness born of days without him. Save for an occasional faint fluttering of his sallow eyelids, Anra did not move, yet I felt that never before had he listened as intently, never before had he understood me as well. It seemed to me that all my previous speech with him had been crude by contrast. Now I remembered and told him all sorts of things that had escaped my memory or seemed too subtle for language. I talked on and on, haphazardly, chaotically, ranging swiftly from local gossip to world history, delving into myriad experiences and feelings, not all of them my own.

'Hours, perhaps days passed – the Old Man may have put some spell of slumber or deafness on the other inmates of the house to guard against interruption. At times my throat grew dry and he gave me drink, but I hardly dared pause for that, since I was appalled at the slight but unremitting change for the worse that was taking place in my twin and I had become possessed with the idea that my talking was the cord between life and Anra, that it created a channel between our bodies, across which my strength could flow to revive him.

'My eyes swam and blurred, my body shook, my voice ran the gamut of hoarseness down to an almost inaudible whisper. Despite my resolve I would have fainted, save that the Old Man held to my face burning aromatic herbs which caused me to come shudderingly awake.

'Finally I could no longer speak, but that was no release, as I continued to twitch my cracked lips and think on and on in a rushing feverish stream. It was as if I jerked and flung from the depths of my mind scraps of ideas from which Anra sucked the tiny life that remained to him.

'There was one persistent image – of a dying Hermaphroditus approaching Salmacis' pool, in which he would become one with the nymph.

'Farther and farther I ventured out along the talk-created channel between us, nearer and nearer I came to Anra's pale, delicate, cadaverous face, until, as with a despairing burst of effort I hurled my last strength to him, it loomed large as a green-shadowed ivory cliff falling to engulf me—'

Ahura's words broke off in a gasp of horror. All three stood still and stared ahead. For rearing up before them in the thickening mist, so near that they felt they had been ambushed, was a great chaotic structure of whitish, faintly yellowed stone, through whose narrow windows and wide-open door streamed a baleful greenish light, source of the mist's phosphorescent glow. Fafhrd and the Mouser thought of Karnak and its obelisks, of the Pharos lighthouse, of the Acropolis, of the Ishtar Gate in Babylon, of the ruins of Khatti, of the Lost City of Ahriman, of those doomful mirage-towers that seamen see where are Scylla and Charybdis. Of a truth, the architecture of the strange structure varied so swiftly and to such unearthly extremes that it was lifted into an insane stylistic realm all of its own. Mist-magnified, its twisted ramps and pinnacles, like a fluid face in a nightmare, pushed upward toward where the stars should have been.

'What happened next was so strange that I felt sure I had plunged from feverish consciousness into the cool retreat of a fanciful dream,' Ahura continued as, having tethered their horses, they mounted a wide stairway toward that open door which mocked alike sudden rush and cautious reconnoitering. Her story went on with as calm and drugged a fatalism as their step-by-step advance. 'I was lying on my back beside the three stones and watching my body move around the little basement. I was terribly weak, I could not stir a muscle, and yet I felt delightfully refreshed – all the dry burning and aching in my throat was gone. Idly, as one will in a dream, I studied my face. It seemed to be smiling in triumph, very foolishly I thought. But as I continued to study it, fear began to intrude into my pleasant dream. The face was mine, but there were unfamiliar quirks of expression. Then, becoming aware of my gaze, it grimaced contemptuously and turned and said something to the Old Man, who nodded matter-of-factly. The intruding fear engulfed me. With a tremendous effort I managed to roll my eyes downward and look at my real body, the one lying on the floor.

'It was Anra's.'

They entered the doorway and found themselves in a huge, many-nooked and niched stone room – though seemingly no nearer the ultimate source of the green glow, except that here the misty air was bright with it. There were stone tables and benches and chairs scattered about, but the chief feature of the place was the mighty archway ahead, from which stone groinings curved upward in baffling profusion. Fafhrd's and the Mouser's eyes momentarily sought the keystone of the arch, both because of its great size and because there was an odd dark recess toward its top.

The silence was portentous, making them feel uneasily for their swords. It was not merely that the luring music had ceased – here in the Castle Called Mist there was literally no sound, save what rippled out futilely from their own beating hearts. There was instead a fog-bound concentration that froze into the senses, as though they were inside the mind of a titanic thinker, or as if the stones themselves were entranced.

Then, since it seemed as unthinkable to wait in that silence as for lost hunters to stand motionless in deep winter cold, they passed under the archway and took at random an upward-leading ramp.

Ahura continued, 'Helplessly I watched them make certain preparations. While Anra gathered some small bundles of manuscripts and clothing, the Old Man lashed together the three mortar-crusted stones.

'It may have been that in the moment of victory he relaxed habitual precautions. At all events, while he was still bending over the stones, my mother entered the room. Crying out, "What have you done to him?" she threw herself down beside me and felt at me anxiously. But that was not to the Old Man's liking. He grabbed her shoulders and roughly jerked her back. She lay huddled against the wall, her eyes wide, her teeth chattering – especially when she saw Anra, in my body, grotesquely lift the lashed stones. Meanwhile the Old Man hoisted me, in my new, wasted form, to his shoulder, picked up the bundles, and ascended the short stair.

'We walked through the inner court, rose-strewn and filled with Mother's perfumed, wine-splashed friends, who stared at us in befuddled astonishment, and so out of the house. It was night. Five slaves waited with a curtained litter in which the Old Man placed me. My last glimpse was of Mother's face, its paint tracked by tears, peering horrifiedly through the half open door.'

The ramp issued onto an upper level and they found themselves wandering aimlessly through a mazy series of rooms. Of little use to record here the things they thought they saw through shadowy doorways, or thought they heard through metal doors with massy complex bolts whose drawing they dared not fathom. There was a disordered, high-shelved library, certain of the rolls seeming to smoke and fume as though they held in their papyrus and ink the seeds of a holocaust; the corners were piled with sealed cannisters of greenish stone and age-verdigrised brass tablets. There were instruments that Fafhrd did not even bother to warn the Mouser against touching. Another room exuded a fearful animal stench; upon its slippery floor they noted a sprinkling of short, incredibly thick black bristles. But the only living creature they saw at the time was a little hairless thing that looked as if it had once sought to become a bear cub; when Fafhrd stooped to pet it, it flopped away whimpering. There was a door that was thrice as broad as it was high, and its height hardly that of a man's knee. There was a window that let upon a blackness that was neither of mist nor of night, and yet seemed infinite; peering in, Fafhrd could faintly see rusted iron handholds leading upward. The Mouser uncoiled his climbing rope to its full length and swung it around inside the window, without the hook striking anything.

Yet the strangest impression this ominously empty stronghold begot in them was also the subtlest, and one which each new room or twisting corridor heightened – feeling of architectural inadequacy. It seemed impossible that the supports were equal to the vast weights of the great stone floors and ceilings, so impossible that they almost became convinced that there were buttresses and retaining walls they could not see, either invisible or existing in some other world altogether, as if the Castle Called Mist had only partially emerged from some unthinkable outside. That certain bolted doors seemed to lead where no space could be, added to this hinting.

They wandered through passages so distorted that, though they retained a precise memory of landmarks, they lost all sense of direction.

Finally Fafhrd said, 'This gets us nowhere. Whatever we seek, whomever we wait for – Old Man or demon – it might as well be in that first room of the great archway.'

The Mouser nodded as they turned back, and Ahura said, 'At least we'll be at no greater disadvantage there. Ishtar, but the Old Man's rhyme is true! "Each chamber is a slavering maw, each arch a toothy jaw." I always greatly feared this place, but never thought to find a mazy den that sure as death has stony mind and stony claws.

'They never chose to bring me here, you see, and from the night I left our home in Anra's body, I was a living corpse, to be left or taken where they wished. They would have killed me, I think, at least there came a time when Anra would, except it was necessary that Anra's body have an occupant – or my rightful body when he was out of it, for Anra was able to reenter his own body and walk about in it in this region of Ahriman. At such times I was kept drugged and helpless at the Lost City. I believe that something was done to his body at that time – the Old Man talked of making it invulnerable – for after I returned to it, I found it seeming both emptier and stonier than before.'

Starting back down the ramp, the Mouser thought he heard from somewhere ahead, against the terrible silence, the faintest of windy groans.

'I grew to know my twin's body very well, for I was in it most of seven years in the tomb. Somewhere during that black period all fear and horror vanished – I had become habituated to death. For the first time in my life my will, my cold intelligence, had time to grow. Physically fettered, existing almost without sensation, I gained inward power. I began to see what I could never see before – Anra's weaknesses.

'For he could never cut me wholly off from him. The chain he had forged between our minds was too strong for that. No matter how far away he went, no matter what screens he raised up, I could always see into some sector of his mind, dimly, like a scene at the end of a long, narrow, shadowy corridor.

'I saw his pride – a silver-armored wound. I watched his ambition stalk among the stars as if they were jewels set on black velvet in his treasure house to be. I felt, almost as if it were my own, his choking hatred of the bland, miserly gods – almighty fathers who lock up the secrets of the universe, smile at our pleas, frown, shake their heads, forbid, chastise; and his groaning rage at the bonds of space and time, as if each cubit he could not see and tread upon were a silver manacle on his wrist, as if each moment before or after his own life were a silver crucifying nail. I walked through the gale-blown halls of his loneliness and glimpsed the beauty that he cherished – shadowy, glittering forms that cut the soul like knives – and once I came upon the dungeon of his love, where no light came to show it was corpses that were fondled and bones kissed. I grew familiar with his desires, which demanded a universe of miracles peopled by unveiled gods. And his lust, which quivered at the world as at a woman, frantic to know each hidden part.

'Happily, for I was learning at long last to hate him, I noted how, though he possessed my body, he could not use it easily and bravely as I had. He could not laugh, or love, or dare. He must instead hang back, peer, purse his lips, withdraw.'

More than halfway down the ramp, it seemed to the Mouser that the groan was repeated, louder, more whistlingly.

'He and the Old Man started on a new cycle of study and experience that took them, I think, to all corners of the world and that they were confident, I'm sure, would open to them those black realms wherein their powers would become infinite. Anxiously from my cramped vantage-point I watched their quest ripen and then, to my delight, rot. Their outstretched fingers just missed the next handhold in the dark. There was something that both of them lacked. Anra became bitter, blamed the Old Man for their lack of success. They quarreled.

'When I saw Anra's failure become final, I mocked him with my laughter, not of lips but of mind. From here to the stars he could not have escaped it – it was then he would have killed me. But he dared not while I was in his own body, and I now had the power to bar him from that.

'Perhaps it was my faint thought-laughter that turned his desperate mind to you and to the secret of the laughter of the Elder Gods – that, and his need of magical aid in regaining his body. For a while then I almost feared he had found a new avenue of escape – or advance – until this morning before the tomb, with sheer cruel joy, I saw you spit on his offers, challenge, and, helped by my laughter, kill him. Now there s only the Old Man to fear.'

Passing again under the massive multiple archway with its ddly recessed keystone, they heard the whistling groan once more repeated, and this time there was no mistaking its reality, its nearness, its direction. Hastening to a shadowy and particularly misty corner of the chamber, they made out an inner window set level with the floor, and in that window they saw a face that seemed to float bodiless on the thick fog. Its features defied recognition – it might have been a distillation of all the ancient, disillusioned faces in the world. There was no beard below the sunken cheeks.

Coming close as they dared, they saw that it was perhaps not entirely bodiless or without support. There was the ghostly suggestion of tatters of clothing or flesh trailing off, a pulsating sack that might have been a lung, and silver chains with hooks or claws.

Then the one eye remaining to that shameful fragment opened and fixed upon Ahura, and the shrunken lips twisted themselves into the caricature of a smile.

'Like you, Ahura,' the fragment murmured in the highest of falsettos, 'he sent me on an errand I did not want to run.'

As one, moved by a fear they dared not formulate, Fafhrd and the Mouser and Ahura half turned round and peered over their shoulders at the mist-clogged doorway leading outside. For three, four heartbeats they peered. Then, faintly, they heard one of the horses whinny. Whereupon they turned fully round, but not before a dagger, sped by the yet unshaking hand of Fafhrd, had buried itself in the open eye of the tortured thing in the inner window.

Side by side they stood, Fafhrd wild-eyed, the Mouser taut, Ahura with the look of someone who, having successfully climbed a precipice, slips at the very summit.

A slim shadowy bulk mounted into the glow outside the doorway.

'Laugh!' Fafhrd hoarsely commanded Ahura. 'Laugh!' He shook her, repeating the command.

Her head flopped from side to side, the cords in her neck jerked, her lips twitched, but from them came only a dry croaking. She grimaced despairingly.

'Yes,' remarked a voice they all recognized, 'there are time and places where laughter is an easily-blunted weapon – a harmless as the sword which this morning pierced me through.'

Death-pale as always, the tiny blood-clot over his heart, his forehead crumbled in, his black garb travel-dusted, Anra Devadoris faced them.

'And so we come back to the beginning,' he said slowly, 'but now a wider circle looms ahead.'

Fafhrd tried to speak, to laugh, but the words and laughter choked in his throat.

'Now you have learned something of my history and my power, as I intended you should,' the adept continued. 'You have had time to weigh and reconsider. I still await your answer.'

This time it was the Mouser who sought to speak or laugh and failed.

For a moment the adept continued to regard them, smiling confidently. Then his gaze wandered beyond them. He frowned suddenly and strode forward, pushed past them, knelt by the inner window.

As soon as his back was turned Ahura tugged at the Mouser's sleeve, tried to whisper something – with no more success than one deaf and dumb.

They heard the adept sob, 'He was my nicest.'

The Mouser drew a dagger, preparing to steal on him from behind, but Ahura dragged him back, pointing in a very different direction.

The adept whirled on them. 'Fools!' he cried, 'have you no inner eye for the wonders of darkness, no sense of the grandeur of horror, no feeling for a quest beside which all other adventurings fade in nothingness, that you should destroy my greatest miracle – slay my dearest oracle? I let you come here to Mist, confident its mighty music and glorious vistas would win you to my view – and thus I am repaid. The jealous, ignorant powers ring me round – you are my great hope fallen. There were unfavorable portents as I walked from the Lost City. The white, idiot glow of Ormadz faintly dirtied the black sky. I heard in the wind the senile clucking of the Elder Gods. There was a fumbling abroad, as if even incompetent Ningauble, last and stupidest of the hunting pack, were catching up. I had a charm in reserve to thwart them, but it needed the Old Man to carry it. Now they close in for the kill. But there are still some moments of power left me and I am not wholly yet without allies. Though I am doomed, there are still those bound to me by such ties that they must answer me if I call upon them. You shall not see the end, if end there be.' With that he lifted his voice in a great eerie shout: 'Father! Father!'

The echoes had not died before Fafhrd rushed at him, his great sword swinging.

The Mouser would have followed suit except that, just as he shook Ahura off, he realized at what she was so insistently pointing.

The recess in the keystone above the mighty archway.

Without hesitation he unslipped his climbing rope, and running lightly across the chamber, made a whistling cast.

The hook caught in the recess.

Hand over hand he climbed up.

Behind him he heard the desperate skirl of swords, heard also another sound, far more distant and profound.

His hand gripped the lip of the recess, he pulled himself up and thrust in head and shoulders, steadying himself on hip and elbow. After a moment, with his free hand, he whipped out his dagger.

Inside, the recess was hollowed like a bowl. It was filled with a foul greenish liquid and incrusted with glowing minerals. At the bottom, covered by the liquid, were several objects — three of them rectangular, the others irregularly round and rhythmically pulsating.

He raised his dagger, but for the moment did not, could not, strike. There was too crushing a weight of things to be realized and remembered — what Ahura had told about the ritual marriage in her mother's family — her suspicion that, although she and Anra were born together, they were not children of the same father — how her Greek father had died (and now the Mouser guessed at the hands of what) — the strange affinity for stone the slave-physician had noted in Anra's body — what she had said about an operation performed on him — why a heart-thrust had not killed him — why his skull had cracked so hollowly and egg-shell easy — he had never seemed to breathe – old legends of other sorcerors who had made themselves invulnerable by hiding their hearts – above all, the deep kinship all of them had sensed between Anra and this half-living castle – the black, man-shaped monolith in the Lost City—

He saw Anra Devadoris, spitted on Fafhrd's blade, hurling himself closer along it, and Fafhrd desperately warding off Needle with a dagger.

As if pinioned by a nightmare, he helplessly heard the clash of swords rise toward a climax, heard it blotted out by the other sound – a gargantuan stony clomping that seemed to be following their course up the mountain, like a pursuing earthquake—

The Castle Called Mist began to tremble, and still he could not strike—

Then, as if surging across infinity from that utmost rim beyond which the Elder Gods had retreated, relinquishing the world to younger deities, he heard a mighty, star-shaking laughter that laughed at all things, even at this; and there was power in the laughter, and he knew the power was his to use.

With a downward sweep of his arm he sent his dagger plunging into the green liquid and tearing through the stone-crusted heart and brain and lungs and guts of Anra Devadoris.

The liquid foamed and boiled, the castle rocked until he was almost shaken from the niche, the laughter and stony clomping rose to a pandemonium.

Then, in an instant it seemed, all sound and movement ceased. The Mouser's muscles went weak. He half fell, half slid, to the floor. Looking about dazedly, making no attempt to rise, he saw Fafhrd wrench his sword from the fallen adept and totter back until his groping hand found the support of a table-edge, saw Ahura, still gasping from the laughter that had possessed her, go up and kneel beside her brother and cradle his crushed head on her knees.

No word was spoken. Time passed. The green mist seemed to be slowly thinning.

Then a small black shape swooped into the room through a high window and the Mouser grinned.

'Hugin,' he called luringly.

The shape swooped obediently to his sleeve and clung there, head down. He detached from the bat's leg a tiny parchment.

'Fancy, Fafhrd, it's from the commander of our rear guard,' he announced gaily. 'Listen:

' "To my agents Fafhrd and the Gray Mouser, funeral greetings! I have regretfully given up all hope for you, and yet – token of my great affection – I risk my own dear Hugin in order to get this last message through. Incidentally, Hugin, if given opportunity, will return to me from Mist – something I am afraid you will not be able to do. So if, before you die, you see anything interesting – and I am sure you will – kindly scribble me a memorandum. Remember the proverb: Knowledge takes precedence over death. Farewell for two thousand years, dearest friends. Ningauble." '

'That demands drink,' said Fafhrd, and walked out into the darkness. The Mouser yawned and stretched himself, Ahura stirred, printed a kiss on the waxen face of her brother, lifted the trifling weight of his head from her lap, and laid it gently on the stone floor. From somewhere in the upper reaches of the castle they heard a faint crackling.

Presently Fafhrd returned, striding more briskly, with two jars of wine under his arm.

'Friends,' he announced, 'the moon's come out, and by its light this castle begins to look remarkably small. I think the mist must have been dusted with some green drug that made us see sizes wrong. We must have been drugged, I'll swear, for we never saw something that's standing plain as day at the bottom of the stairs with its foot on the first step – a black statue that's twin brother to the one in the Lost City.'

The Mouser lifted his eyebrows. 'And if we went back to the Lost City . . . ?' he asked.

'Why,' said Fafhrd, 'we might find that those fool Persian farmers, who admitted hating the thing, had knocked down the statue there, and broken it up, and hidden the pieces.' He was silent for a moment. Then, 'Here's wine,' he rumbled, 'to sluice the green drug from our throats.'

The Mouser smiled. He knew that hereafter Fafhrd would

refer to their present adventure as 'the time we were drugged on a mountaintop.'

They all three sat on a table-edge and passed the two jars endlessly round. The green mist faded to such a degree that Fafhrd, ignoring his claims about the drug, began to argue that even it was an illusion. The crackling from above increased in volume; the Mouser guessed that the impious rolls in the library, no longer shielded by the damp, were bursting into flame. Some proof of this was given when the abortive bear cub, which they had completely forgotten, came waddling frightenedly down the ramp. A trace of decorous down was already sprouting from its naked hide. Fafhrd dribbled some wine on its snout and held it up to the Mouser.

'It wants to be kissed,' he rumbled.

'Kiss it yourself, in memory of pig-trickery,' replied the Mouser.

This talk of kissing turned their thoughts to Ahura. Their rivalry forgotten, at least for the present, they persuaded her to help them determine whether her brother's spells were altogether broken. A moderate number of hugs demonstrated this clearly.

'Which reminds me,' said the Mouser brightly, 'now that our business here is over, isn't it time we started, Fafhrd, for your lusty Northland and all that bracing snow?'

Fafhrd drained one jar dry and picked up the other.

'The Northland?' he ruminated. 'What is it but a stamping ground of petty, frost-whiskered kinglets who know not the amenities of life. That's why I left the place. Go back? By Thor's smelly jerkin, not now!'

The Mouser smiled knowingly and sipped from the remaining jar. Then, noticing the bat still clinging to his sleeve, he took stylus, ink, and a scrap of parchment from his pouch, and, with Ahura giggling over his shoulder, wrote:

'To my aged brother in petty abominations, greetings! It is with the deepest regret that I must report the outrageously lucky and completely unforeseen escape of two rude and unsympathetic fellows from the Castle Called Mist. Before leaving, they expressed to me the intention of returning to someone called Ningauble – you are Ningauble, master, are you not? – and lopping off six of his seven eyes for souvenirs. So I think it only fair to warn you. Believe me, I am your friend. One of the fellows was very tall and at times his bellowings seemed to resemble speech. Do you know him? The other fancied a gray garb and was of extreme wit and personal beauty, given to . . .'

Had any of them been watching the corpse of Anra Devadoris at this moment, they would have seen a slight twitching of the lower jaw. At last the mouth came open, and out leaped a tiny black mouse. The cub-like creature, to whom Fafhrd's fondling and the wine had imparted the seeds of self-confidence, lurched drunkenly at it, and the mouse began a squeaking scurry toward the wall. A wine jar, hurled by Fafhrd, shattered on the crack into which it shot; Fafhrd had seen, or thought he had seen, the untoward place from which the mouse had come.

'Mice in his mouth,' he hiccupped. 'What dirty habits for a pleasant young man! A nasty, degrading business, this thinking oneself an adept.'

'I am reminded,' said the Mouser, 'of what a witch told me about adepts. She said that, if an adept chances to die, his soul is reincarnated in a mouse. If, as a mouse, he managed to kill a rat, his soul passes over into a rat. As a rat, he must kill a cat; as a cat, a wolf; as a wolf, a panther; and, as a panther, a man. Then he can recommence his adeptry. Of course, it seldom happens that anyone gets all the way through the sequence and in any case it takes a very long time. Trying to kill a rat is enough to satisfy a mouse with mousedom.'

Fafhrd solemnly denied the possibility of any such foolery, and Ahura cried until she decided that being a mouse would interest rather than dishearten her peculiar brother. More wine was drunk from the remaining jar. The crackling from the rooms above had become a roar, and a bright red glow consumed the dark shadows. The three adventurers prepared to leave the place.

Meantime the mouse, or another very much like it, thrust its head from the crack and began to lick the wine-damp shards keeping a fearful eye upon those in the great room, but especially upon the strutting little would-be bear.

The Mouser said, 'Our quest's done. I'm for Tyre.'

Fafhrd said, 'I'm for Ning's Gate and Lankhmar. Or is that a dream?'

The Mouser shrugged, 'Mayhap Tyre's the dream. Lankhmar sounds as good.'

Ahura said, 'Could a girl go?'

A great blast of wind, cold and pure, blew away the last lingering of Mist. As they went through the doorway they saw, outspread above them, the self-consistent stars.

The world's greatest science fiction authors now available in paperback from Grafton Books

J G Ballard

The Crystal World	£2.50	☐
The Drought	£2.50	☐
Hello America	£2.50	☐
The Disaster Area	£2.50	☐
Crash	£2.50	☐
Low-Flying Aircraft	£2.50	☐
The Atrocity Exhibition	£2.50	☐
The Venus Hunters	£2.50	☐
The Day of Forever	£2.50	☐
The Unlimited Dream Company	£2.50	☐
Concrete Island	£2.50	☐
Myths of the Near Future	£2.50	☐
High Rise	£2.50	☐

Philip Mann

The Eye of the Queen	£1.95	☐

To order direct from the publisher just tick the titles you want and fill in the order form.

All these books are available at your local bookshop or newsagent, or can be ordered direct from the publisher.

To order direct from the publishers just tick the titles you want and fill in the form below.

Name _____

Address _____

_____

Send to:
Grafton Cash Sales
PO Box 11, Falmouth, Cornwall TR10 9EN.

Please enclose remittance to the value of the cover price plus:

UK 60p for the first book, 25p for the second book plus 15p per copy for each additional book ordered to a maximum charge of £1.90.

BFPO 60p for the first book, 25p for the second book plus 15p per copy for the next 7 books, thereafter 9p per book.

Overseas including Eire £1.25 for the first book, 75p for second book and 28p for each additional book.